Carinian's Seeker

TJ Michaels

A Samhain Publishing, Ltd. publication.

Samhain Publishing, Ltd.
512 Forest Lake Drive
Warner Robins, GA 31093
www.samhainpublishing.com

Carinian's Seeker
Copyright © 2007 by TJ Michaels
Print ISBN: 1-59998-429-6
Digital ISBN: 1-59998-328-1

Editing by Sasha Knight
Cover by Anne Cain

First Samhain Publishing, Ltd. electronic publication: February 2006
First Samhain Publishing, Ltd. print publication: May 2007

Dedication

To my children, the greatest substitute cooks and tea makers in the world, thank you for your never-ending support. To my boss, Mizz Stud—I could never have done this without your support. To my editor, Madam Knight, a living example of the word patience. To Bix and Carin for trusting me with their story and providing lots of middle-of-the-night ideas. Blessings to you all.

Chapter One

Carinian Derrickson wondered for the millionth time what nutball was responsible for sending her here in mid-January. She was a San Diego scientist, not a blasted snow bunny.

She snatched her gym bag out of the trunk of her rented Mustang GT and, shivering down to the little hairs on her toes, absently slammed it shut. The dark, cloud-covered sky threatened to dump on her but at least the snow had stopped for now. Wrapped in a down jacket, wool pants and a pair of low-heeled pumps she couldn't wait to get out of, she quaked all the way through the front door of the fitness club. The foothills of Colorado might look like a nice place to live with its panoramic views of soaring snow-capped mountains, but Carin didn't care for five-below-zero anywhere. At least she wouldn't have to miss a workout in this godforsaken tundra.

She clenched her teeth, trying to stop them from chattering as she made her way to the check-in desk. Head tilted in wonder, she was unable to stop her brow from flying upward at the teenybopper dressed in a cropped T-shirt and short-shorts at the front desk. If the girl showed any more skin, she'd be stark naked. It was so cold outside Carin was sure the kid would be a popsicle by the time she made it to her car once her shift was over.

Numb fingers fished a guest pass out of her jacket pocket. With mumbled thanks she thrust it at the teenybopper and all but ran for the warmth of the locker room to change.

An average height of five-foot-seven, Carin loved her body—toned, cut and nicely muscled. Maybe she would enter the natural bodybuilding contest next year. She certainly had the build for it and could pull off feminine-but-strong any day of the week.

Through the loud Shania Twain remix and clang of weights came a brush against her mind. The gentle touch was a deliberate but unfamiliar whisper quickly swallowed up by the emotions whirling around the place, bombarding her empathic senses. Spine stiff, she glanced up from the free weight rack into the mirror. Had she become the center of attention of a few of the sweating, straining gym-goers reflected behind her?

The rough edges of the consciences of others sawed into her—too many women hated their shape, too many men were determined to grunt away their midlife crisis and too many of both sexes strutted around for nothing more than getting noticed. It was times like this she missed her gym at home, a small private facility where she rarely had to interact with more than a few members at a time. Easier on her mind that way.

Carin's gaze settled on the width of her hips and the tiny bit of bulge around her middle. Nothing she could do about the hips. Her mother used to tell her, *"Honey, you may as well relax about your hips, 'cause as long as you're living in that beautiful cinnamon skin, your booty ain't going nowhere."* Then the woman would shove a slice of butter-smothered cornbread in her face without remorse, knowing Carin was constantly in the gym.

The memory brought a smile to her lips as she settled on an incline bench with a pair of twenty-pound dumbbells and lifted the weights smoothly. After pressing out eight good reps, the twenties hit the floor on a wince. Her shoulder was acting up again. Damn. She closed her eyes against the sudden pain radiating just underneath the scars from the arthroscopic shoulder surgery she'd had a year ago.

The sharp ache seared through the tendons where her left shoulder met the top of her biceps, then twisted through the bone and down her arm all the way to her wrist. It hurt like hell. Damned arm was supposed to be healed by now.

Abandoning the free weights, she sat on the leg extension machine, stretched out her legs and...her entire body screeched to a halt. The hairs on the back of her neck stood on end when a presence, this one standing out from the others, seemed to surround her. Caressed and stroked, as if seeking a way in, instead of the constant beating of feelings she was used to. Hmm. This was more than a brush against her mind. Someone focused on her, strongly.

Goofball, she chided herself. The place was packed, a veritable meat market. Everyone was checking out everyone else, so of course someone focused on her.

Head lowered in concentration, prepared to launch into another set of leg extensions, Carin frowned. The tips of a pair of Nike's stared back up at her. Someone else's Nike's.

Carin looked up to a solid, thick set of calves, and up some more to the nicest pair of thighs she'd seen on a man who wasn't on TV. The muscles were large, well-developed and went on forever before finally reaching the hem of his shorts. An obvious bulge declared the owner of said shorts as well-endowed. *Look at that thing, and he's not even hard. Oh Lord, what am I thinking?* She compelled her gaze to make the rest of the journey up to his face and blinked twice. Okay, he was still there. Not a dream.

This had to be the most striking masculine face this side of heaven. She'd never been attracted to a man outside her race before, but it was instantly there for this man. His features were strong, chiseled, like some kind of rare marble sculpture with nicely tanned skin. A clean shaven face allowed her to see the smoothness of it. No five o'clock shadow. No scars. No wrinkles. Not a pretty boy, but ruggedly handsome with midnight black hair tastefully cut shorter at the sides and back, and just a little longer on top with a hint of wave.

Carin pulled in a swift intake of breath. His eyes were the color of...well, what? She couldn't quite decide. They seemed to have trouble choosing whether to be hazel, or light honey brown with a hint of silvery gray. He towered over her with a friendly expression, a bit of humor etched into an easy smile.

"Excuse me." Oh, she liked his voice, too. "Mind if I work my sets in between yours?"

Without a word she forced her stare to leave his face, shifted her butt on the seat and hopped off the machine.

He leaned over, set the machine to two hundred pounds— obviously a moderate weight for a man his size—and settled down to work. Carin stood with her arms folded over her chest and watched his legs extend and lift the weight with ease, thigh muscles flexing sinuously, smoothly. The man made it look easy.

Every nerve in her body snapped to attention as she admired him from head to toe. She tried to stop looking, she really did, but just couldn't help it. Biceps and forearms bulged under his tight long-sleeved Coolmax workout shirt. Those arms were folded over a wide chest with nicely pronounced pecs. Sculpted abs tapered down to a trim waist. Rock hard, everywhere. Dayum!

Gorgeous face. Killer body. Beautiful smile. He was, in a word, perfect. But there was no such thing as a perfect man, or a perfect anything else. So he was probably an asshole.

Turning smartly on her heel, she walked away and left the dark-haired, *Lord of the Rings* action hero look-alike behind her.

೫ಆ

She'd been gracious, almost friendly, when Bix asked to work his sets in between hers. Then she went all aloof on him and stalked off in a huff. After that he kept a close eye on her from a distance.

So *this* was Dr. Carinian Derrickson? The picture stashed in the back pocket of his shorts didn't do the woman one whit of justice. She was clearly the finest milk chocolate skinned woman he'd ever seen. Damn, she had a killer body. Cut, well-defined muscle. Nice curves in all the right places. Her features were classically Afro centric—firm full lips, mysterious smoky brown eyes, and thick naturally coiled hair. It was pulled back into a long ponytail. The casual style allowed him plenty of opportunity to memorize the lines of her beautiful face. The woman was, in a word, hot. Too bad she was his target.

Thankful for his psychic abilities, Bix brushed gently against her mind and was puzzled. For some reason the woman was extremely uncomfortable in this place. He'd have to be smooth if he wanted to get anywhere with her and made sure their meeting on the way to the front door was perfectly timed.

Carin looked his way and smiled, her deep brown eyes expressive, warm. Then, as if she'd caught herself doing something she shouldn't, those eyes glittered as cold and frosty as the sheet of ice covering everything in the parking lot.

Bix ignored her body language. Then he caught her scent. He hadn't noticed it before in the midst of all the sweaty bodies moving around the fitness club. It was times like this he wished his senses weren't so keen. Something about the way this woman smelled made his gums tingle and burn. Made his incisors threaten to slip free. He clamped down on the strange reaction, willed his fangs to cease their mutiny and turned on the charm.

"Hey there," he called, plastering on his innocent-as-a-newborn smile. "You're leaving, too?"

"Yep." Her answer was short and definitely intended to send a go-away message. He purposely didn't get it.

"I'm going across the street to get a bite to eat. Care to join me?"

"I'm sorry, but I have an early day tomorrow." The flat quality in her voice made it clear his charm wasn't working.

Oddly enough, her rebuff hit him square in the gut and he felt his facade slip just a hair. Ruthlessly squashing down the unexpectedly strong instinct to conquer, Bix got back to business. Carinian's business. "Are you going to skip dinner altogether?"

"I don't mean to be rude, but are you always this nosy with people you don't know?"

She stopped underneath an illuminated lamp in the parking lot and planted her fist on her hip. When her tennis shoe began to tap out an annoyed rhythm on the cold, icy ground, he cut her off before she could get her reprimand—and he was sure that's what it would be—out of her mouth.

Hands held up in the universal "you win" gesture, he backed up a step and kept right on smiling. "Look, I'm not asking you out on a date. We both just worked out and unless you've already had dinner, I'm sure you want to eat before it gets too late. I'm going right over there," he said, pointing to the Village Inn restaurant across the street. "If you care to join me, please do. By the way, my name is Jon, Jon Bixler. My friends call me Bix."

He extended his hand and waited patiently for her to take it. She looked down at it like she expected it to turn into a Gila monster, but he held steady. Finally, she placed her smaller hand in his with a firm grip, though her face said her first impression of him hadn't been decided yet.

"Carinian," she offered softly, eyeing him askance.

"Nice to meet you," he said casually, pumping her hand up and down. His smile remained plastered in place even when she didn't say the same. Something inside of him wanted her to soften up a little, maybe even see him as a...as a what? Hell, he wasn't sure. No, that wasn't true, he knew exactly what he wanted. Her. But in his heart he knew it was impossible. This woman should never trust him.

Bix turned away and started towards his car. After three steps, he turned back again. One side of his mouth tipped up when Carinian's right eyebrow rose a good inch. She probably wondered if he'd forgotten something.

"I forgot to mention." His voice lowered to a conspiratorial whisper as he looked right and left. "I'm having the ribs."

His insides warmed when laughter bubbled right out of her. With a wink, he disappeared across the parking lot, leaving her shaking her head. But at least she was smiling. For the life of him, he couldn't figure out why he cared.

Chapter Two

A few minutes later Carin found herself seated in a booth across from Mr. Damn-You're-Fine, laughing her head off like she was outside at a ballgame or something. He, of course, ordered the ribs with a simple side salad, just as he'd promised in the parking lot. She had the rice pilaf with a no-frills grilled chicken breast.

"So, Carin, where are you from?"

"San Diego."

"What are you doing in Colorado this time of year?"

A giggle bubbled up past her lips at his raised eyebrows and look of chagrin. Yeah, exactly how she felt about being in the arctic that some people called the Midwest.

"Here for training. I, uh, work for a biotech company. We just bought some new analytical software and I was sent here to learn how to use it."

"I'm sure you'll be having a talk with the person responsible for sending you here as soon as you get back to the coast." Then he laughed. It was the first time she'd heard him do it, and the sound rumbled up out of his chest in a controlled boom. Deep, sensual. Damned sexy.

And he just seemed to get more appealing as the minutes slipped by.

He told her the funniest stories about his hillbilly Arkansas family and friends, and their antics growing up in the South. Like the time he and some of his cousins decided to have a footrace and see who could make it to the bottom of the hill first. With their eyes closed. Bix ended up in the hospital with stitches from his forehead all the way down to his chin after running headfirst into a neighbor's fencepost at full speed. Or the time he'd jumped off the roof of his mother's house with a sheet tied around his neck to see if he could fly. It was amazing he had no scars from any of it.

A ten year stint in the military followed by several years of exploring the world led to the loss of his country bumpkin accent and the acquisition of a bit of sophistication.

In between chuckles, the way those smoldering hazel-gray eyes took her in made her belly flutter nervously, but she didn't feel uncomfortable or afraid. She was attracted. It had been an eon since a man had caught her attention and the feeling was rather foreign. She was glad when she spotted their waiter approaching, desperate for something other than his yummy mouth to concentrate on.

The second their plates met the table her stomach responded. Loudly. Oh Lord, she was beyond embarrassed as the stupid organ gurgled and grumbled, telling anyone within earshot it was well past mealtime.

"I'm glad I asked you to come and eat dinner with me. Seems your stomach is, too."

Whoa, was he teasing her about how much food she'd ordered? They'd been having a perfectly good time, but the bottom line was she didn't really know him. There'd been plenty too-brainy-too-curvy comments growing up. The last thing she was in the mood for was some strange guy, no matter how friendly or gorgeous, to throw subtle darts about not being a skinny little stick figure.

Carin looked up from her plate and searched his eyes, but what she expected to see wasn't there. No snarky, turned-up lips, no condescending flat stare. Instead, his carefree expression held a hint of mischief. And she felt it. *Felt* him good-naturedly poking fun at her. A warm wash of humor emanated from him. A slight brush against her mind, just like the one she'd felt in the gym, urged her to reach for the same emotions and embrace them.

Instead she pushed them aside and dug into her food, wondering if Bix felt her apprehension towards him build and then melt away. She'd known since she was a child that she was an empath but never actually explored her abilities. However, she knew enough to realize folks typically projected their emotions. But this was different. Bix's emotions streamed out of him in a controlled manner, not rushing at her like most people's. Maybe she should explore this a bit.

"I'm glad you're eating," Bix mumbled around a bite of spicy smoked meat. "Most women don't actually eat anything when they're out at a restaurant. They just kind of push the food around on their plates."

"Well, I've never been the frilly-froo-froo, too-cute-to-eat type," she said, taking a healthy bite of juicy chicken breast. "Besides, if I want to stay healthy I have to give my body plenty of good food, not starve myself to death."

He gave her a slow, intense once-over, conveying exactly what he thought about her body. From the top of her head down to the tasteful peep of cleavage showing through the scoop neck of her T-shirt. He lingered there for a moment. "I agree. And you look like you take care of your body very well. Very well, indeed."

The man eyed her like she was a tasty morsel on his plate. Unused to such attention, all she could do was look down at her slowly disappearing chicken and rice and mumble a shaky, "Thank you." His expression was too hot to handle and left her wishing she'd worn more clothes. *Or less.*

Blushing like a schoolgirl, she was thankful he couldn't hear her heart speed up every time he leaned forward and gave his full attention as if her words were the most important in the world.

Then he seemed to back off a bit, relaxing against the backrest of their booth with a lazy smile. Thank goodness. One more heart-stopping grin or wickedly hungry look and she'd go up in smoke. Lord, this was ridiculous. But it sure felt nice. Too bad she was leaving in the morning.

"What time is it?" she asked, glancing down at her bare wrist. She'd forgotten her watch was already packed in her overnight bag at the hotel.

"It's almost seven-thirty." Bix raised his hand to get the waiter's attention and paid the check. "I have a plane to catch, so perhaps I'd better go."

"Yeah, me too. I'm packed, but I have to...uh, yeah. I have a plane to catch, I mean," she rambled. She hated when she rambled. It was a nervous thing. She clamped her lips shut, and then remembered her manners. "Oh, goodness, I'm sorry. I didn't thank you for taking care of my dinner, Jon."

"Bix."

"Right, sorry. Uh, I mean Bix," she blurted out nervously. *Geez, I'm a babbling idiot with this guy.* On a subtle but steadying breath, her chin went up as she took, well sort of took control of her nervousness. "Listen, I've gotta run. It was nice to meet you, Bix." She pulled a business card out of the PDA case in her purse and pushed it across the table. "If you're ever in San Diego, give me a call. Good night."

"Wait, I'll walk you to your car."

She frowned at his commanding tone. Not harsh, but as if he expected her to simply obey him, and do as he wanted with no question. Strangely, she wanted to yield to his wishes, but shook it off with practiced ease. Besides, she was going home tomorrow and would probably never see him again in her life, so why start something she had no intention of continuing? But damn she wanted to so badly. Scooting out of the booth, her body cooled with an unexpected sense of loss.

"Thanks, but that's okay. I'll be fine. Good night." Coat in hand, Carin headed for the front door, needing to reconcile her reeling emotions and put some space between herself and this all-too-alpha male who made her want to forget all measure of self-control.

She reached out to push open the glass doors when a large, slightly calloused hand landed gently on top of hers. Bix. She turned around and glared at him.

"It's dark out and I'm a bit old-fashioned when it comes to a lady walking alone in the dark." Bix felt her shock at both his presence and her reaction to his touch. Her shiver of fear was arousing. The scent of it tickled his nose and... Wait. Her fear was arousing? What the hell was wrong with him? He reluctantly removed his hand from hers, backed up a step and pushed the door open. Shooing her through and into the parking lot, he allowed himself a half-smile as Carin projected her confusion.

She didn't understand this flicker and buzz between them any more than he did. He let his concern flow out of his mind and concentrated instead on the way her tight butt moved underneath her workout clothes as she walked to her car. Oh God, not good. Perhaps looking up at the lamppost was a better idea.

℘℘

Carin's stomach dropped into her shoes when a glance into the rear-view mirror told her Bix still tailed her. She felt hunted, yet strangely exhilarated by his pursuit, if that's what it was. An odd combination of fear and eagerness warred in her mind. With the restaurant a mile behind her, good old-fashioned fear pushed everything else aside. Her cell phone rang just as she considered dialing 9-1-1.

"Hey there. Where are you staying?"

The medium bass of his voice floated across the airwaves and through her earpiece, soothing and massaging her senses. Her panic dissipated but didn't disappear.

"At the Ramada, right off of I-25 and 120th."

"You're kidding," he continued in the same relaxed voice. "I'm at the same hotel. I'll bet you were getting worried wondering if I was last week's hatchet murderer following you around."

"I was *not* worried," she growled mutinously, glaring daggers at him through the phone. When his chuckle grew into outright laughter, her frown gave way to a reluctant smile. "Okay, fine, I was getting a little nervous. There, you happy?"

Her grumbling made him laugh harder. "Yes, actually, I am happy. Means you have common sense, woman."

Once at the hotel, he parked right next to her, got out of his car and waited while she shut off the engine, popped the trunk and hit the automatic locks on the Mustang. As soon as she cracked her door, he was there to open it for her. She knew her expression was openly skeptical as she secured the vehicle and dug her gym bag out of the trunk.

"I'll take that for you." With an easy manner, he reached out and took the duffel from her fast freezing fingers. She stiffened as his hand brushed hers and her bemused expression set him off on a new round of laughter.

"What's the matter now?" he teased. "Never met a gentleman before?"

She rolled her eyes and gave him her best "what do you think", one-sided smirk. In all her thirty-six years, she'd never met a man who held doors, pulled out chairs or offered to carry her bag. Or set her blood pulsing in her ears, and sent butterflies winging up and down her spine. And the simmering, appreciative looks he'd passed her way over dinner. Lord, it was too much.

"May I see you to your room, Carinian?"

Hell no. She just didn't think she could continue to act right if he got anywhere near her room. But by the time she'd managed to stutter out all her arguments they were standing in front of her door.

Bix set her gym bag on the typical hotel-brown carpet, reached out and gently took her by the hand. She looked down to where his fingers stroked hers, liking the contrast between his lightly tanned skin and her darker cocoa tones.

"Carin?"

"Yes?" she answered absently, her mind focused on the slightly roughened palm holding hers securely. And what happened to the formal Carinian of only a few seconds ago? The more informal he became the more her goose bumps came out to play. What was up with that?

"May I kiss you good night?"

Always the gentleman. She nodded and waited anxiously as his head descended at a leisurely pace, like one big slow-motion picture. When he finally reached her lips she was almost giddy with anticipation, wondering what his gorgeous mouth would feel like, taste like.

He pulled her close and took her lips in a sweet caress. The kiss began innocent enough, but she knew, *knew* he wanted more than a chaste meeting of the mouths. He wanted to deepen the kiss, to ravish her. To press her up against the wall as his blood pounded through his body.

Now how the hell did she know that?

His hands slipped from her waist up to her shoulders and held her there a moment before he broke away, his breathing harsh and unsteady.

Bix couldn't believe the tremendous amount of effort it took to hold himself in check. He wanted nothing more than to rip her clothes off and take her right there in the hallway up against her door, and then hold her to his heart while his fingers tenderly stroked through the cottony curls at her nape. To softly kiss a path down the side of her neck, reveling in her natural scent as he made his way to her pulse point. He locked his knees to keep them from shaking as he forced his body to obey his mind. God, his fangs throbbed and hummed beneath their sheaths. The fine tendons that controlled their movement pulled taut, begging him to bare them, to sink them along with his throbbing cock deep into the sweet depths of her body.

What was it about this woman that made him want to rut like some untamed animal, then treat her with such tenderness? It was damned strange. *And sexually frustrating.*

He bid her good night, licked his lips and grinned at the dreamy-eyed look on her face. With a gentle kiss to her palm, he stepped away and strode down the hall. For the first time in his life, Bix wished he wasn't well-endowed. His damned dick rubbed painfully against his zipper as Carin's loudly projected thoughts followed him down the hallway.

You're so sexy. Stay and make love with me.

Twice he almost stopped and gave in to her unvoiced wishes. Her next thought slammed into his brain and his back stiffened in anger as his feet ground to a halt.

What would be the harm? I'll never see you again in my life anyway.

What? Anger welled up in his gut, sudden and fierce. A feral growl erupted from his throat as he whirled around and glared back towards her hotel room door. It closed with a quiet snap and he stood there a moment just to make sure she stayed inside, alone. The urge to scout the hotel for any other male vamp in the vicinity overwhelmed him. Not an ideal inclination for an undercover Seeker.

Bix's mouth dropped open as he looked down at himself in alarm. His chest was puffed up, his teeth bared and his lips pulled back tightly at these sudden feelings of possessiveness. His fangs had slipped free and were visible to anyone who might happen to walk down the hall. Was he in someone else's skin? He hadn't bared his fangs "accidentally" in, what, a hundred years? What the hell was going on?

Walking the short distance to his own door, he dug down into his jacket pocket for the keycard to his room as he thought on Carin's last words.

The woman thinks she'll never see me again, eh? We'll just see about that.

Chapter Three

Before he could close the door to his unexceptional hotel room, his cell phone rang. He knew it wasn't Carin calling him back. The special ring tone identified the caller as a member of V.C.O.E.—the Vampire Council of Ethics.

He shrugged out of his jacket and tossed it carelessly over the only chair in the room, and then sat on the edge of the bed and toed off his shoes before answering. A silky sweet voice reminiscent of smooth jazz music floated across the line to him. Deep for a woman, but sensual. It fit her perfectly. Too bad Bix couldn't stand the bitch.

"Have you acquired the target?"

Bix ground his back teeth on a deep breath and ignored the implied insult. God, he didn't feel like doing this right now.

"You will not question me, Natasha. I'm more than capable of doing my job. In fact," he said for probably the fiftieth time, "I've been dressing without my mother's aid for quite a long time. Longer than you've been alive, actually."

"Now, now, Jon. You're getting testy in your old age," Natasha purred. "As the V.C.O.E. Liaison for the Western territories, I'm just doing my job. You know that, don't you, lover?"

Lover? Would she ever give up? Resting his elbows on his knees, he stretched his neck from side to side and forced his body to relax. When he tuned back in to the voice on the cell phone it was droning on about some boring piece of nothing or another. He took charge of the conversation with his annoying Liaison and brought it back to business.

"I have acquired the target, Natasha. You may report to the Council that she is scheduled to fly back to San Diego tomorrow, just as they arranged," he drawled in the most bored voice he'd ever heard himself speak. "I'll be sure to contact you as soon as Dr. Derrickson leads me to Sidheon."

"Dr. Derrickson, is it? Surely you've gotten past the formality of last names with her, Jon," Natasha said cattily.

Bix didn't bother to answer. He put the phone on speaker mode and tossed it on the bed. His pants hit the floor, followed by his shirt and underwear. Naked, he ducked into the small bathroom and turned on the shower.

While the water warmed, he strolled to the closet and pulled out his only set of clean clothes for tomorrow. The dirty laundry was stuffed inside a duffel bag and left near the door for easy retrieval before his jaunt to the airport in the morning. After a lengthy silence, a hard, angry female voice crackled over the phone line. Natasha. Hell, he'd almost forgotten she was there.

"The temporary house in San Diego is all set up, Jon. Alaan will pick you up at the airport and assist you as needed."

Bix called over his shoulder with a distracted, "Fine," glad his best friend would work this case with him. Excellent. Back in the bathroom again he flipped on the faucet over the small sink. "What about the territory leaders in California? They know I'm coming?"

"All taken care of. I don't have any additional intel other than what I sent you yesterday before you flew to Colorado. If anything else comes up, I'll try to get it to you before you board your plane to San Diego tomorrow."

"Yep," he mumbled his response around his toothbrush.

"Good luck, Jon. I look forward to seeing you when you report back to headquarters."

"It may be a while," Bix mumbled, wrinkling his nose in distaste. "If there's nothing else, Natasha, good night."

"Good night, lover."

Bix clicked off the speakerphone and snapped the unit shut. It landed on top of his bag at the door as he headed for the shower. His hand settled on his left shoulder, digging into the muscles there. Odd. It was tight, sore and pulsing. He hadn't worked his shoulders this week at all, but the pain was acute.

The bathroom filled with a fog of soothing steam. He stepped into the tub and yanked the shower curtain closed. The strong, hot spray of water pulsed over the muscles of his back and thighs as he searched inside himself for the source of his discomfort. His keen senses dipped below his skin, into his veins and slid along and through his muscles. When he searched the connective tissues of his throbbing shoulder there was nothing unusual. But if it was perfectly fine, why the hell was it so sore?

He shut off the shower and headed to bed. Under the cool sheets and scratchy blankets, his thoughts settled on a beautiful woman with dark brown eyes and skin, and a body to die for. A body he wished he could cuddle up to right now.

His fingers had itched all through dinner to bury themselves in her thick, curly hair to see if it was a soft as it looked. The short-sleeved tee she wore let him look his fill at smooth-as-velvet skin over sleek muscle. His thoughts strayed to the elegant curve of her neck. Keen ears had picked up the strong pulse beating there as they'd talked and laughed over their meal. He imagined the same beat now. Strong. Steady. His cock swelled and pulsed in time with the imagined thump of her heart.

Hell, it was going to be a long night.

ᏦᏬᏣ

"You fool. Incompetent, idiotic fool," Sidheon roared, not bothering to hide the sharp points of his fangs from the human trembling in front of him.

"I'm sorry, Dr. Sidheon, but I thought this cart was yours," the little man stuttered, shrinking away from the very strong hand capable of snapping his neck like a chicken's.

"Well, it is not mine. If this is not my specimen cart then where the bloody hell is it?" Sidheon thundered. If it weren't for the fact this man could be trusted to keep his secrets he'd have replaced him a long time ago, brilliant or not.

"They were all lined up next to one another in the hallway. Everything looks so much alike. I—well, someone else must have taken your specimens by mistake. Or maybe the quality folks just got them mixed up. Don't worry. I'll find them, Dr. Sidheon. I'll find them." The little man bowed and scraped.

"You had better, Dan, or I promise to peel your hide," Sidheon hissed on a promise of pain. Lots and lots of pain as his incisors glowed a muted orange from the flame of the Bunsen burner on the lab table. He shooed the human away and watched him scurry towards the door, knowing the puny man was on the verge of peeing his pants.

Sidheon strode out of his lab door, locked it behind him and made his way down the hallway. There were only four labs on this level and security up here was airtight. The cart couldn't have gone far. He discreetly peeked through the small square window of each door, trying the handles as he passed. Where the hell were his experiments and all of his samples?

He looked through the window of the last lab and caught sight of his cart, identifiable only by the purple bands around some of the tops on the glass vials tucked neatly into dozens of small boxes. The stainless steel cart sat unobtrusively off to the left side of the door leading into Dr. Carinian's labs. Bloody hell.

He pressed his forehead against the cold reinforced glass of the window, not bothering to try the door handle. If Dr. Carin wasn't in her lab the doors stayed locked and dead bolted, even if she was in the building. Sidheon's cool breath steamed up the window, momentarily obscuring the cart on the other side of the steel door. He needed to get it back before the good doctor had a chance to explore too much.

He hoped he wouldn't have to kill her, at least not before he had the chance to fuck her. A perfect picture of her equally perfect body formed in his mind, prompting a bulge to form at the crotch of his pants. Sidheon licked his lips at the thought of her luscious curves and miles of smooth-looking skin. And her scent. Spicy, clean, invigorating. Like allspice and ginger. He'd seen her working out a couple of times in the company gym when she was working late. Smart and beautiful, a rare combination these days, the woman had the firmest, sexiest ass he'd ogled in ages, literally. Though he'd enjoyed her from a distance with only an occasional polite hello, perhaps he'd take it a step further, reveal his desire for her. Then maybe show his true nature? Play with her awhile, like a cat waiting to pounce on its favorite toy. Something he'd never contemplated with a human. But if she played nice, maybe he'd bless her with some of his cock before he gorged on her blood.

Chapter Four

Carin pushed the call button on the shiny double-doored elevator, smiling wistfully. Her mind drifted back to her trip to Colorado where she'd sat in a restaurant with Jon Bixler and talked about everything from favorite football teams to friends with fake boobies. She couldn't recall the last time she'd felt so free or drawn to anyone who wasn't family.

An unexplainable sadness crept over her, realizing she'd probably never again see the man who'd made her laugh like a loon and treated her with so much kindness. She shook her head at her pity party, stuck her key into the elevator panel and pushed the button for the nineteenth floor. The doors were closing when someone called her name.

"Dr. Derrickson? Hold the elevator please."

Damn it, not now. She groaned inwardly, immediately recognizing that voice. Her boss, Charles Martin, the last person she wanted to see. In all the years they'd worked together she'd always blown off his advances as nicely as possible, even when she'd returned his many gifts of flowers and chocolates. The man was oblivious of her lack of interest and as long as she smiled and remained cordial he seemed to believe he had a chance with her. Did he? Hell no. But his unspoken hope kept her in a position to get what she needed—access to the most sophisticated materials and equipment for her projects. In spite of the fact he was a total pervert who only wanted a piece of her ass, Carin almost felt guilty for using the bastard.

"Good morning, Charles." Her voice was pleasant as she plastered a patient expression on her face and smiled into his black beady little eyes. Funny, they didn't quite fit into his pasty face. While his eyes were too small, his skull seemed too large for the rest of his body. The combination of picking up his lecherous emotions and looking at him came close to causing her physical pain. Charles might be a certifiable genius, but Carin didn't think she'd ever seen a more ugly man. It took all her willpower not to scrunch up her face on a wince.

"Thanks for holding the elevator, Dr. Derrickson. By the way, what are you doing here? I thought you were going on vacation right after your training. You're not scheduled to return until next week. In fact, didn't your flight from Colorado land just an hour and a half ago? I know you're eager to catch up on things but..."

Lord, the man sure could talk. She should be used to his chatter by now but it still irritated her like a bad rash. *God, he makes my butt itch.*

Just before they glazed over, her eyes lost focus on Charles and riveted on the tall man entering the elevator behind him. Her mouth fell open and her wits flew right out of her head. Bix? And damn, was he wickedly handsome, the epitome of masculinity with silky dark hair and lightly tanned skin. Her dark eyes met his honey laden silver-streaked ones, and her heart slammed up into her throat. She couldn't help but stare as she took in the cut of his black tailored suit set off by a cream silk band collared shirt. A tailored trench fell from his neck to well past his calves. The man was impossibly wide across the shoulders. The clean lines of the leather coat accentuated his powerful build, even if he was probably the only person in all of San Diego walking around in a real winter coat. Expertly cut, it made her think of the cool garb worn in the movie, *The Matrix.* On his feet were polished black...Doc Martin boots? Now *that* was an eyebrow lifter.

Curiosity finally overrode the initial shock of coming face-to-face with the tallest, most impressive man she'd ever had the pleasure of spending time with. What the hell was he doing here? Still standing behind a blithering Charles, he winked at her.

"Hi, Carin. How are you?"

Oooooh, this was bad. The smooth tenor of his voice brought visions of him kissing her senseless in a hotel hallway into her suddenly empty head. She looked down at the floor, examining her shoes as she tried to get her thoughts together. *Deep breath in. Now let it out slowly.* Okay, back to the original question—what was he doing here?

"I'm fine, Bix. Thanks for asking. And what brings you here?"

"You two have met already?" Charles asked, his whiny voice laced with something akin to suspicion.

"Yes, we met in Colorado while I was at Aegis for software training." The elevator doors closed and Charles stood next to her while Bix moved to an unobtrusive spot behind her. Confined areas had never bothered her before, but Bix's presence filled up the small box speeding her upstairs to her labs. He even seemed to take up all the air, let alone the space.

Carin discreetly breathed a sigh of relief when Charles pushed the button for the tenth floor. At least he wouldn't be getting off with her. She stiffened as a purely sensual feeling slid over her skin. Instinctively, she knew it was Bix's gaze burning through the back of her suddenly too-tight royal blue silk blouse. Her breasts began to swell and the nipples pebbled against the sheer lace of her bra. *This is insane,* she thought, even as her body reacted to the mere presence of the man standing behind her. Just like in the hallway of the hotel in Colorado. She hadn't understood it then and didn't understand it now.

A light sheen of sweat formed under her arms. She folded them over her chest and held her lab coat closed. It wouldn't do for Charles to see her nipples stabbing through the fabric of her blouse. Though he'd probably like the show, damned perv.

"Well, I'm glad you two have met, Cari," Charles said happily, his voice a little too high-pitched. She hated when he called her Cari. Charles' expression cleared while Carin's brows scrunched together. Why would Charles be pleased she'd met someone? A very good-looking someone she hadn't expected to see again, ever.

"Mr. Bixler flew in this morning, too," Charles continued, oblivious to her mood, as usual. "He's going to oversee your current gene therapy project." He grinned, expecting her to be pleased with the change of oversight.

"What?" Lab coat and swollen breasts forgotten, Carin rounded on her boss, hands on hips and her eyes wide with a mix of anger and shock. This would ruin everything. If looks could kill, she'd see Charles six-feet under by noon.

"The company is sending me to Puerto Rico to oversee the building of the new biotech plant. Since you're the consultant for the gene therapy his organization is paying us to develop, you're on loan to Mr. Bixler starting Monday morning. Internally, you'll still report to me, just from long distance."

Carin blanched. Aw hell, there was still equipment in her lab she'd, uh, "borrowed" from Research and Development, like the cell transfection machine she hadn't signed out properly. In fact, she'd skipped going on vacation after Colorado for the sole purpose of making sure the thing wasn't missed. Besides, she'd planned to spend the extra days working on her private project, but with Bix in play she'd have to make an unplanned trip back to R&D. She'd have to move fast.

Jingling the set of spare keys to her lab, Charles said, "Mr. Bixler and I were just on our way up to your lab to look at some of your documentation. But since you're right here, why don't you take him up with you and show him what you've been working on? I've already provided him with some of the information, but I figured a look at the real thing might better get him prepared to jump right in on Monday."

"Uh, yeah. Sure." *Shit.* So much for having the weekend to clear the things out of her lab that shouldn't be there. All she could do was hope Bix didn't know what he was looking at. Like Charles.

"Excellent. I'll check in with you later, all right, Cari?" Charles crowed, then turned to Bix and said, "Mr. Bixler, it was nice to meet you. Please feel free to tell Dr. Carin if there's anything you need help deciphering. She's one of the most brilliant minds in her field."

The elevator doors whispered open and Charles stepped off, whistling. She wanted to punch him in the nose. The dolt was completely unaware of how anxious she felt right now. Carin narrowed her eyes behind Charles' back, resisting the urge to stick her tongue out at him as he left her alone in silence with Bix.

৪০৪৪

Sidheon's assistant had alerted him the moment Dr. Carinian walked into the facility. He didn't waste any time making his way down the long hallway to wait in front of her

31

door. His testing was only two days behind. As soon as he had that cart back, he could get on track. Then sometime this afternoon, he'd inform Carin she would be having dinner with him tonight. And perhaps a bit of animalistic fucking...

His head snapped up, his brow pulled down on a scowl. He sensed her coming, could almost hear her footsteps, but something was...different. And she wasn't alone. Suddenly an air of caution streaked over and through him. He needed to move. Now. Away from her lab door and down the hall in a blur, he ducked out the nearest exit and into the stairwell. Easing the door closed just as the doctor stepped around the corner, Sidheon froze as she stopped to unlock the metal door in the exact spot he'd stood only moments before.

He watched the other man's head swivel from side to side as if he were looking for something. He didn't move like a human and the intensity of his eyes reminded him of...shit, a Seeker.

His contact had told the truth after all. The Council had put a Seeker on his tail, a so-called dispenser of justice. But it didn't matter. Once he got his specimens back he'd be able to finish testing his serum and make enough to put his plan into action. All he needed was a few more weeks, a month at the most, then every one of those arrogant V.C.O.E. bastards would be sorry they'd ever labeled him a rogue.

Yes, every Elder and stooge of the V.C.O.E. would pay. Starting with the damned assassin vamp walking into Dr. Carinian's labs right now.

৯৩

Bix reached out to Carin with his senses and tried to touch her mind. He jerked his neck back subtly when he slammed into a solid wall of anger. He didn't think she realized it, but she was blocking him with her ire. He backed off the gentle, unsuccessful probing and settled for directing his keen senses to her heart and lungs. Damn, she was pissed.

He had to admit, she was good at maintaining an illusion of control. Her heartbeat and breathing said she was royally upset about him being here, but her expressionless face and relaxed shoulders said she couldn't care less if he dropped off the face of the earth just now.

Carin pulled a ring of keys from her lab coat pocket. They jingled furiously in her hand as she jammed the key into the deadbolt.

"It's nice to see you again, Carin," Bix said, trying to work past her defenses. "Like Charles said, I'm not officially your boss, just your project coordinator. I'd like to go out some time while I'm in town," he suggested, flashing his most charming smile. But it wasn't working, not today. Carin's disposition was as chilly as the winter night they'd met in Colorado. In spite of the wonderful time they'd had, it was rather obvious she wasn't happy to see him now.

"I don't date guys I work with." Her voice was clipped and hard. She turned her back on him and went back to fiddling with the lock on the door. She turned the handle and the heavy steel door swung open.

"I don't work for your company, beautiful. I work for an organization with a vested interest in the new gene therapy and cancer drugs you're developing. So technically..." He almost ran into her back when she stopped abruptly in the middle of the doorway and rounded on him. One hand fisted on her hips as the other one pointed a stiff, angry finger at Bix's chest.

"Technically," she snapped, "you led me on in Colorado by keeping your affiliation with my job a secret. My work happens to be very important to me, damn it."

"The organization I represent has stakes"—he hated that word—"in many pharma and biotech companies. I had no idea I was being sent here until I was on my way to the airport early this morning." The lie stung his tongue as he forced it out of his mouth. Over the decades he'd always done whatever was necessary to protect his species, including lie to beautiful women. But this time it just didn't feel right.

She tossed her head and moved fully into the lab, flipping on a series of lights before her keys landed on one of the many tables with a loud clunk. Anger rolled off her in waves as she stood in the middle of the room and pointed out what was what. The place was huge, filled with the most sophisticated equipment money could buy. There were several stations of both stainless steel and graphite topped tables. Some of the stations had various types of microscopes along with computers to record results. The DNA sequencer, centrifuges and fermenters had their own stations and programmable logic controllers to automatically turn them on and off. Six large basin-style sinks took up a third of one long wall, again, all stainless steel. Near the front door, a long oak desk with a matching hutch and a row of bookcases broke up the monotony of the shining steel.

At the back of the lab were two doors. Carin walked back and unlocked the one on the left. She stepped into a full private bathroom, showed him where supplies were kept, soap, towels and the like, and then left him alone to look around. While she sat at her desk checking her voice mail, Bix peeked through the window of the door she hadn't bothered to open. The ideas that popped into his head caused a roguish smile to play at the corners of his mouth. The room contained a full-sized bed made up with lots of pillows and comfortable-looking blankets, linens and throws. With Carin this close, that bed looked a lot like paradise.

"You sleep here, Carin?" he called over his shoulder.

"Sometimes." Her words were clipped and somewhat distracted. "When I'm close to a breakthrough, I'd rather just keep working at it."

He frowned, but quickly schooled his features when she didn't bother turning around when she answered. Rude wasn't something he had to put up with often. Because she was upset, he'd overlook it. This time.

"Don't your pets get lonely?" he asked, knowing he was probing but didn't care.

"I don't have pets or anything waiting at home so sometimes I just stay here," she mumbled, writing down yet another message on a small notepad next to the phone.

No one at home waiting? For a second he wondered why a woman as smart and beautiful as Carin didn't have a lover. Bix moved away from the bedroom door and looked around. Her workspace was free of any scent but hers. He inhaled deeply, taking in the rich, natural spice and immediately regretted it when his cock started dancing around in his pants. Deliberately facing the bookcase, he snatched one of the many books about blood diseases off one of the many shelves. Bix flipped through it without seeing a single word on any of the pages. All he could think about was the way Carin's legs gripped the edge of the chair she sat in while checking her messages. Those thighs should be gripping him. He snapped the book closed and shoved it back into its spot with enough force to make the bookcase tremble, cringing when the thing rocked against the wall.

Carin's head popped up at the noise, and those expressive deep brown pools searched his face. Though still angry, she seemed concerned for him. Bix turned away, he had to. Every drop of blood in his body dive-bombed for his dick from just a glance of those beautiful eyes of hers. When the aroma of her luscious body stole to him from across the room, Bix was ever thankful for the leather trench denoting his Seeker status—it hid his bulging erection. Damn it, he'd been in hundreds of relationships over the years and here he was losing it over a woman's eyes and the way she smelled? This was insane. Besides, Carin was off limits. She was a target whose sole purpose was to lead him to a rogue. End of story. He mentally kicked himself in the ass and got back to business.

"Who else has labs on this level?" he asked, changing the subject.

"Dr. Lee and Dr. Rene have labs across the hall. Dr. Sidheon's labs are next to mine, right down the hall. Our four labs are more extensive than the others in the facility so we have the whole floor."

Sidheon was right next door? Perfect. Exactly what he needed to know. Natasha had sent him a new lead this morning—Sidheon had been spotted at an address across town. Perhaps after he checked it out, he could track the rogue back here. In the meantime, he had an angry woman to deal with. A woman he happened to need if he was going to get close enough to Sidheon's research to figure out what the rogue was up to.

Carin threw down her pen, pushed away from the desk and stalked across the floor. She buried her head in one of the file cabinets and started tearing through it. Bix walked up behind her and, with a gentle touch, laid his hands on her shoulders. The connection between them was instantaneous and powerful. Powerful enough to make his fingertips tingle with the need to touch while his head screamed at him to take a step back and do his duty. His head lost the battle.

"Come on, Carin," he crooned as he leaned forward to whisper against the nape of her neck. "Don't be mad at me, sweetheart. This is all out of my control." Hell, *he* was out of control.

"Out of your control? Yeah, whatever," she snapped, tearing the manila folders out of the file drawers. "You're here to do a job. Let's just get it done so I can get back to work." The words were pushed through gritted teeth as she snatched the last two folders out of the cabinet, slammed the drawer and turned to shove the files at him.

"Carin," he called softly, taking the documents and setting them down on the nearest lab table. "I didn't send myself here, sweetheart, I promise." Well, at least part of his explanation was true. "But I must admit, I am very glad to see you." His fingers teased over her shoulders and down her arms with a gentle but firm grip.

The shield she'd unknowingly erected with her anger dropped like a stone. Her mind was bare to him now, wide open and exposed. His keen hearing caught the sudden intake of breath, heard the hitch in her throat and the sigh that followed as his hands moved over her skin. But it wasn't her reaction he was gauging. It was his own.

Awareness like nothing he'd ever experienced shook him down to his black boots, assailed him and overloaded every one of his senses. This went well beyond the ability to scent a woman. He could smell the faint musk of her sweat as it made its way up through her pores. Could hear the oxygen in her lungs mix with the blood before it thumped through her heart and swirled through her body. He could smell her hair, her skin and the fragrant arousal just beginning to pool between her legs.

His fangs ached in response to the sweet blood pulsing underneath her skin. What the hell? He'd never smelled blood *under* skin before. God, he desperately wanted to taste her. Instead, he clamped down on his lips and chanted to himself, *No teeth, no teeth, Bix!*

And stranger still was his ability to *feel* her confusion; it hung like a cloud over his head as Carin tried to puzzle out this thing between them. This attraction—was it just a squall of emotional lightning destined to fade away, or would she always be caught in the vortex of such a potent storm? She was baffled by her reaction to him, but one thing he knew for certain—she wanted him. Wanted to push him away. Wanted him to hold her closer.

"Carin, sweetheart."

"Yes."

Shit, she heard him?

"Of course I hear you. You're speaking to me."

But he hadn't said a word. Not with his mouth anyway. His whole body stilled as his mind wrapped around the answer. It was crystal clear. He couldn't believe he hadn't figured it out the night he met her. Idiot. Carin was his mate. His woman. His damned *target*.

Wasn't this a fine mess? He'd never be able to resist her allure, knowing she was meant for him, to bond with him. But the Council would have his balls if he took a target, an *assignment*, to his bed. Bloody fucking hell.

She gazed up at him, taking in his expressions, questioning. She didn't understand any more than he did. But when her plump lips parted invitingly he couldn't resist a second longer.

Bix slowly lowered his head, taking in the look of wonder on her face as he eased in closer. He rubbed his lips against hers, enjoying the silky slide of skin on skin. It just made him want more. Damn, she smelled so good. Today, a light mist of vanilla and allspice overlaid her musky tones. He deepened the kiss until he was lost, drowning in the essence of Carin.

Her fingers tightened over the tense muscle of his forearm and the slide of the leather tantalized the skin underneath. There was nothing sweet about the way he took her mouth in the potent caress. No, this was hungry, desperate, and he was man enough to admit he needed it more than anything or anyone. He dug into the thick hair at the base of her skull, just barely able to keep from yanking the pins out of it so he could run his fingers through the cottony curls.

"Mmm, Bix, why do I like kissing you so much?" Her thoughts projected into his head. Knowing how she felt turned him on until he was nothing more than a glowing ember in the fire of her sweet kisses. When his tongue touched hers, it was a melding of the mouths, a fusion of the senses. And she tasted damn good, just like his favorite fruity candy. He took her lips, her tongue, tried to steal her very breath. She gave back a roaring flame and all but consumed him, body and soul. He'd waited all his life to feel like this with a woman, but...

"Dr. Carin?"

Yaaaah! She jumped a mile out of her skin, frazzled and panting. At the first gasp of distress, Carin found herself sheltered behind Bix's wide back. One of his strong arms pinned her hard against his body until her face was muffled between his shoulder blades. Tense and ready to spring, he stood between her and whoever had walked into her lab unannounced. The man was so still, the play of muscle on his back was the only movement.

Too short to look over his shoulder, Carin tapped his forearm. He relaxed just enough for her to wiggle free of his hold.

She stepped around him and nervously straightened her already straight lab coat. One glimpse of his face had her struggling between the urge to draw back in amazement or let her own hackles rise and make it known that she ran the show around here.

Bix's lips were drawn tight into hard lines and the hazel-gray of his eyes glinted through narrowed slits. He was a predator ready to pounce, a contradiction of the demanding but tender man who'd been kissing her mere seconds before.

The tech at the door backed up two steps. Her gaze traveled from Carin to the tall, menacing man and her eyebrows rose in comprehension.

"Sorry, Dr. Carin, the door was open, and, uh... Sorry, I should have knocked anyway."

"No worries, Shell." She smiled sheepishly at the lab technician. Great, now she was blushing like a schoolgirl who'd just been caught making out with her first boy. What had she been thinking, kissing her project coordinator? Let alone kissing him in a lab with an open door, knowing the quality techs ran in and out all day. The answer—she hadn't been thinking at all. She'd been feeling. The last time she'd done such a thing was...well, in Colorado when he'd kissed her good night outside her hotel room. Okay, no more kissing in the lab. In fact, she was supposed to be mad at him, so no more kissing period.

"Now wait just a minute. You can't just cut me off now," he protested into her mind as his neck snapped sideways to look down into her face. *"Are you fucking kidding me?"*

"Who the hell are you cussing at, damn it? And will you frickin' get out of my head, Bix?"

Lifting his hand, he smoothed a bit of smeared lip gloss off her bottom lip. With a cheeky grin, his tone smooth as ice, he promised, "I'll check in on you later, Carin." Turning away, he moved slowly towards the door.

She wanted to cut him off? When they'd just found each other she thought she'd nip him in the bud? Carin had a lot to learn about how much a prime male would take from his mate. May as well start her lessons now.

On his way to the door, he sent her a few private thoughts. A triumphant grin spread across his lips at her swift intake of breath. In his mind he imagined a warm caress beginning at the top of her head, then sent the heat simmering down each individual bone of her spine until he'd weaved a smoldering trail all the way to her little toes. Bix filled her head with thoughts of what he'd have from her in addition to such sweet kisses. And those thoughts were deliberately nasty.

A backward glance revealed a wavering smile plastered on her face as the lab tech handed her a clipboard. The pen moved shakily across it. He wondered if she had any idea what she was signing. But he heard her clear enough.

"Oh Lord, how do you do that?" she wailed, shifting her weight from one foot to the other.

"Same way you can, sweetheart. Like this." The thoughts he bombarded her with transformed into images. Naked, sweaty, straining images.

She blushed a deep shade of caramel. He was sure the space between her legs was growing moist and her panties getting a bit uncomfortable. All in the space of a few seconds.

"Oh good gracious. Oh, my God. This is so *not fair,"* she protested hotly.

"I know, sweetheart, but I don't play fair." He looked back just long enough to wink, then disappeared out the door and down the hall.

"Dr. Carin, you all right?"

"Uh, yeah. Sorry, Shell. What?" Okay, not only did she feel on horny-toad overload, she sounded like she'd had crack for breakfast. Damned man.

"Where do you want me to put these?"

"Huh?"

"The DNA results from the samples you submitted before you went out of town. You just signed for them, but where do you want me to put them?"

Carin absently pointed to her desk, thanked the studious lab tech and hustled over to the sink to wash her hands. Warm water splashed over her fingers as she stood weak-kneed with every thought on Bix and the soul-searing kiss he'd laid on her, among other things. And he had psychic powers, very strong, very kinky ones. She'd never met anyone like herself, someone with those kinds of abilities, but for some reason she wasn't shocked to learn he had such talents. And boy did he know how to use them.

She moved away from the basin and the automatic water spigot turned off as she strode towards her private bathroom. She'd look at the test results later. Right now she needed a shower. An arctic cold one.

ဆဆ

Bix strode out of Carin's lab smiling wickedly. He'd been a bad vamp, sending his thoughts, feelings and images into her brain with such intensity. But since he realized what she was to him, he felt entitled to let her know just how much he wanted to get next to her skin.

But first he had a rogue to catch.

He'd sensed another vamp on this floor when he and Carin had gotten off the elevator. The presence had been strongest near her door. Earlier while scouting the facility he'd also picked up and followed the trail of several other vampires. None of them matched Sidheon's description.

The territory leaders and local Seekers were notified ahead of time and expected Alaan and him in their city for a hunting expedition, but he didn't want the information to get to anyone else. Especially someone who might be in league with Sidheon. Since every territory and region had Seekers, he and his partner wouldn't stand out too much, but there was one small problem—Natasha's intel made no mention of other vamps working inside this particular biotech company. His brow furrowed as he wondered what else he didn't know.

Once out of the building he glanced down at his watch and picked up his pace. Damn, it was hot. He tugged at the band collar of his specially cut, jet black, leather trench. He loved his coat, the symbol of his hard-earned status as a Seeker. But it was still made of leather; more precisely, made-for-Montana-winters leather. Not ideal for walking briskly in seventy-degrees under clear skies and unimpeded sunshine. He unzipped the long coat to the waist and dug around in the inner breast pocket until his fingers wrapped around his favorite candies, a wireless earpiece and a neatly folded handkerchief. Unwrapping a couple of watermelon Jolly Ranchers, he popped them in his mouth, then mopped his brow with the hankie.

With the earpiece in place, he spoke quietly into it, "Dial Serati." A few seconds later, Alaan responded on the other end of the line.

"Damn, Alaan, you sound like Barry White," Bix chided.

"Yeah, and I'll kick your ass while singing like Barry White, too," Alaan quipped at Bix's wry humor. The man hated Barry White jokes. The platinum blond, curly-haired, six and a half foot, lean fighting machine's voice just didn't match his fair god-like looks. Someone was bound to throw a "deep voice" joke his way at least once a day. But Bix knew he was the only one who got away with it.

"Keep dreaming, beautiful," Bix snorted back. "I'm walking out in back of Building A7. Where are you?"

"Two blocks west, top level of a public parking structure. Got a clear view of Idac's rear entrances. I can see you from here. On the way."

Bix heard the engine of their big SUV roar to life through his earpiece. A few minutes and a few streets later Alaan picked him up in an alley and the two Seekers headed down Mission Blvd.

"What's going on, Bix?"

"Not sure yet," he said, his tone serious as he peeled off his trench coat. He tossed it into the backseat, accepted a cold bottle of water from his partner and downed all twenty ounces in five big swallows. He repositioned one of the overhead vents and leaned his head back. Boy, was he ever appreciative of air-conditioning.

Eyes closed, enjoying the cold air blasting directly into his face, he asked, "Did anyone by chance mention there were other vamps hanging out in this camp?"

"No," Alaan responded thoughtfully. "I spotted a few going in and out while you were reacquainting with your target. No sign of Sidheon yet."

"We knew Carin could get us close to Sidheon, but it turns out the bastard's lab is right next to hers. I didn't spot him the entire time I was in the building. This whole situation concerns me big time. I expected to see other vampires in town, but not this many working in one building. We have no idea where their allegiance lies. Call Natasha. See what you can get out of her."

"Done."

The SUV screeched to a halt in a seedy part of town that anyone with good sense would avoid even in broad daylight. Not wanting to be easily recognized as a Seeker down here, Bix left his trench in the backseat and hopped out.

Both men automatically raised their watches and synched up. "Rendezvous at the intersection of La Jolla and Turquoise around six o'clock?" Alaan asked seriously.

"Works for me. Later, Barry." Bix heard a deep *"Kiss my ass"* echo through his mind, and chuckled as he took off walking down the street to check out another lead on Sidheon.

Chapter Five

Carin had conducted a number of quality-control tests over the past several months. The results had been consistent, though less than desirable. Now, they were all skewed, almost the exact opposite of what they'd been before. What the hell was going on?

Before, the serum had made the skin cells resistant to the viruses introduced to them. In fact, after the initial mutation each virus had been unsuccessful in penetrating the skin cells at all, dying within seven days. It had been several days longer than she'd hoped for, but the cells were left healthy and whole. Now, the exact same virus was actually hijacking the cell signals causing infection to occur within hours.

She returned the vial to the specimen cart when something about the contents of the cart caught her eye. There was no name on the side to identify it and the labeling on the vials was inconsistent with her coding system. These weren't her specimens.

Curious as to what she'd stumbled onto, she retrieved three vials from the cart. One held what looked like skin samples, labeled discreetly on the bottom with a small v. The second vial contained a viscous liquid. Except for the slight purple tint, it looked exactly like her serum. The third vial was clearly blood. But whose, she had no idea.

With a v-skin sample secured on a glass slide, she placed a single drop of whatever the purple-tinted liquid was on top of it. Upping the power on her microscope to cellular magnification, she put her eye to the eyepiece.

Holy shit, the tissue cells were changing. But changing into what? After a few seconds she noted the color of the tissue as a pale pink. After two minutes, a strange, dead-looking gray. At five minutes the tissue was charcoal black with the consistency of ash. It was dead.

Running over to the small refrigerator tucked in the corner of the huge lab, she carefully retrieved a petri dish with several samples of skin taken from her own scalp. The purple-tinted serum didn't do anything to her skin. After five minutes, the sample looked no different than it had when she'd put it on the slide. So what was the difference between her skin and the one in the vials from the specimen cart?

She slipped a sterile pair of tweezers into the mystery vial and retrieved more skin. Her brows drew together against the lens of the microscope's eyepiece. What the hell kind of skin was this? To the naked eye, the mystery sample looked to have the same properties as her own, except her skin was darker. But under the microscope, the molecular structure was different. The v-skin was denser, stronger somehow. Perhaps it wasn't human skin at all? Maybe from some kind of animal?

Noting the difference between the skin cells and the destructive power of the tinted serum on the mystery skin, she was curious what the blood would do. She put a single drop on the glass slide with her own skin, and a single drop on a second slide with the v-skin. She pulled back from the microscope, shaking her head. If she was puzzled before, she was stumped now.

The blood didn't affect the v-skin at all, but the results on her skin were nothing short of miraculous. Her skin had changed and the cells multiplied. The dry sample was now more elastic and healthy looking. Her final note in her notebook reflected the results.

The sample of my skin is not only more healthy looking, it actually appears to be younger, stronger and more resistant to stress and viral activity. The molecular structure of my sample skin now mirrors the v-skin. It is dense and not easily punctured. When a virus was introduced to my modified skin, it was unable to penetrate. The blood had regenerative effects on my skin, but was not effective on the v-skin.

In short, the test results from the blood were close to the tests she'd run with her experimental serum, only the blood worked better. How in the world did this mystery blood work better than her synthetic serum? No human had blood like this.

She nicked some of the skin, purple liquid and blood, and stashed them in a refrigerated safe. With everything else back in the trays and boxes exactly the way she found them, the cart was returned to its spot next to the lab door. The skin on the back of her neck pebbled as the sixth sense she'd never quite understood kicked into high alert. Someone was coming.

Hurrying across the lab to the nearest stainless steel worktable, Carin hopped up on a stool and had just put pen to paper when a knock sounded on the steel door right before it opened.

Carin looked up and almost cringed. Dr. Aleth Sidheon stood in her door. The man was sinfully good looking, but boy did he make her skin crawl. He'd never said more than a passing hello and was always strictly professional in his dealings with her, but something about him creeped her out. He was tall and lean, not as tall as Bix, and certainly not as muscular. Where Sidheon was almost platinum blond and pretty, Bix's hair was the blackest black and his features rugged. Sidheon's eyes were a bright vivid blue and his skin looked like he'd never seen the sun in his life. Bix was golden-skinned and golden-eyed with mysterious, sexy streaks of silvery gray.

Hold up. Why in the world was she sitting here comparing Sidheon to Bix? *Girl, get it together and deal with the man standing in front of you.* She painted on a sugary smile and motioned for him to come on in. Wanting to get back to whatever was on the specimen cart, she really wished he would just go away. Boy did his timing suck.

"Hi, Aleth," she said in the friendliest tone she could muster.

"Hello, Dr. Derrickson. How was your trip to Colorado?"

"It was cold. Training was good, though. What can I do for you, Aleth?"

"My assistant misplaced my specimen cart. Do you mind if I check yours to see if you received mine by mistake?"

She motioned to the cart she'd just wheeled over to the door. "Sure have at it. I had time to take a few of the specimens out, only to put them all back again." She watched his face tighten almost imperceptibly, and went on chatting. "I'm so far behind, Aleth. Haven't had time to analyze anything. A new program coordinator showed up this morning and I've been trying to get him up to speed."

"New program coordinator?" Sidheon asked.

"Yeah, some guy from Venture Pharma Biotech Capital is here. He's taking over one of Charles' projects while he gets the new plant up and running in Puerto Rico."

"How many projects is this new person going to oversee?"

"So far, just mine. Venture has a large stake in the new cancer drug I'm developing."

Carin almost breathed a sigh of relief when Sidheon's brow cleared and a small smile appeared across his thin lips. Something told her to be very careful with him.

"Do we know anything about this Venture Pharma person? Like his name?"

His voice was just a bit too syrupy for Carin's taste. She knew a snow job when she heard it. After all, she was delivering one herself.

"Oh, I guess it is a he, isn't it?" Along came her smoothest impression of a scatterbrained scientist. The man was fishing. Fine, he'd come up with nothing on the hook. Her words somewhat breathy, she said, "Let me think, what was his name?" She tapped her pen against her chin and looked towards the ceiling. "Geez, I can't remember. Give me a minute and I'll think of it, I'm sure." She instinctively cleared her mind of thought, looked ridiculously distracted and went back to writing in her notebook. All he got out of her was an occasional absent-sounding "Hmmm" and "interesting" followed by a "What was I doing again?"

She could feel Sidheon's patience begin to run thin when it became obvious she wasn't going to elaborate on this new addition to the staff.

With an annoyed huff, he asked, "Do you mind if I have a look at the specimens?"

Carin raised her head, her expression clear and bright. "I'm sorry, what did you say, Aleth?"

"I asked if I could take a look at—"

She cut him off with a wave of her hand. "Oh sure, sure. It's all yours." She went back to writing, then said as an afterthought, "Actually, if you want, just go ahead and take it. I won't get to it before tomorrow afternoon anyway. If it's not yours, leave it in the hall. The QC lab folks will come and get it, and maybe we'll both find our stuff in the process."

"Excellent suggestion. Thank you very much, Dr. Derrickson."

"Please, Aleth, when are you going to start calling me Carinian?" she chimed, her expression as sweet and as syrupy as his voice had been moments before.

A knock sounded on the open door. Carin glanced up and flashed a genuine smile to one of the QC lab techs. Reyna was a sweet girl, fresh out of college. Short with reddish-brown hair, creamy fair skin and a nose dotted with an abundance of freckles, Carin thought she looked a lot like Heidi with a haircut.

"Hi, Reyna. Come on in."

"Hi, Dr. Derrickson. Dr. Sidheon," she said with a polite nod. "We left the QC carts in the hall as we always do, but somehow they got all mixed up. Dr. Lee brought this one back downstairs to us. It looks like it belongs to you, ma'am."

"Thanks, Reyna. Just put it over there." She motioned to the spot next to the door where Sidheon's cart had been sitting.

"Sorry for the mix up, doctors."

Carin replied with a gracious, "No problem."

Sidheon looked at the girl like she was a complete moron and said nothing. Instead, he smiled tightly, wheeled his cart out into the hallway, and disappeared.

Reyna twisted up her mouth and snapped in disgust, "Well, don't some of us think we're all that?"

Carin smiled, let out a sigh of relief at his departure and went back to work as Reyna closed the door on her way out.

After a few moments of unease, she got up and threw the deadbolt home.

ꕤ

Sidheon chuckled all the way to his own rooms, locked the door and began checking the contents of his spec cart.

The good doctor had always been friendly, though somewhat cool towards him. Now he knew why since Dr. Derrickson wasn't very good at hiding her thoughts. She'd projected them so loudly, even a young, untrained vampire could have picked them up before she'd cleared her mind and tried to play dumb on him.

Sidheon had suspected there was some latent psychic talent there, but he couldn't recall any time when she'd blasted her thoughts out in a torrent like she had today. She was obviously shaken by something, and her anxiousness magnified her psychic abilities. Luckily she had no idea or he wouldn't have learned of her wariness of him. He wasn't offended, but rather impressed. Carin was a smart woman not to trust him.

Based on the cheesy explanation she'd given for handling his vials, it made sense for her scent to be all over the little glass containers. Made perfect sense, in fact. Would have even been believable if she hadn't been so worried about getting caught.

And now she posed a problem. It wouldn't take Carinian Derrickson much time to figure out how the serum and blood affected the skin samples. But if she figured out both the blood and skin came from his body, and neither specimen was human, he'd have a mess on his hands.

For all he knew, she could be working with the tall man he'd spotted entering her labs earlier. She'd claimed he was a new project coordinator, but Sidheon had immediately sensed the man was a prime male vampire. Damn it all to hell and back. He couldn't afford to have Carinian spill what she knew. Especially not to a fucking Council assassin.

After each glass vial was secured in the safe, he pulled out his cell phone and dialed.

"I've found the cart, you imbecile. But there's a mess you're going to clean up."

The voice on the other end of the line ratcheted up a few octaves. "What? Why? If you found it then there's no need to—"

"Shut up, you idiot," Sidheon growled into the phone. He clamped his thumb and forefinger over the bridge of his nose and sighed. He would never understand how such a brilliant biochemist like Dan could lack the most common sense. "There *is* a need, and since you lost it in the first place you're going to take care of it. Do you understand me, Dan?"

A long silence followed. His ridiculous assistant was all ears.

"Dr. Derrickson had the cart. I want you to make sure she doesn't have a chance to tell anyone what was in it," Sidheon said, his tone somewhere between bored and condescending.

"But why—"

"Because, there's a prime male vamp on the biotech campus I've never seen before. The same vamp happened to be in Dr. Carinian's labs today. Any further questions?"

"No, sir. I'll take care of it, sir."

"You'd better, Dan, or you'll be my next biotech experiment."

Chapter Six

Carin's plan was to stick around this big blue ball they called Earth for as long as she could, not die at an early age like all the rest of her family. Not only did she plan to enjoy life well past ninety, she wanted to be here until she met up with Jean Luc Picard and the Starship Enterprise. Hell, she wanted Jean Luc to play a song on his flute for her, then take her on a romantic interlude on the holodeck. And after she'd screwed Jean Luc's brains out, she'd dump him for Commander Data.

Who the hell wanted to die? Nobody in their right mind actually looked forward to the day when they discovered what it was like to slip from this life into...into what? Most people believed death was a great step into the beyond, a step we all must take. Carin didn't agree. As far as she was concerned, death was overrated.

Her grandmother had succumbed to a flesh-eating disease at age sixty-two, her mother to lung cancer at forty-seven. Her sister died at thirty-nine from a freak blood clot that developed in her leg on a long flight and traveled up to a major artery to block it. Carin had no grandparents, no parents, no aunts or uncles. No one. The thought of loving someone just to lose them overwhelmed her with a grief too profound for words. Every person close or important to her had been taken one way or another.

As tired as she was, Carin forced herself to keep working. She would find a way to become something other than destined-to-die-young if it killed her. A type of vampirism seemed to be the best option, and she was close.

Although something inside of her reached out for Bix, trusted him, he would never understand her reasons for secretly tampering with her own genes. He'd probably tell his superiors on her, like anyone else in their right mind would. But she couldn't let that happen, couldn't afford to lose her job, her reputation, and most importantly, access to the lab. Her secret had remained safe for years and it would stay that way. Connection, attraction, or not, Mr. Bix would remain in the dark along with everyone else. Now, if she could just get her thoughts off the man and under control before she let something slip.

She was on the verge of a breakthrough when her cell phone rang. Whoever it was had shitty timing. Snatching it off the lab table, she flipped it open without bothering to check the caller ID.

"Derrickson here," she said shortly, shifting the phone from one ear to the other.

"Hi, sweetheart."

Sweetheart? Ooooh, yummy. Bix's sexy voice floated through the earpiece and made its way down her body. She glanced at the ceiling as her stomach danced with a mix of longing and annoyance. Hadn't she just seen him this morning, and not under the best of circumstances? The bastard was her project coordinator and would be snooping around her lab. She didn't like the idea one bit, so why was she so damned happy to hear his voice? The grin melted off her face and she rolled her eyes on an impatient sigh.

"What do you want, Bix? I'm kind of busy here."

"You working late?" he asked.

"I'm always working late," Carin said absentmindedly as she reached for yet another notebook to place the results of the improving tissue and serum tests.

"Great, I picked up some dinner. I'll bring it over."

"Wait..."

"Be there in half an hour."

"But, Bix..." The line went dead. Damned man. She didn't have time for this right now. She catapulted out of the chair and grabbed onto the edge of her heavy wood desk as her stomach went one way while her head went the other. Lord, she was dizzy. Perhaps eating would be a good idea after all considering it was now evening and she hadn't bothered to take a proper lunch. She made her way across the room, loaded her arms with beakers and glass containers, and moved to one of the large sinks. Her hands in a pair of non-latex gloves, she wiggled her fingers in front of the sensor to get the hot water running and started giggling. Bix was coming over. She couldn't wait to see him. No, wait, that wasn't right. One minute she was glad to see the man, the next she wanted to stick him in the ass with a pitchfork. Yep, she was definitely working too hard. And definitely horny, er, hungry. For food, damn it.

৪৩০৪৪

Bix eased open the door to Carin's lab, made his way to a table off to the side of her work area, and watched her jot notes into a thick notepad. After looking into the microscope, she rolled her eyes up to the ceiling with a loud, frustrated grumble. Rubbing her temples, she muttered to herself before taking more notes.

Concentrating on whatever was under the microscope, she screwed up her face into a fierce frown. She peered harder at the specimen as if her gaze could make the anomaly correct itself. He could tell, no, could *feel*, she was at a total loss.

"What am I doing wrong? I've modified this blasted serum twenty times already."

She huffed out a frustrated breath and pushed away from the lab table, taking her temper out on the top of the stainless steel surface. Cursing, his little hellion smacked it loudly with the flat of her hand. He smiled as she rubbed her palm on a wince, stood abruptly and turned to retrieve a new sample from the specimen cart beside her.

She almost ran smack into him.

"Damn it, Bix, will you please stop moving around here like a damned cat? You scared me half to death," she growled, reaching past him to get the vial she was after.

"Sorry, sweetheart." But he knew his grin told another story. Her little show of temper amused him, but she didn't look like she'd appreciate knowing that right now.

Bix's eyebrows inched up as he listened to her speak into a little digital voice recorder. What the hell was the woman up to?

"Skin cell sample has stabilized. Collagen and melanin content increased significantly, which is good. Toxins in fat cells underneath the skin decreased. Before application of serum, vitamin D level was normal. After application, absence of vitamin D occurs and affects the epithelial layer."

She barely looked up when he set an assortment of plastic bags filled with containers on one of the cleared lab tables. He'd selected something he hoped would appeal to her senses and was pleased when he heard her stomach growl. But she didn't budge from her stool, determined to figure out whatever was puzzling her.

Bix let her work while he removed paper plates, napkins, cups and plastic forks out of one of the bags and made a place setting for both of them. Cups were filled with cold cranberry juice and several take-out boxes were arranged in the middle of the table. A couple of Bunsen burners rummaged from one of the supply cabinets took the place of candles.

He turned and watched her hand make its way to the small of her back to massage the tense muscles there. All the while, her eyes remained plastered to the microscope lens as her fingers worked their way into the hollow of her spine, just above the curve of her ass. His gaze dropped to that sensual slope where toned thighs gripped the stool she sat on. His mouth started to water.

Carin had no idea how long he'd actually been tailing her, and he'd sure as hell make sure she never found out. Every night since she'd become his target, he'd done nothing but dream about those legs wrapped around his waist as he buried his dick deep in her body. His mind was constantly filled with the thought of Carin's smooth, warm flesh glowing sweetly as she lay in front of the fireplace in his home, her hair in a wild tangle as she rode him hard, taking him fully inside her tight heat.

He'd enjoyed kissing her, but knew when they finally made love it would be mind-blowing. And they would indeed make love. Addicting, hot and fulfilling love. Before he could stop himself, his legs carried him across the room to stand right behind her tall metal stool.

His fingers found several knots in both her shoulders and the tender muscles stretched tight from her neck to the base of her skull. She sighed with pleasure, lifted her eyes away from the microscope and let her head fall forward as Bix worked on her. The breathy quality of her moans wrapped around his cock and squeezed. He shifted uncomfortably as his swelling flesh strained against the zipper of his pants. *Resistance is futile*, he thought, leaning forward to bury his nose in her hair where the clean scents of rosemary and peppermint made his cock jump. So much for dinner. He needed more than a nice meal right now. He needed some hot, wet woman. This one in particular.

"Carin?" he breathed harshly, his fingers still digging into her neck muscles.

"Mmmm?" she responded lethargically, not bothering to look up.

"Is there any tape around here?"

"On the desk over there." She motioned lazily across the room. A smile inched up one side of his mouth when she groaned at the departure of his talented fingers from her tired muscles.

With a roll of tape and a piece of paper he covered up the small window on the lab door, slid the deadbolt home and returned to the delicious sight of Carin, legs spread on her stool, eyes closed with her chin on her chest. His fingers eased back to her shoulders and kneaded the flesh there.

He was unworthy of her trust, knew she had no idea why he was really here in San Diego. But when she shrugged out of her lab coat and let it fall to the floor, his strength of will flew out the nearest window. He couldn't have forced himself away from her tempting body if he'd wanted to. Carin's pristine white jacket pooled on top of his boots, and when she leaned her head to the side, baring her neck to him, a long, deep groan rippled down from his chest and vibrated a path to the underside of his balls. Damn, he was toast.

He let his thoughts run free, not bothering with any shields or precautions. Instead he wanted her to understand, to see and feel how much he longed to strip off her blouse so he could tease her bare skin. Her breath hitched when his fingers teased her throat then moved to unbutton her top. The blouse joined the lab coat on the floor and his heightened senses felt her body infuse with heat as his head dipped forward over her shoulder so his lips could travel across the length of her collarbone. She reached back and buried her hands in his hair. His head moved in an erotic dance as his chin pressed into the stiff, sore muscles of her neck between erotic nips and kisses.

The scent of her body wafted up to tickle his nose and her blood called to him. His tongue flicked out to taste and tease her sensitive skin, and her passion blossomed under his knowing touch. Quiet sighs a thing of the past, she moaned constantly now, her back pressed tight against his chest as he nibbled and sucked all the little erogenous zones on her neck and shoulders. His hands roamed at will and pleasure pooled deep in his loins when her tight abs jumped and fluttered under the pads of his fingers. Pleasure-pain caused his eyes to drift closed when her hands tightened at his scalp and pulled his mouth more firmly against her neck. Her flesh was sweet, smooth, like the richest chocolate.

Her pebbled nipples reached out to him as he explored her lush body. He wasn't sure where he got the ability to hesitate, but hesitate he did. Even when Carin's hips squirmed on the edge of her lab stool and her sweet faint moans became needy whimpers, he wouldn't touch her breasts. Suddenly the act of touching a woman there had never seemed more intimate. He wanted to brand her, mark her, but he needed something else first. Something he'd always assumed with every other female.

"I need your permission, sweetheart."

"You have it. Please...please touch me." She guided his palm away from her stomach and up to her swollen, tempting breasts. Caught up in the escalating pleasure as deeply as Bix, she hadn't even flinched at communicating psychically.

"You're going to be mine, baby. After this, you're mine alone."

"Mmmm, yes," she purred as he turned her around on her stool to face him.

Bix eased Carin's knees open and stepped between them. He lifted her from the stool and groaned when her legs automatically encircled his waist. He walked with her hot core centered directly over his throbbing erection all the way to the back of the lab to the door she hadn't bothered to open for him earlier.

Bix pressed her hard up against the door, taking her mouth in a brutal kiss until she gasped and squirmed in his arms. Her desperate plea echoed in his head when he set her to the floor on shaky legs.

"Don't you dare let me fall on my ass."

Her telepathic words were as shaky as the fingers trying to fit the key into the lock. While she frantically searched for the correct one he lowered his lips with one thought in mind—drive her insane with desire. He caressed the full globes of her ass and she empathically reached for him with a longing so openly wild it made total chaos of any remaining sanity. By the time she got the lock open, he wanted nothing more than to run to the bed, strip her bare and spread her wide.

He crowded her inside, closed and locked the door behind them. She moved around the small room, flipped on a couple of soft lamps, and pulled the covers back on the bed. And he was on her heels every step of the way. Never stopped touching her. Never stopped stroking her. He just couldn't help himself. Her body and soul enchanted him. Her blood called to his with such strength, it scalded his veins as it pumped through his body, craving to mix with hers.

Bix tortured himself by slowly stripping her where she stood. Very slowly. Every bit of skin he exposed made him swallow convulsively. Every moan and intake of breath was precious to him. She was projecting her emotions again. He was glad to know she'd pushed aside any anger at his unexpected arrival, or apprehension about his special abilities, and given in to her need. Her need to be filled, to be taken...to be loved? No, she still fought that one. But he was a patient man.

With an arm under her knees, Bix lifted her up against his chest. Her fingers eased under his coat and slid over the muscles covered by his white silk shirt. His skin caught fire. Bix didn't miss the wicked gleam in her eye nor the self-satisfied smile when his pec muscles jumped and twitched under her touch. Eyes on Carin, he tossed her into the middle of the bed with a bounce, sending several of the plump pillows flying. He unlaced and toed off his boots without ever taking his gaze off her, allowing his burning need to zing from his eyes to hers with laser accuracy. Carin stretched and preened while he watched her rub her bare arms and legs against the bedding. Mmm, he couldn't wait to get his hands on her.

He growled like the hunter he was when Carin went still as a statue, her full attention on the movement of his fingers as the black leather trench dropped to the dark blue carpet in a pile. Button by button, his shirt parted to reveal more and more of his body. His golden skin glowed in the dim light, and she couldn't seem to tear her gaze away from the muscles bunching and releasing with each movement. The shirt was laid neatly at the foot of the bed before he turned to let her look her fill.

He ran his hands over his flushed skin, tweaked his own nipples, and licked his lips while he pinned her with a sensual stare. The man was such a tease, but a beautiful tease. His chest was baby smooth, with not even a light sprinkling of hair.

God how she wanted to feel that skin, stretched over such perfectly developed muscles, sliding against hers. And he was moving too damned slow. Carin sighed with relief when he finally unbuckled his belt, followed by the button and zipper holding his trousers closed. He spread the top of his pants, buried his hand inside and stroked himself, keeping his silver-streaked eyes on her face.

Carin held her breath as the garment was pushed over his trim waist, down his powerful legs to settle on the floor. A nice-fitting pair of black silk boxers was left behind. The guy obviously liked black. She couldn't blame him, he looked damned good in it. Ooh, he had such a tight ass. Taut and perfectly rounded. And his legs were to die for. Legs even a woman would be jealous of. They were heavily muscled, smooth and lightly tanned, just like the rest of him.

His boxers hit the floor and Carin gulped. Oh my GOD. Her heart rate had been beyond elevated the moment he kissed her, but it was nothing compared to the thrumming in her chest at the sight of Bix's impressive cock. Thick, ridged with veins and pulsing with a life of its own, it was so hard and long it tapped against the planes of his stomach. Despite being concerned about his girth, Carin's mouth watered at the thought of what he tasted like. Soaking wet, she wondered for a second if her pussy and her mouth were having some kind of contest to see which could get wetter the fastest. Again, his hands found his stiff rod and stroked. She moaned as his thoughts pushed into her mind and her head filled with the pleasure he felt as his hand moved up and down his hardness.

He released his cock and Carin watched it bob up and down as he approached the bed. His movements were sinuous and sleek. Oh Lord, he was doing the predator thing, and it was so damned sexy she stayed there on her back, lifted her legs up in the air and purred like a lioness in heat. He kneeled between her thighs on all fours, and leaned down to take her mouth in a wild openmouthed kiss that left her panting and hungry.

She shivered from the inside out when Bix lowered his head and feasted on the underside of her breasts, nudging the full globes with his chin and nose, taking in her scent as he moved over her body. Carin arched against his mouth, fingers tangled in his thick midnight hair. She wanted him to gobble her up. To take every bit of her into himself. Never in her life had she wanted to be devoured like she wanted it right now.

Bix cherished every moan, every shudder. Her reaction to his touch overwhelmed him. He could hear her, smell her, *feel* her. And it made the tasting that much more acute, deep. He loved knowing how much she wanted his hands, mouth and tongue all over her. Focusing on her breast, wrapping his lips around the crown, he pulled it deep into the heat of his mouth. After one taste, he was like a starving man. Couldn't get enough of her sweet Hershey's Kiss nipples.

While he licked, tasted and lavished attention on her swollen, full globes, Bix rubbed the head of his throbbing cock against the slick, pink folds of her pussy. He shook with his own need, but no matter how great his want, her pleasure came first. As his mate, it would always be this way.

As gently as he was able, he slid the sensitive head into her creaming opening. She was amazingly tight. The feeling of her honeyed walls squeezing him was exquisite and sent his senses reeling. The sound of her aroused panting inflamed his own desire as he pushed slowly into her hot, warm sheath, inch by torturous inch.

The sleek caress of her sheath told him she hadn't given herself to many men. Hell, she gripped him so hard if not for the absence of a hymen, he would have thought she was a virgin. Well, he might not be the first to take her, but damn it, he would be the last. The feelings of possessiveness and desire were headier than any he could remember in all his long years. Her smooth, cinnamon thighs were spread wide in invitation when her body suddenly stiffened beneath him. Bix looked down at her face and froze.

Her eyes were squeezed shut and he could feel her warring with herself, trying not to tense. There was no true pain, but she projected a slight stinging sensation as her body stretched to accommodate him. He knew he was a large man and a distraction was probably a good idea right about now.

His lips moved softly over hers, then over her ear, coaxing her out of her fear with words so erotic she blushed.

"Carin, you taste so good. I love the sweet heady scent of your pussy. It calls to me, begs me to sink my tongue inside and feast on your dewy center. God, I want you so bad, baby, I can barely control myself."

When he returned to her mouth he dove right in and kissed the care right out of her head. The tickle of his teeth scraping back and forth along the sweat-slickened skin of her throat caused a delicious shiver to work its way through her body and infuse into his.

He barely managed to maintain control over his body, but his fangs? Hell, there was no controlling them at all. They just plain wouldn't listen to him and extended with a mind of their own. He hoped she wouldn't notice the sharp incisors, because heaven help him, he couldn't stop now. He felt her wonder at the pleasure-pain of the little scratches and revel in the ripples of pleasure they sent down her spine. Pleasure she wanted to experience again and again.

"Is he...biting me? Mmm, I like it."

The second he heard those thoughts form in her head, Bix obliged and let his fangs scrape lightly across the column of her neck. Questing fingers slipped down to play in the close-cropped curls of her mound, then after a few torturous moments, drifted lower to skim over and around her clit. There was no ability to think at all now. The shared rush built and hummed, sending a blush from the cheeks of her face clear down to the cheeks of her ass.

Bix chose that moment to push fully inside and settle to the hilt. The slick walls of her sheath were agonizingly tight around his hard cock. The pressure was exquisite, squeezing him on all sides of his staff until the blood pulsed through the veins twined around it. He gritted his teeth and forced his body to remain still to allow her a moment to get used to his girth.

"Oh yes, this is what I want," she crooned silently. His woman wanted to be full to bursting with his cock. To be well and truly sexed. Done up, done right. Heat ravaged his body where their skin touched, where he filled her. Shaking with urgency, Carin gasped roughly against his throat, pressing steamy, openmouthed kisses against his Adam's apple as Bix swallowed convulsively. But the little knot at his throat was the only thing moving.

"Bix," she whispered against his skin, holding him tight, her arms and legs wrapped around his taut body. "Oh, Bix. Baby, please."

He didn't reply. Couldn't form the words against the barrage of sensation traveling from his cock to his brain, down to his toes and back. God, she felt so good stretched around his straining erection. His body was tense, every muscle tight. Sweat ran down the sides of his face to weave a trail of moisture down his neck and chest. The rocks of his biceps trembled with the effort of staying still. But he would cut off his arm before he hurt Carin.

"Damn it, Bix. Move, please."

Instead he pressed his lips together and ground his back teeth.

"Lord, if you didn't move soon I'll blow a gasket," she yelled this time, urging him to stroke deep inside her body. Instead, he let her feel his need, his urgency, and the iron grip he exerted over himself to make sure this was enjoyable for her. She needed to understand how much her pleasure meant to him.

Strong, warm fingers caressed his bulging arms and up to the solid, flexing pecs of his chest. Her fingers left little patterns in the sweat pouring over his skin. She pulled him down to her until her nipples stabbed into his chest, sending a jolt of pleasure through his entire torso. Suddenly, Carin stretched up as much as she was able and sank her teeth into his neck where the thick muscles met his shoulder.

The second she clamped down on his neck a shaken growl made its way out of his throat and he threw his head back on a loud yell. Something primitive, primal snapped and sent him careening over the edge. She didn't have the apparatus to pierce his skin, but the sensation of her biting, licking and sucking him in that sacred spot made him hotter 'n hell. So hot, the beads of moisture on his skin threatened to sizzle and steam like drops of water tossed into an overheated dry skillet. He couldn't have kept still a second longer if she'd begged him to.

He eased his throbbing cock slowly out of her, then slammed home. Her cries of pleasure pulled hard at his already slipping control. Her words were wild, untamed, telling him what she wanted him to do to her, and how hard and long she wanted it. Her body twisted and wrapped around his, gave him pleasure, and took much more. Carin's hips rose to meet his as she tugged and yanked on his hair, spurring him on.

"Harder, Bix," she pleaded, half out of her mind. Her chest heaved, her breathing heavy and labored. "More, baby. Oh, yes, give it to me."

Damn, she was sexy and hot for him. Only for him. How could he not give her what she wanted? Hard, fast, then harder still. One hand held her hip firmly against his groin as he plunged inside. He arched his body and buried his nose between her lovely breasts. The sound of her heart thundering underneath the plump orbs was hypnotic. Her blood. He could smell it, almost taste it. The urge to bite her, to savor the sweet nectar of her body, and then lick her from neck to knees was almost unbearable.

No teeth, no teeth! Oh shit! He clamped his lips closed and tasted blood on his tongue. His blood.

She met him thrust for thrust, pounding against him. Her slick, cream-coated pussy tightened and fluttered, milking him. Taking him. Her sweet channel had a vise grip on his engorged cock. If she squeezed any tighter he'd just give up the ghost and die. Panting out his pleasure, he pushed deeper and felt the ring of her cervix encircle him. His pants became growls. Bix went buck wild. Dominated her in their loving.

"Yes, take me."

He reached down, his finger unerringly finding her thick, sensitive clit. The little bundle of swollen nerves pulsed under his questing fingers. He rubbed, tugged and stroked until she was delirious with pleasure. Until he was more than aware that every muscle between her toes and her head pulled tight, then tighter still as she strained against the pressure of the orgasm building within her core.

The spring snapped and she came on a scream. Bix, his balls drawn up against his body, was right behind her. He exploded in molten release, his thick load rocketing against her womb.

It was an endless loop of built and shattered ecstasy, both physical and psychic. His pleasure streaked through him, slammed into her, and back again, over and over until they were blinded with the sheer joy of it. In all his long years, he couldn't remember anything quite like being with Carin. And he hadn't even taken her blood yet. The thought of what that would be like made him dizzy all over again.

When his eyes regained the ability to focus, Bix just couldn't bear to part with this woman. He rolled with her to one side of the mattress, still planted firmly inside her sweet treasure. The thick comforter at the foot of the bed was pulled over them and they settled into the plump pillows. Even when he could finally make himself pull out of her warm body, Carin remained sprawled on his chest, clinging sweetly to him as he stroked her back and placed light kisses at her temple. Together, they floated in the afterglow of their lovemaking.

After long moments, Bix finally spoke softly against her cooling skin.

"How long have you been psychic?"

"Psychic? I'm not sure if you can call it that," she whispered on a sated sigh.

"There are different types of psychic abilities. Some people can detect thoughts. Others are empathic and can feel other people's emotions. Which one are you?"

"Well"—she yawned—"I've always had a kind of sixth sense. Sometimes I can pick up people's feelings. But until I met you I couldn't hear them speaking in my head. Earlier, when you were leaving the lab you spoke to me in my mind, then ducked out before I could ask you about it. How did you do that?"

Bix didn't answer right away, needing to know a little bit more about where she stood on her abilities. Just because she had them didn't mean she accepted them. "Did anyone ever try to help you develop your ability?"

"Are you kidding? Puh-lease. I learned to keep it quiet, especially growing up. People thought I was weird. By the way, handsome," she crooned, stroking a single finger across a flat male nipple, "you didn't answer my question."

"How did I speak to you in your head? Well, I have a little bit of psychic ability, too." He left out the part about her being able to hear his thoughts because of their newly forming bond.

"But I've never been able to hear anyone's words in my head before, Bix."

He changed the subject. "Why did you bite me?" he asked, dropping a kiss on the side of her face.

"I don't know," she replied quietly, honestly. She tilted her head to the side, pondering, as if she didn't understand it herself. "It just kind of felt right. Is that okay?"

"Baby, you have no idea," he drawled, lowering his mouth to hers. He nibbled on her bottom lip before sucking the plump cherry, then rolled her onto her back and slid home in one smooth stroke. Bix was sure the loving would be easy, slow and tender this time. After all, he'd been sated, right? Wrong. With each slide into Carin's wet folds, a coal-hot spark shot straight from his dick to his fangs. And the more he sank into her body, the more powerful came the need to join with her, to bond mind, body, blood and soul.

He couldn't stay easy and slow with her. His thrusts came faster and harder. The writhing, panting woman with her smooth cocoa legs wrapped around his waist, urging him on didn't help. He looked down to where the skin of her calves brushed against his thigh. The contrast between her beautiful dark skin and his fairer golden hues was stunningly sensual and strongly erotic. Her pussy fluttered around him and her calves pushed into the meat of his ass, pulling him deeper.

"I love it when you lose it inside of me. Come with me, baby," she cried into his thoughts.

And lose it, he did. Taking her just as deep and hard as the first time. She exploded around him, bathed him with her juices as her pussy tightened and flexed so strongly it felt like she would rip off his dick if he pulled out too fast. The woman milked his come right out of his balls until it blasted against her cervix with such intensity his vision blurred.

Damn, would he ever have the strength to leave her lush body? He sure as hell hoped not.

Chapter Seven

Carin awoke in the dark. She stretched, then winced as muscles she'd forgotten were capable of becoming sore protested her movements. She rolled to her side, her hands roaming over the cooling sheets where Bix had lain. His natural masculine scent greeted her, but he did not.

Why had he left her? She couldn't help feeling disappointment at finding him gone. She thought he'd enjoyed their little tryst. She snorted to herself as she sat up and snapped on the lamp. Well apparently not.

She rose, padded out of the bedroom and into the bathroom next door. There, taped to the glass shower stall, was a note. She snatched it down and felt her cheeks heat. Her lips parted in a wide grin as she read it.

Sweetheart,

Had to run out and get some work done on another project. Thank you for a fabulous dinner. I have no regrets that we never got around to eating it. I wrapped everything back up and put it in your little fridge. Enjoy. It's Thai. You're something special. Can't think of a single evening I've enjoyed more in a long, long time. I'll see you again very soon.

Always,

Bix

PS—Charles gave me the spare set of keys to your lab. I made sure I locked up on the way out. Wouldn't do for someone to step in and see all that sweet, beautiful skin of yours.

Boy, does the man have a way with words, she thought as she folded the note and laid it on the small counter next to the equally small sink. She hopped into the shower with a lot more pep in her step. Since he hadn't hit it and run, maybe they could spend time...whoa, stop right there and hold the door. Regardless of the weird connection between them, it was still just sex.

In college there'd been no frat parties, no nights out with the girls, not if she wanted to finish her doctorate early. In between the death of her mother and grandmother she'd foolishly indulged in a disastrous relationship with a womanizing idiot. After a devastating and painful end, she'd given up trying to decipher men and focus on school at the same time. As a result she'd earned her bachelor's in medical science by age twenty and gone on to complete her Master's and PhD, all in less than ten years. All by herself.

A lonely road to say the least, but even now she couldn't afford to get all tooty over the man or try to recapture all the fun she'd let pass her by.

And here she was again with a dilemma—a biological problem to solve and no time to be distracted with a relationship. Maybe they could just have some more good hard sex? Perhaps. But fall for him? No. Or at least that's what she told herself.

There was no way she could afford to put much stock in anything developing between her and Bix. For some reason she felt like she was running out of time on figuring out the shortcomings in her serum. And she still hadn't figured out all the properties of the blood and samples she'd stumbled on in Sidheon's cart.

After a good mental shake and a steaming hot shower, Carin pulled on clean sweats, changed the bedding and stuffed all the dirty laundry into a dry-cleaning bag. The bags and containers full of food packed up, she carried it all to the door, locked up and headed to the gym.

She pushed the fabulous loving Bix had laid on her to the back of her mind, and prepared to throw herself into her workout. Yep, by the time she was done, she'd have forgotten all about her little Lady Chatterley experience. She had it all under control. Well, except for being unable to ignore the sweet ache between her thighs. Damn.

৪୦৫৪

"I can't believe you didn't shower first. I smell her all over you," Alaan quipped.

"What's wrong with that?"

"Are you serious? I'm getting the hard-on from hell just from her scent on you, Bix. That's just wrong, you bastard. What kind of friend are you, anyway?"

Bix had teased his best friend since the day he'd sworn off women two years ago. Alaan used to be quite the lady's vamp, but he'd pretty much cut sex out of his diet altogether. Nobody understood it except Bix. But then Alaan hadn't bothered to explain it to anyone but Bix.

Being a Seeker was dangerous business, and being the mate of a Seeker could be just as risky. Years ago Alaan had found a mate, only to lose her to the well-aimed blade of a rogue he'd been hunting. Now, as the single son of the Matriarch of

Clan Serati, he was one of the most eligible and wealthy bachelors in the western territory. With the number of women who'd claimed to be mated to him, if even half of the stories had been true Alaan would have had his own mega-harem. Plain tired of playing games with the unmated females of the ten clans and their ambitious mamas, he'd cut off every female who wasn't a relative. Two years of no pussy had the poor devil horny as hell. Bix totally understood how Carin's spicy scent affected the man. After all, he'd sported his own semi-hard erection since leaving her asleep in the lab an hour ago.

"It's not my fault you haven't had a woman in two years, Alaan. You're a healthy vamp of breeding age, and no sex? That's just not normal, man," Bix teased unmercifully, flashing an impish grin, fangs and all.

"Oh, shut up," Alaan grumbled at Bix's ribbing while they both tried to rearrange the bulges in their pants. "Damn, this is uncomfortable. Now I can't even leave my trench in the SUV while I tail Sidheon."

"That's for sure. We can't have your dick waving at every female who crosses your path while you're trying to work, now can we?" Bix chuckled as Alaan flipped him the one-fingered salute.

He stopped the vehicle around the corner from a little sushi place where Sidheon was reported to eat several times a week. Alaan hopped out and Bix drove away to a good spot for surveillance. He raised a sleek pair of modified, non-reflective, digital binoculars and positioned them on Alaan as he walked down the street. Seconds later their prey passed him by. Sidheon was right on time.

"All right, there's our man," Bix whispered into his mouthpiece. "You on him?"

"Right behind him." Alaan strolled behind Sidheon. His pace was easy and unhurried, with the occasional stop to peer into a window at some overpriced item or another. Dressed in black jeans, a dark gray fine-gauged wool sweater and the black leather trench coat of a Seeker, Alaan looked like an overdressed tourist window-shopping on the boardwalk. To humans, anyway. To the vamps congregating in the warm night air to enjoy the ocean breeze and the last of an orange-tinted sunset, he looked like a prime male vampire. A Seeker with a fat attitude.

"Why am I doing this again?" Alaan whispered sarcastically.

"Because," Bix replied dryly, "I think the vamp I scented near Carin's door this morning may have been Sidheon. He could have easily spotted me while I was scouting out the building. He wouldn't automatically suspect you since there are other Seekers on the boardwalk, that's why." Bix smiled at Alaan's none-too-subtle snort and popped a couple of watermelon Jolly Rancher candies into his mouth.

Following Alaan's progress from his parking spot down the street, Bix watched his partner stop briefly and clasp hands in respect with two Seekers apparently patrolling the beach. Nodding his thanks when they pointed him to a restaurant that catered to their special needs, Alaan was off again, careful to keep his prey within his sight at all times. After a few uneventful minutes, Alaan walked past his target and stopped at the pre-designated surveillance point. Pretending to study the menu posted on the door, he stepped aside to let Sidheon enter the building.

Alaan's deep voice came through Bix's earpiece. "He's awful pretty looking. You sure Sid's not a woman?"

"If anyone can tell the difference, it's you my friend."

"Kiss my ass, Bix," Alaan hissed into the small flesh-colored mouthpiece barely visible against the side of his face.

"Sorry, handsome. Ass kissing's not possible. I'm taken." Bix chuckled at his partner's deep growling response. "Keep me posted. Bix out."

Alaan crossed the street and grabbed a table at a seafood house directly across from Sid. With schooled features and thoughts, he ordered a glass of red wine and a light dinner. Repulsed that Sidheon even breathed the same air he did, what he really wanted was to walk across the street, pound the shit out of the pasty-faced pretty boy, and truss him up for a trip back to V.C.O.E. headquarters for sentencing. There was nothing he hated worse than a rogue, a vampire excommunicated from clan life for betraying his own kind.

Alaan watched the hostess seat Sidheon at an outdoor table facing the street. The skinny, too-pretty traitor sat alone for almost half an hour when suddenly he flashed a predatory grin as his gaze locked on a good-looking woman passing by. A woman with cinnamon skin, a tight, killer body, and endless legs. Dressed for a casual evening, she sported a pair of formfitting, dark green capri pants, low-heeled pumps and a hunter green short-sleeved sweater. Her hair was pulled back into a long, curly ponytail. If she'd been a bit taller and a little more muscular, the woman could have passed for Carinian Derrickson. Definitely not good.

Sidheon looked after the woman as she smiled her thanks at him for what was probably some lame-assed compliment and kept walking. Was that a hint of fang? Was he crazy, letting his incisors slip free in public? It didn't matter if nobody noticed but Alaan. No vamp, rogue or otherwise, was to bring attention to their kind under any circumstance. Idiot.

"Please, please screw up so I can take you down right now. Screw finding out whatever you're scheming."

"I heard that. What the hell's going on, Alaan?" Bix whispered through their security link.

"I'm watching Sid eyeball a fine-assed sistah who looks a lot like your girl. Five-foot-seven, dark skin, similar facial features, and legs like I don't know what. Damn, she looks good. Could be a pattern here."

"Aw, hell. That might be a problem."

"Exactly what I was thinking. Wait, someone else just showed up. A mousy-looking human male just joined Sid at his table. The guy looks like a subordinate or something. Sending you a digital now," Alaan said as he raised his vid-phone as if he were making a call.

"Hold on a minute," Bix whispered. "Okay, I've got the digital transmission. Yep, he's Sidheon's assistant. Name's Don or Dan, or something like that. I saw him talking to Carin in her lab while I scoped out the place earlier. Seemed to spend a lot of time either watching her or running back and forth between Sidheon and Carin's labs, and the quality-control rooms downstairs."

"Well that didn't take long," Alaan muttered. "The mouse is leaving and Sid looks pissed."

"I see him. You stay on Sidheon. I'll tail the mouse and catch up with you at the house later."

"What's up with dinner?"

"Depends on how long I have to tail Sid's go-fer. Hopefully, I'll be having chocolate tonight." Bix chuckled, as thoughts of Carin continually inserted themselves into his mind. God, the woman was like a drug. He wanted her as much now as he had only hours before. Their marathon loving this evening hadn't done a thing to slake the urgent need to be with her, to touch

78

her. To bind her to him. He could also use a little bit of blood, but he was pretty sure she wasn't up for that yet.

"Tell Dr. Carin I said hello, you horny bastard."

"Smart ass," Bix gritted out between clenched teeth, striving to get a hold of himself. He couldn't afford to allow a woman, any woman, to interfere with his concentration while on a mission. Besides, he was still dealing with being far gone over her. Carin was his mate, and yes, he was supposed to be crazy for her. But it didn't mean an independent prime like himself would immediately adjust to such a strong need for anything other than blood, sex and action. Aw, who the hell was he kidding?

Alaan's quiet voice interrupted Bix's brooding. "Sid is on the move. And by the way, there's a half-pint bag of AB-negative in the cooler under the backseat. You know, just in case the chocolate thing doesn't work out. Catch up with you later. Serati out."

"Good luck, partner. Bix out."

ℬℭ

Bix followed Sidheon's idiot crony for hours. The man's errands seemed typical enough, stopping to pick up prescriptions from the local Walgreens, get some takeout from a restaurant on La Jolla Blvd. Bix was bored out of his mind until the man finally stopped somewhere interesting.

Don, Dan or whatever his name was, parked across the street from a warehouse in the industrial district. It looked newly built and awaiting an occupant. Bix drove past and disappeared around the corner before circling back to park down the street. He watched the little mouse of a man look over his shoulder as if he expected to be followed. Maybe the guy wasn't willingly helping Sidheon? From the terrified expression on his face as he looked around, it wasn't hard to guess where the man's loyalties lay—on the side of self-preservation. He seemed a bit green about the gills as he slid a key into the lock on the front door of the building and disappeared inside for the better part of two hours.

From there the man had gone straight home and stayed there. By the time Bix met up with Alaan at the house designated for their use, it was well past one o'clock in the morning. Spending the night in Carin's arms was obviously out.

Chapter Eight

Other than a glimpse of him from a distance around the facilities, Carin hadn't seen Bix in three days. Why she'd expected him to pop up everywhere, she had no idea. Even at the gym she'd looked over her shoulder every now and again, hoping. Finally, she'd reprimanded herself for refusing to accept she'd been the recipient of a one-night stand. Okay time to forget him.

She was almost home when a sharp jolt of pain shot through her lower back as the muscles spasmed. Thoughts of Bix's strong hands kneading the tension away popped into her head. So much for the two grueling hours spent throwing herself through every lower body exercise she could think of, all in an attempt to get her mind off the man. Obviously it hadn't worked.

Rolling her eyes at her own ridiculousness, she screeched to a stop in her driveway and dragged herself into the house. She'd been alone for years, but she missed this man so much the only word she could think of to describe it was hollow. All this drama for a man she knew nothing about, other than he was a great lay? Yeah, a great *one-time* lay.

"Now see, that's exactly what you get," Carin grumbled to herself as she kicked off her tennis shoes inside the front door. "Getting all worked up 'cause you thought that damned man was serious about you. Now look at you, feeling all stupid and disappointed."

After a quick wash up she settled back in the thick, overstuffed cushions of the couch. A plate of untouched food congealed on the coffee table while her thoughts flew all over the place. One second she was thinking about the next steps for her serum, then her head filled with the images of a tall, dark-haired, gorgeous manly-man who'd put it down on her in the bedroom at the back of her labs earlier this week. She didn't like it at all.

Carin sat up on the couch, snatched out of a comfortable doze by the ring of the doorbell. Startled, heart in her throat, she glanced towards the unlit fireplace at the clock over the mantle. Eight fifteen. Who the hell would come by her house after dark without calling first? Moving with silent caution she rose, grabbed the sturdy baseball bat next to the door and peeked through the viewing hole.

Bix? How dare he show up after three days of no visits and no phone calls. Bastard.

She snatched open the door, perched a fist onto her hip and tapped a bare foot on the hardwood floor.

"How dare you show up here, damn it. After...ommph..."

As his mouth took hers in a swift, dominating kiss, Carin forgot her desire to talk, and only wanted to taste. In an instant, the yearning was there for the slick slide of his tongue against hers, the sweet taste of watermelon candy, and the nibble and nip of strong, white teeth. The spice of his unique scent floated out from under his leather trench and up to her nostrils. Oh Lord, she couldn't see, couldn't breathe, and didn't want to. Kiss now. She could fuss at him all she wanted later.

When he finally released her, she snatched her fingers away from the leather covering his solid, muscled chest, amazed at how off balance she was by the unexpected eagerness to see him again. Overwhelmed by the strangest combination of anger mixed with sudden shyness, Carin stepped back and away from him.

The soft crinkle of a plastic bag swinging on the end of Bix's fingers caught her attention. Yep, it was definitely the bag causing her breath to quicken. It had nothing to do with the hungry glitter in his silvery honey eyes or that damned come-hither smile.

"I know it's a little late for dinner but thought I'd bring you something anyway."

She threw up her hands, exasperated when her stomach flip-flopped at his sexy lopsided grin. "What is it with you always trying to feed me?"

"I can be quite the demanding lover, sweetheart. I've got to make sure you keep up your strength."

Demanding? Loving every three or four days was demanding? He didn't crack a smile as he winked. Her eyes went wide. Oh goodness, he was serious.

"Are you going to invite me in?"

"Huh? What? Oh, yes, of course."

Bix took one step into the house, toed off his shoes and kicked them aside. He followed her into the living room in his stocking feet, set the plastic bag on the coffee table and unloaded it as Carin sat on the couch.

"I hope you like Mexican food." He smiled, so at ease he didn't even bother looking up.

She nodded dumbly and stared at him as if one of them was crazy. How could he appear so calm after laying such a carnal kiss on her? And how dare he dive into her pussy like he couldn't live without it, then not call or come by her labs for days. Then there was the issue of him coming by her house unannounced. How had he known where she lived, and why wasn't she calling him on the carpet instead of sitting here like some dimwitted high-school chick?

"You're projecting again, Carin." He grinned. Her expression confused, she peered up at him. What the hell was he talking about? When he tapped the side of his head, she dropped her gaze to the floor, embarrassed he could so easily pick her thoughts out of the air.

"Bix, it's after eight o'clock. It's too late to eat, and I'd like to know what you're doing here."

He moved around the coffee table and peeled the soft leather coat from his body, then carelessly tossed it across the arm of the sofa. Sitting beside her, he took her smaller hands in his and stroked the center of her palm with his thumb. "Let me put you at ease, baby."

Baby? Her forearm muscles flexed involuntarily at the sudden urge to smack him.

"Working for a multibillion dollar organization has its downside. Unfortunately, I'm here in San Diego for more than just the cancer drug you're working on for us. I wanted to see you but my choices were to either wake you up past midnight after I was done working, or come by when I could...which is now."

"So, it wasn't just a one-night stand?" she asked boldly, needing some closure once and for all. Sure, she was upset the man hadn't called, but if she had any sense she would leave well enough alone. Hell, a single bang was the way to go with him, or anyone else. She had work to do and couldn't afford to be distracted. But damn, she really wanted to be distracted by him. Badly.

"One-night stand? Not on your life. You're addicting, baby, and there are some things I'd like you to consider, but we'll talk about that later."

"How did you find out where I live?"

"I have my ways," he teased with a sheepish grin. She wasn't buying it and her well-practiced "come again" glare must have gotten her point across. He threw up his hands in the universal "I give" salute.

"My organization always asks for the personal information of any person working on research for us. Besides"—he leaned forward to plant a silken kiss across her forehead—"do you really mind that I didn't call first?"

Well, no, but it was the principle of the thing, though she hadn't said as much. This psychic stuff would take some getting used to.

"I'm sorry, baby. I didn't mean to disappoint you. Let me make it up to you?" At her subtle nod he pulled back the cardboard cover from one of the foil tins and revealed her favorite food in the whole world. Chile rellenos. And he'd even left off the cheese. Like many black women her age with lactose intolerance, she had a deep abiding love for dairy but couldn't touch the stuff. How had he known? She guessed the same way he knew everything else about her—he was damned nosy. She wasn't sure whether she should be pissed off at his intrusion into her personal information, or flattered because he'd paid attention to such small details.

She couldn't resist eating just a little bit of the delicious food, considering she hadn't actually eaten any of the hard, cold fare still sitting on the table. After a round of chile relleno, homemade tortilla chips, and a spicy cilantro salsa so hot it reminded her of Bix's sizzling kisses, Carin sat stiffly on the couch next to him trying to keep her hands to herself.

Lord, it was the strangest sensation, this urge, this hunger. And for a man she didn't really know, who'd banged her, and then disappeared? Not to mention his knowledge of her personal tastes bordered on creepy. So...why wasn't she creeped out?

"Would you mind helping me clean up this stuff?" Bix asked, motioning to the aluminum trays and bowls, some of which she'd emptied in a hurry. Glad to have something to do other than search for unease where there wasn't any, she agreed, snatched up a few of the containers and hustled out of the room.

Once in the kitchen he led her right into her element by bringing up a single, but in no way simple, subject.

"Tell me your solution for the drug you're developing for Venture."

While they washed dishes and filled Tupperware with leftovers, he gave his undivided attention as she explained her vision for the development of an effective cancer drug. The cancer treatment should take a two-step approach. One part of the therapy involved introducing a biological agent into the body to find and destroy cancer cells directly, almost like a reverse virus, or retrovirus. The second part would inject altered, perfected DNA to hopefully identify and change the pieces of the patient's DNA strand, whether damaged or just predisposed to disease. It was all hypothetical at this point, with only a few small samples of an experimental solution to test with.

But if her serum worked, all this would be moot. If it worked on her, it would work on a cancer patient. However, she kept that bit of information to herself.

She'd royally impressed him with her knowledge of what affected the human body, both positive and negative. Warming quickly to the subject, she was completely relaxed now. An excellent time for bed.

Bix stepped up behind her as she rinsed the last fork and put it in the dishwasher. The second his hands touched the curve of her shoulders, her spine went rigid. Easing closer, he slid his fingers up to the tense muscles above her collarbone, and squeezed gently until she moaned. Only then did he dip his head and nibble on a spot where her neck sloped upward. A light scrape across her sensitive skin elicited a groan that wrapped around his dick and called his name.

"Feel good?" he asked, still nipping and massaging.

"Mmm-hmm, very."

Peeking into her mind, he knew his fingers felt heavenly, but she thought his mouth was beyond divine. If he kept this up she'd be nothing but a puddle of aroused woman on the kitchen floor. He rather liked the image.

"For what I have in mind, the floor might be a bit uncomfortable," he drawled in her head, working his way up to her ear with his lips and down to her smooth stomach with his hands. Her head fell back against his chest with a sigh.

"Bix, I'm supposed to be mad at you. How do you drive me crazy so fast?"

"Same way you do me, sweetness." He weighed her beautiful breasts in his hands and loved feeling the transition of her berry nipples from compliant juicy areolas to firm suckable points as his thumbs grazed over them repeatedly. All her weight was back on her heels as she wriggled against his very hard cock nestled between her butt cheeks. She totally trusted him not to move. If he did, she'd hit the floor like a sack of flour.

"Carin, I need to feel you. No clothes, just you."

She cried out and writhed against him when his entire palm closed over her swollen breasts and squeezed. No words came out of her mouth in response to his need, but her thoughts were unmistakably clear. She wanted him, but adamantly refused to have another one-night stand. But there was something deeper, so deep it made his heart ache as he empathized with her wild tangle of thoughts and emotions. On one hand, she could really get used to being touched like this. But then again, she had to hold a little bit of herself back, or at least try to. She couldn't afford to lose herself in him, or anyone else.

He wasn't sure what she meant by that, but he was sure he'd been an idiot. While he was secure in what was developing between them, Carin didn't have a clue they were connected in ways beyond her experience or understanding. Bix could have kicked himself for being so focused on work he hadn't taken two minutes to call and just say hello.

"Carin, I'm sorry I didn't take the time to call you earlier this week." No response, other than a barely perceivable stiffening of her spine. "Look up at me, baby."

The second she turned her head enough for him to see her smoky brown eyes, he took her mouth with a kiss so open and hot, it dwarfed the one he'd laid on her earlier at the front door.

The woman was on fire and all he'd done was fondle her breasts and massage her neck. Well, he'd nibbled there a little bit, too. His blood pumped to the same cadence to which the muscles of her belly fluttered. Damn, the need to be naked rolled off her in waves, pushed at his mind and wrapped around him until he wanted to tear her clothes off and have at her right here in the kitchen.

Bix smiled as her thoughts hit him square in the chest. She wanted to have at him first, eh? He could live with that. Steadying her on her feet, he eased away from her warm body. She turned around to face him, eyes ablaze with a longing almost as raw as his.

He peeled his jeans down his long legs and kicked them off, then stood there and let her watch his dick bob underneath his black silk boxers. Her tongue flittered nervously across her top lip, then the bottom one. Knees gave way and she dropped to the floor, taking his boxers with her. Her gasp was audible as his rigid staff bounced up and tapped her on the chin.

She looked up in amazement as the thing seemed to take on a life of its own. He didn't blame her one bit. His cock had never been this hard. Engorged to the point of bursting, it bobbed and jerked, completely out of his control.

Wanting nothing to impede her progress, Bix yanked his shirt off over his head and dropped it to the floor.

His eyes closed on a sigh when her warm, wet tongue snaked out and flicked the tip of the sensitive skin. He shuddered at the contact. Damn, it felt beyond good. And was even better when he was abruptly surrounded by wet, mind-boggling suction. Oh God.

Carin wrapped her whole mouth around the crown with no further preliminaries. The pleasure of her assault was so intense he had to lock his knees to keep them from buckling. Obviously finished sampling the wares, she put her back into it as she sucked and pulled at him hungrily. Her mouth sank down until he felt himself butt against the back of her throat. Pulling back, she pressed her tongue underneath and took him with her, then relaxed her jaw and slid back down again. Damn, she gorged on his cock like he was her favorite dessert, swallowing him eagerly until he couldn't help but pump his hips as she moved her lips over his hardness.

"Mmm, you taste so good." Her thoughts slid over and surrounded his, caressing him, mind and body. *"I think you're now my favorite piece of candy."*

Hell, if she kept this up, he would explode down her lovely throat.

In the middle of a particularly long, loud moan, Carin pulled away. Bix's eyes popped open. Her hands, once urgent and needy, now gently stroked his shaft and toyed delicately with his balls. What the hell? Damn it, he didn't want soft and easy. Not after she'd built him up with such fierce play. The woman must totally be into torture. When she grinned up at him, her eyes filled with triumph at his obvious distress, he knew he was right. Yep, definitely into torture. Fine, because he sure as hell wasn't too proud to beg—but only with her. If it had been anyone else trying his patience, he would have pulled his jeans on and stepped right out the door.

"Carin, baby...I can't take the teasing. Not now," he pleaded, grinding his back teeth together as he forced the words out past his tingling fangs. He spoke to those damned fangs, too close to losing it. *Stay in there. Stay sheathed, damn it.*

Her mouth covered him again, taking him deeply. He yelled to the ceiling, yanked the ponytail out of her hair and buried his fingers in the cottony softness. Touching her face, her neck and everywhere his fingers could reach, he loved the play of muscles in her mouth and throat, all hot, warm suction as she went down on him. Almost as exquisite as being inside her pussy. Almost.

Carin let out a startled yelp when it was Bix's turn to play. He pulled her off her knees, swept her up in his arms and headed for the bedroom. He grinned at the deer-in-the-headlights widening of her eyes when she landed in the middle of the bed with a bounce. She may have been a bit surprised at his manhandling, but he knew she liked it. Carin didn't want a wuss for a man. She wanted an alpha, like him. Stalking her slowly, he walked around the entire bed, growling low in his throat when her eyes went all misty and desperate. Then he was on her, stripping her T-shirt and sweats off, followed by a sheer piece of underwear that should have been illegal to wear, even under her clothes. With a single yank, it was history, along with her bra.

When she was naked, trembling and reaching for him, Bix pulled back the curtains and adjusted the blinds to allow the moonlight to stream in without anyone seeing into the house. The pale beams set her perfect skin aglow.

He climbed onto the bed next to Carin's writhing body with one goal—to hear her say she wanted him always.

"Up on your knees, sweetheart." Instead she lay on her back, rolled her hips and looked him dead in the eye as she stretched her arms up over her head. She wasn't projecting any thoughts right now, her mind void of everything except the need to be challenged, taken. Mounted.

"Carin, up on your knees. Now." His voice was hard with passion, not anger. When she didn't comply, the prime male rose up in him. Bix flipped her over on her stomach and instinctively clamped his teeth down on her neck when she struggled. She immediately stilled. He licked the same spot to soothe away the sting and felt her arousal bloom again. But the firm slap on her bare ass made it skyrocket.

"Ooh! Do it again," she hissed. "Yes, just like that, Bix." Up on her knees now, she pushed back against him with an urgent swivel of her hips. Was she ready? Oh yeah, and it was not like him to keep a lady waiting. He positioned the head of his cock against her weeping slit and slid in slowly. After an inch, he stilled and clamped his lips together. Perhaps the danger of his fangs piercing through the flesh would give him some measure of control. Carin turned and snarled at him and he felt them pierce his lips. Damn, this wasn't working.

He gave her another inch and she dropped her shoulders down on the bed, hiking her ass up in the air. Rubbing her breasts against the comforter, she slid her hands all over the soft bedding, mewling frantically until he gave her some more cock.

"Bix, stop playing with me, damn it. Fuck me already." She didn't care that she yelled at a man who towered over her, and was strong enough to pick her up and toss her around. Her pussy was on fire and only he could put it out. And he knew it.

"You want me, sweetheart?" He eased in and out, peppering her back and shoulders with hot but gentle kisses. Everywhere his lips touched went up in flames.

"Yes, I want you," she cried.

"But that's not enough. I want you to *need* me, Carin." He slid out of her, slammed home and then stilled.

"Oh God, I do but...I-I can't," she screamed, but he sensed her mind fighting what her body and heart really wanted.

"You're mine, Carin. Say it, baby."

"Yes. I mean no. I can't be yours, not yet."

Bix was puzzled at the intensity of her fear. It was well-hidden, but there was very little she would be able to keep from him. She was genuinely, truly afraid of giving all of herself to him. Through the link he sensed something akin to terror snaking through her consciousness like a frantic disease. Eating away any chance for happiness or companionship. What was she afraid of? Sensing her near-panic warring with her arousal, he backed off. For now.

"But you are mine, Carin. I don't plan on going away, sweetheart. We belong together and in time you'll know it like I do. Until then, feel me, feel this." He buried himself to the hilt and rocked against her ass with sure, solid strokes. Making sure she hit her peak at least three times, he reveled in her pleasure as each climax tore through her. Then he let himself join her in the delicious madness of orgasm. And even after they'd both regained their senses Bix touched, teased and tasted until she was a slumbering heap of warm, happy female.

Chapter Nine

One arm over his head and the other wrapped around Carin's sleeping form, Bix listened to her quiet breathing. He idly stroked the dark curls on her head. He loved her hair, all naturally thick and soft, not chemically straightened or plastered against her head. Her rich, coffee skin reminded him of espresso with a measure of Irish Cream stirred in, deliciously beautiful, inside and out. Like chocolate filled with golden caramel. Mmm, he liked caramel. He could eat it for hours, just like the tips of her lovely breasts and sweet succulent pussy.

But Carin had a problem, and as her man he felt compelled to help her solve it. But at what cost? He'd filched several tablets of notes from her lab and read them in disbelief. The woman wanted to be a vampire and was trying desperately to find a way to turn herself. She didn't know vampires really existed but had gathered enough research on the various attributes of his species and was pretty close to piecing together a genetic replica of their DNA. The woman was terrified of death, totally and completely preoccupied with it. At only thirty-six, she was more concerned with extending her life than people twice her age.

Of course, it was impossible to be turned into a vampire, but she could extend her life by mating with one. Correction, mating with *him*.

According to her notes, Carin had been using her own blood to experiment with skin cells introduced to the serum she'd created. It already had the ability to combat aging and introduced an incredible resistance to disease to the original cells. Unfortunately, the cells absorbed too much iron from her blood, resulting in a slight toxicity.

What she'd discovered and engineered so far was beyond amazing for someone who'd started from scratch with no firsthand knowledge of vampires. Even if she was the most sought after and brilliant mind in her field, what she'd accomplished was unheard of, especially for a human.

If what she was doing ever leaked out, uproar in both vampire and human communities would follow. But V.C.O.E. could use Carin's research to find a way to fight their enemies. She looked soft and submissive in her sleep, but her disposition wouldn't last long when he broached the subject of her research. May as well get this over with.

Bix nudged the top of her head with his chin. She moaned softly and turned into his body, instinctively seeking his warmth. "Wake up, sweetheart," he whispered against her hair. She groaned and nuzzled deeper under the covers, trying to bury her head underneath his body.

"Carin," he spoke a bit more sternly, "wake up, baby."

She stretched with a well-deserved yawn, her nipples and breasts deliciously sore, still swollen and heavy. Her body felt well used, the strong muscles of her legs protested her movements, fatigued after spending so much time wide open under Bix while he pushed into her, filled her. Her eyes fluttered open reluctantly, and she scrunched her eyebrows together in an attempt to focus on the face mere inches from hers.

"Bix, whaaaat?" she grumbled, trying to roll back underneath his arm. Bix's calmly stated words snapped her out of any remaining slumber.

"I know about your vampire research, Carin. What do you think I should do about it?"

Her dark brown eyes met his silver streaked honey ones as she bolted straight up in the bed. She dragged the covers up and over her bare breasts while running a hand through the tangled mass on her head that was supposed to be hair. Her mouth fell open, but she recovered in a flash and painted on a mask of indifference while her emotions reeled.

"You know about my research?" she asked as calmly as if he'd informed her the moon was full in the sky.

"Yes, sweetheart, I know all about it."

"B-But how," she sputtered, unable to believe all her hard work would be flushed down the drain now. After all, it was his responsibility to make sure the project his organization funded was on track. They held the purse strings and she doubted they'd appreciate their lead scientist deviating from what they were paying for.

"I took a peek at some of your notes. When you're onto something, you're like a dog with a bone, love. You didn't even notice."

"I-I, uh..." She paused and took a deep breath. Stuttering wouldn't win the fight here. She appeared steady, but was far from it. Her mind ran a million miles an hour trying to figure a way to get him to keep her secret. Hell, nothing came to mind. Well, she'd just have to take it like a woman. Carin squared her shoulders and faced him boldly, trying to ignore the slightly hairy leg rubbing against hers under the covers.

"Bix, I take full responsibility for my actions."

"I expected nothing less. But responsibility is not what I want from you."

She arched a brow in question. He didn't hesitate to explain.

"I want you to help me find out what Sidheon is doing."

Sidheon? Hell, that was simple, even welcome. Just the mention of the man's name sent nasty chills up her spine. After she'd accidentally ended up with his specimen cart, she'd seen some test results that hadn't made any sense at first. Now she was beginning to make serious headway on it.

"So, you want my help? Is that all?"

He looked up at her from his pillow and traipsed a single finger up her arm, sending a chill of anticipation clear down to the back of her knees.

"Oh no, baby. That's not all I want."

Whoa, hold the door. If her cooperation wasn't all he wanted, then what exactly *did* he want? Her thighs spread wide with him between them in some sort of permanent arrangement, perhaps? Not bloody likely. Well, at least not the permanent part.

Ignoring the goose bumps his caress inspired, Carin climbed out from under the covers, wrapped a quilt from the end of the bed around her body and went to stand in front of her dresser across the room. She needed some space if she was going to think straight. Anywhere within arm's length of Bix and she forgot any coherent speech. Facing the mirror perched on top of her dresser, she shook her head on a snort and a smile. A solid, hard-muscled body reflected boldly back at her from across the room. Damn he was just too sexy for words, all golden and hunky and damned delicious. Thick, black, bed-head hair called to her fingers, even from way over here.

But something was going on here, especially if the man really knew about her research and wasn't freaked out about it. Maybe he was bluffing. Turning to face him, she backed up against the dresser and crossed her arms over her chest. Bix sat up in the bed and leaned against the headboard, watching her from beneath hooded lids. In spite of the conversation he appeared at ease, his interlaced fingers cradling the back of his head.

"Why don't you think I'm insane for researching how to exhibit the traits of a non-existent species? How come you aren't tripping out because I want to be a vampire?"

"Because, Carin, *I'm* a vampire."

"What? No way." She laughed and waved him off. Until she noticed he wasn't laughing with her. Oh, hell, was he serious? She sobered quickly.

"But you can't be...I mean, I would know, right? I'd have bite marks or something by now, right?" It was times like this she wished she was truly psychic instead of just an empath, damn it.

His legs swung off the bed and he rose slowly. A half grin formed on one side of his mouth on her swift intake of breath. The man had the nerve to look down at the huge erection dancing healthily at his groin. "Bite marks?" he asked silkily. "Well, not necessarily." He smiled like a rogue and let his incisors lengthen. Every muscle along her spine tingled erotically as his cock and teeth both reached for her.

He watched her closely while she eyeballed his fangs, her temper getting hotter by the second. The expression across his tight brow seemed a bit puzzled. What, he expected her to panic or something because he had elongated incisors? Well, panic wasn't what he was gonna get, the bastard. Instead, her brows snapped together in a boiling frown. Her hand balled up into a strong fist and settled into the hollow of her hip with her toe tapping a mile a minute. She was pissed.

Bix's eyes widened just long enough to recognize what flew towards his head. Moving with the speed obviously born of a vampire, he avoided the object. Barely. The empty crystal vase that had been sitting on her dresser shattered into a million pieces against the wall in the exact spot his head had been only seconds before.

"You son of a bitch. You knew what I was trying to do all this time? You're the very thing I'm trying to create in myself and you didn't say anything? Didn't offer to help me? You bastard!"

One of several glass beakers sitting on her dresser flew. Damn, she wished her aim were better. She'd only clipped his shoulder that time.

"Look, Carin..."

"No, you look! I've worked my ass"—another beaker sailed towards him—"off for years trying"—a small metal specimen tray full of glass vials took off—"to figure out how to become a fucking vampire!"

Carin couldn't believe it. Endless years of beating her head against a wall trying to find the keys to making herself long-lived and here she was sleeping with a damned vampire? How stupid could she be?

Her eyes went wide when he reached her side just as she picked up a heavy ten-gram scale weight from on top of a stack of magazines. He bared his fangs again, but this time a threatening snarl erupted from deep in his throat. In a flash he maneuvered around the bed and had her sandwiched between his hard naked body and the wall.

"Don't ever, *ever,* do that again, Carin," he ground out in clear warning. "I don't care how mad you get at me, you will respect me at all times. Do you understand?"

His hands were gentle and the words spoken at a whisper, but the honed muscles stilling her movement, along with the tick in his jaw, made it pretty clear he'd reached the end of his tolerance. Never mind the fact he held her six inches off the floor. But she was no punk bitch. Hell, she could make her jaw tick, too.

"Fuck. You," she hissed into his face. Pushing away from the wall, and away from Bix, Carin stuck her chest out and acted big and bad, but she knew her back left the wall because he'd let her. Her instincts told her Bix would never hurt her, but the man was no pushover. Inwardly acknowledging her inability to walk all over him freed her, made it all right to loose the reins of her carefully controlled life and give them to the bossy, protective, stubborn male. Carin never realized she liked that in a man. The knowledge brought with it a rush of steaming arousal and the urge to be thoroughly ravished.

But she wasn't going to tell *him* that. Then, he'd be an overbearing ass all the time. A gorgeous overbearing ass... *Oh, snap out of it, girl. You can't do this noodle-spined stuff right now.*

Then again, if she was nice maybe he'd bite her and...and what? Because of the characteristics and behavior of DNA strands, her research concluded it was unlikely humans could be "turned" by simply introducing simulated vampire genes, but perhaps she could be enhanced? Wait a minute, the specimens she'd stolen from Sidheon's cart... And Bix was after Sidheon. It all clicked into place in one *a-ha* moment. Sidheon was a vamp. It was his blood she'd stumbled on in the specimen cart, the blood with regenerative properties. But if she hadn't recognized

Sidheon or Bix as vamps, what else, and who else, had she missed? What else did she *not* know about his kind?

Carin paced back and forth in front of Bix as he half-sat on her dresser, oblivious to what his beautiful body was doing to her ability to think straight. She slowly got her wits together and urged Carin-The-Scientist to surface. Just as she opened her mouth to ask another question, he pressed against her mind, telling her what he'd rather be doing right now. It involved no talking, lots of honey and a little bit of rope. And so hot she couldn't keep her lips from forming a surprised little "oh" as the wicked details streamed into her head.

A crooked, cheeky smile spread wide across his lips at the dark blush creeping up her chest. Arrogant man. Carin's fingers wrapped around something new to throw when he sent another thought.

"You smell like my come, but not nearly enough. Come over here and get some more." Oh Lord, she was going to explode on the spot, his nasty thoughts enough to cause goose bumps to form on her bare arms at the same time her nipples drew up into tight little aching buds. Her gaze followed the large hand he lowered to his groin and slid up and down his hard cock.

Carin focused on the carpet. She tried to keep her gaze there, really she did, but she had a mutiny on her hands with her damned eyeballs. They were supposed to listen to her, not go off on their own to watch his fingers wrap around his magnificent rod. It was too hot in the room and her knees threatened to join her eyes in the whole mutinous business. Swallowing convulsively, throat tight with such a blitz of emotions that she couldn't pin them all down—anger, hunger, and embarrassment at being so needy. Even with his fangs gleaming under the moonlight streaming in through the open blinds, he was such a handsome devil. *Her* handsome devil. She turned away and shook her head in an attempt to clear it. Yep, it was time to change the subject and hopefully get some answers. *And sound convincing when you open your mouth, girl.*

Turning to face him, she said, "Look, Bix, I have some questions. Can you tell me..." Her mouth snapped closed. Without a sound he'd moved up behind her, close enough to rub her nose against his chest.

"Not now, baby. Later." He backed towards the bed, crooking his finger. Her body started moving like a puppet on a string. Rubbery legs and all, she shuffled the short distance to where he stood with his cock waving at her. The man was a walking aphrodisiac.

Her ass clenched when the arousing scent of her sex mingled with his filled her nostrils. Sitting on the edge of the bed, she grabbed hold of his forearms, sank trembling fingers into his vein-roped forearms and held tight as her head fell back. His fangs, followed by his warm, wet tongue traipsed up her neck. The tickle-scratch set off a sweet shiver along her nerve endings, through her breasts, and down to her soaked pussy. With his thick mushroom-shaped tip positioned at her door, legs spread as wide as they could go, her belly did the butterfly dance, spurred by his deep, satisfied groan as he entered her willing body.

What had she wanted to know about vampires again?

⁎∘⁎

Bix cradled her against his chest, tracing a relaxing path up and down her spine. Carin's finger drew little circles around a tight male nipple. He sighed contentedly for the tenth time in the last ten minutes. Sated enough to think halfway straight while holding her securely in his arms, he felt sleep tug at the corners of his mind. Groaning inwardly, he winced when she rose up on her elbow and peered at him with clear determination. It was question time and he obviously wasn't going to distract her.

"Bix, tell me about vamps? I never did buy into the whole undead theory. I've also seen you out in the daytime. Are we talking Blade the Daywalker or what?"

He chuckled, his fingers continuing their easy exploration of her body. He couldn't stop touching her. If she wanted to talk about the consistency of pig shit, the woman would still manage to make it sound sexy.

"Forget everything you ever heard or saw in a movie, sweetheart. There are a lot of misconceptions about my kind," he crooned, dropping a lazy kiss on the top of her head. She must have figured where his lips were headed next when she scooted away, dragging the blankets up to cover her nakedness. She pinned him with an excited but serious stare.

"Well, what kind of misconceptions?"

Bix swore he heard the gears turning in her head as the scientist re-emerged with logic, reason and tons of inquiries. And she was off to the races.

"I think I've figured out the biconvex structure of the red blood cells and how to recreate them in human genes, and how to deal with the hemoglobin deficiency and iron absorption. I can slow the deterioration and aging of organs, but the regenerative properties—"

"Whoa, whoa." He chuckled, holding his hands up in man's most effective "I surrender" gesture. "Slow down, Carin. One thing at a time."

"Okay, what about blood?"

"There are rules to bloodletting. While the meds we ingest help, we can't get around the need for blood. It's hardwired into our DNA. But the V.C.O.E..."

"V.C.O.E.?"

"Vampire Council of Ethics," he continued, "decreed thousands of years ago that we must never *take* blood. It has to be freely given. The same rule stands today."

"But what if there's no convenient human around willing to give their blood?"

"Well, why do you think we have such hefty investments in pharmaceutical and biotech companies?"

Her eyes went wide and he practically saw the light switch on in her head.

"You've got other pharma and biotech companies working on the very thing *I'm* working on, right?"

"Yeah, sort of. We own blood facilities, which is key since human blood can't be reproduced. Hemoglobin and Factor Eight, which are used to treat hemophilia, can be manufactured but not the actual blood. So we have blood sources available in every major city if there are no handy humans."

"What about other Council rules?"

"We must never draw attention to ourselves, which is one of the only reasons we have survived this long. And we can't kill a human. If we have to feed from a human instead of a plastic donor bag we must only take enough blood to survive. No gorging allowed. And, here's the big one." He hesitated for drama's sake. "Never, ever, steal another vamp's mate or bond a mate against their wishes."

The last was spoken with a bit more heat than he intended. Carin cocked her head to the side, her curiosity at the intensity in his voice simmered along the bond.

"It makes sense but why is this particular rule so important?" she asked.

"That damned rule, or the lack thereof, has been the reason for some of the worst battles in history. Look at all the trouble Helen of Troy caused. And all because she'd been stolen from her vampire mate, though history has never identified the man as one of us."

"So, no vampire bed hopping, eh?"

Bix's brows rose at her choice of words, but he didn't interrupt.

"But you don't get diseases like normal humanoids, so what's the harm in spreading the love?"

Spreading the love? He'd kill any man, vamp or otherwise, who set eyes on her. He'd skin 'em alive and...

"It's not my type of gig," she said thoughtfully, her expression museful. "But if others want to fool around it's none of my business."

He breathed a sigh of relief. Good, he wouldn't have to kill anyone after all. He'd better explain mating to her a bit more. But only a bit. "Vampire mates are special, Carin. First, we don't typically fool around with human women. The chance of accidentally exposing our kind is too great. Second, just because a prime male sleeps with a female doesn't mean they're mated. It just means they're fucking. Nothing more."

"Really?" she asked. Her face was calm enough, but she was suddenly projecting. Now he felt like a cad from the stab of pain resonating just underneath her rib cage. She wondered, *So is that what we're doing? Just fucking?*

Bix reached out and smoothed her hair back behind her ears. He felt her sadness and wanted to tell her she'd already met her mate—him. All they had to do was share blood, truly desire the bondmating, and the bond would be complete. Right now it was strong but could still be broken if she met and mated another prime male vampire. But there was no way in hell he'd allow such a thing. He wasn't ready to tell her she was stuck with him. Not because she couldn't walk away, but because he couldn't afford to let her.

"Listen, baby, when a vampire male finds the perfect woman for him, he knows. We all have some psychic ability, but he's attuned to her like nobody else. It's more than being able to read thoughts and communicate telepathically. It's almost like they meld, become part of one another. Feel each other's joy, pain, wants and fears. Once mated, bonded, they can't bear to be apart. Losing a bondmate is said to be close to experiencing death. I hear it's a pretty deep thing." He left his expression wide open, ending his thoughts on a whisper, peering into her soul. He felt her throat clog with unshed tears. But did she really understand what he was trying to say?

Pushing her unruly tangle behind her ears again, she plunged back into the conversation. "So what about daylight? Silver? Garlic?"

He knew the moment her emotional wall went up but decided not to push. She would understand soon enough. He would see to it. In the meantime, he would give her what she wanted. Information.

"We've always been able to move around during the day, though it's not our natural time. It's uncomfortable but we can build up a strong resistance to sunlight, though it takes a long time. It's basically an allergy. Too long in the sun and we get a nasty rash. There are plenty of drugs to help us tolerate it. Allergies to silver are real, but we can usually control it with meds. Exposure to silver or sun doesn't cause us to blow up or turn into ash like on the movies. As for garlic? I actually like garlic."

She giggled. He loved the sound of it.

"So, sweetheart, vampires are cousins to humans, not a different species altogether. Our bodies need food just like yours, but not quite to the same extent."

"What about your senses? You know, sight, hearing and the like?"

"It's true we have keener sight, hearing, smell, the whole nine yards."

"But how? How do you regenerate? And more importantly, if you bite me it won't do a damn thing, right?"

Oh, it would do something all right. It would make him hot and horny and begin to close the circle of their bond. But he wasn't ready to go there. Instead he said, "I can't turn you, Carin." Well, it was sort of true. And as much as he was into the woman, he still had a job to do. Catch or kill Sidheon at all costs. "Back to business, love. Are you going to help me with Sidheon or not?"

"Talk about spoiling the mood. Damn," she snorted. "Well, if I help you what do I get out of it?"

"How 'bout I keep all your secrets?" He chuckled. He was only kidding, but soon realized it was definitely the wrong thing to say. If looks could kill, Carin would have him drawn and quartered faster than he could form his next thought.

"How 'bout I spill all yours, Bix," she fumed in a tight voice. She scowled for all she was worth but he couldn't let her anger move him. Not one iota.

"Who'd believe you, Carin? Modern-day vampires who can walk around in the daylight? You're too smart a woman to risk your reputation just because you're pissed off at me. I can deal with you being pissed off. If it takes down Sidheon and keeps you safe, I can handle it, baby."

"Keeps me safe? Oh, please. You've got your own agenda, here. What the hell do you care about keeping me safe?" She swung her legs off the bed, stormed to the closet and tore through the hangers, snatching down a pair of jeans and a soft sweater off the shelf.

"Come here, Carin."

"Kiss my ass, Bix." She yanked on her clothes, sans underwear, and grabbed a pair of sneakers from the closet floor.

"Carin, I said. Come. Here." His voice was louder and definitely harsher. She couldn't have cared less.

"I don't give a damn what you said." Hell, two could play this game. She was the queen of stubborn piss-off-ivity.

She stilled, dropped her tennis shoes to the closet floor with a loud thump and stood there stiff with anger, cheeks blooming with embarrassment. What in the world was she doing? There was a vampire lounging in her bed. *Her* bed, in *her* house. If anyone should be getting dressed and getting the hell out, it was him. She flung herself around to face him, hands on hips. Damn it, he did it again. Suddenly, he was right there, his nose not three inches from hers. Well, this part of the vampire myth was definitely true. He hadn't made a sound, yet he moved so fast it was dizzying.

"I am not used to being disobeyed, Carin."

The quiet menace in his voice was more disconcerting than if he'd just yelled at her. But she was no punk. "Get over it." She refused to show the intimidation she felt to this oversized, muscle-bound clod of a vampire. Who she happened to be falling in love with. Aw, hell.

"Carin, I'm sorry. I was only kidding when I suggested I'd rat out your research. Really, baby, I didn't mean it. But I did mean it when I said I need your help."

"What are you, crazy? Why the hell should I trust you?"

"If you don't trust me, then trust your heart. Carin, you know I won't ever hurt you." He went down on one knee and she felt her resolve melting like snow during a San Diego summer while her knees started to do the Jell-O thing again.

"B-But what if I lose my job? Or Sidheon gets wind of all this?"

"I've got your back, sweetheart. With Sidheon, as well as anything and everything else you face in life from now on."

Now that sounded a bit permanent to her. Did he really see this thing between them going further?

"I meant what I said, Carin. You're mine, and I take care of my own."

"How do I know I can count on you to be there for me, Bix?" she asked, never taking her eyes off of his.

"Sweetheart, if there's anything you don't have to worry about, it's me being there. I have a whole lot of years in front of me. I can't imagine not spending them with you."

"Right. Say that to the girl you were just trying to blackmail," she said mutinously as he stripped her naked with blurring speed. Only he wasn't silent about it this time. Every inch of skin he bared elicited a groan or an intake of breath. The way he looked at her made her feel like the most beautiful woman in the world.

He shook his head. A clear look of regret marched across his handsome face. "I said I was sorry, sweetheart," he crooned, sliding up her body, brushing his hair along her bare skin as he moved. He stood, looked down at her and waited patiently.

Carin had wondered all her life if she would ever find someone who touched her deeply like this mate business Bix talked about. Well, it hadn't happened so far. Probably never would. Too bad she and Bix couldn't... She cut the thought off, not wanting to dwell on what would probably never be. She adored Bix, but that didn't mean he wanted to do the bond thing with her. Painting on a calm façade, she forced herself to appear indifferent. A moment passed. Then two. Sigh...this wasn't really working. Not with all the honey-sweet emotion pouring out of him to ooze down through the strange link they shared.

Then again, he'd made it clear that vamps knew when they met their mate. Surely he'd have said something by now, right?

Sighing with a mix of regret and pleasure as Bix sank down to his knees, her anger melted.

"I'll think about it, Bix. Really, I promise."

"That's all I ask, sweetheart."

Bix's talented tongue traced lazy circles around her navel. It tickled, making her squirm under his touch. He smiled against her soft skin. Lifting her high in his arms, he carried her back to bed. A loud smack filled the room where his lips planted a playfully sloppy kiss against her forehead.

"I have to go meet a friend. Let's have lunch tomorrow, all right?" he murmured, tracing imaginary lines across her cheek. His words were low, deep, sending the bottom of her tummy into a flutter like the tail of a kite whipped along by a stiff breeze. And she didn't want him to leave.

"It's Friday night. Can't you just spend the night and let's make it breakfast-in-bed instead?"

After trailing tender kisses from cheek to cheek, he rubbed noses with her and sighed.

"I'd love to stay, but I can't. Why don't you come over to my house right around noon tomorrow? Brunch? I make a mean French toast. Always covered with cinnamon." He waggled his eyebrows. She giggled.

"Mmm-hmm," she mumbled, nuzzling the side of his neck. He smelled so good. "I'm a sucker for a milk toast, uh, I mean French toast man."

"Milk toast? I'll show you milk toast, damn it." Bix commenced to tickle her silly. She'd never been tickled by a man before. She decided she liked it.

"I give up, I swear. Go away already," she cackled, holding her aching stomach.

Pressing a flat palm against her chest when she started to rise, he gave her one last kiss and whispered against her mouth, "I'll leave directions on the coffee table for you. Don't get up, sweetie, I'll see myself out. Can't wait to see you tomorrow. And be prepared for some deep conversation concerning you and me."

Whoa, now that sounded serious. And his gaze, hot and smoldering, slid all through her until holding his stare was impossible. She looked away for a moment, then felt his fingers under her chin. Lifting her face for a final peck, Carin watched in amazement as he dressed in a flash and was gone without a sound. Wow, this vampire stuff was pretty cool.

Chapter Ten

Bix and Alaan sat outside of the small warehouse Dan-The-Mouse had slunk to several times this week. He was sure to show up any moment now. Sid had been scarcely seen around the biotech facility and they'd lucked out when an anonymous tip came in. Whatever Sidheon was doing, this was the place to get the goods. There was no one around. While Bix would rather have someone to interrogate, a quick scout of the building would do for now.

"What about Carin's family? Are they going to care you're a white guy?" Alaan asked around sips of blood-laced cranberry juice.

"Carin doesn't have any family. And actually, now that I think about it, the subject hasn't come up between us at all," Bix said thoughtfully, closely surveying the shadows around them. "She doesn't seem to care one way or the other," he mouthed around a handful of watermelon Jolly Rancher candies.

"She's a beautiful woman, Bix. Smart, bold. You're a lucky man. When are you going to tell her she's your mate?"

"I'll tell her when the time is right. I can feel the bond between us, but we haven't shared blood. I want her to have a choice, Alaan." Knowing he couldn't bear to ever let her go, he'd said all he was going to say on the subject. Besides, the woman hadn't agreed to even date him, let alone mate with him. The completion of the bond required a true commitment and the exchange of blood. He wouldn't take a drop of hers without her permission or her promise. As a vampire, he knew hot sex was the assurance of neither.

Alaan nodded and Bix knew he understood the drive to bond, as well as the anxiety of keeping his potential mate safe by not bonding. A rogue vamp with a grudge against the Serati Clan, couldn't get to Alaan, so he'd stolen Sher instead. The beautiful, dark-haired beauty hadn't survived. Bix wondered if his friend would ever find another female like her who could satisfy him on all levels. And if he did, would he be willing to take the risk?

Bix shook the thoughts away, suddenly restless. The possibility of anything happening to Carin made his blood run hot and his muscles ache for action. He needed to do something. Anything.

"We've been watching this place for an hour, Alaan. Let's go check it out."

They drove a couple of blocks down the street, circled back and pulled into the alley behind the building they'd been casing.

Bix broke the lock on the back door and eased it open. The next instant, the hair on the back of his neck rose to full attention. A creeping feeling of dread pushed at him the second he stepped over the threshold. He looked over to Alaan. "Did you feel that?"

Alaan's blond brow pulled down into a fierce frown as he nodded.

Thankful for keen sight and hearing, the two vamp Seekers took a quick look around, moving silently through the huge building. What the hell was going on? The entire first floor of the warehouse was deserted. No boxes, no crates, nothing. Just a new-smelling, dusty cavern of darkness. Why would Dan keep making trips to an empty warehouse? It didn't fit Sidheon's clean-cut image at all. In fact, the whole situation felt off.

"Something's wrong. Let's get the hell out of here," Bix whispered.

Filled with a sudden sense of urgency, Bix moved out into the alley, keeping his back flat against the wall until he was clear of the door. Their contact had claimed Sidheon was on to them, or at least on to *him*. This whole thing could be a set-up.

Alaan headed for the SUV, but stilled at his friend's hissed call. Bix motioned for Alaan to take the left side of the alley while he took off on silent feet to the right. They met up in front of the building.

"Look there," Alaan said, motioning his head towards someone darting across the street.

Sidheon's assistant, Dan, was running towards a dark, late-model vehicle as fast as his short little legs could carry him. Alaan was on him in a flash, reaching the vehicle before Dan could get his whole body inside. He wrapped his large arms around Dan's torso, smashed the man back against his chest, and held him tight enough to partially inhibit his breathing. It had the intended effect as Dan's panic escalated, making him instinctively try to take deep, thick breaths between whimpers.

Bix joined them in the shadow of a doorway. "Was this a set-up?" he demanded.

"I can't tell you. H-He'll kill me."

Alaan let his fangs slip free and lengthen menacingly. He lowered his head to Dan's ear and whispered, "Don't worry about Sidheon. I'll kill you. I'll just enjoy it more because of who you've sold yourself to." Alaan rubbed his incisors against the back of Dan's neck with a satisfied growl. The little man shook like a loose shutter in a storm, and would've been a crumpled heap on the sidewalk if Alaan hadn't been holding him up.

Alaan let go of the panicking human and Bix grabbed him by the collar and lifted him clean off the ground. "Tell us." His voice resonated with menace. He wasn't in the mood to be fucked with, and if he had to skin the simpering toad to get what he needed, then let the skinning commence.

Dan sobbed now, blubbering with wonder about how he could have gotten himself into so much trouble. "Oh please, please don't kill me."

"Then tell me what I want to know. You have ten seconds, then the skin starts coming off an inch at a time. Clear?"

"Yes, yes. Crystal clear. It's all Sidheon's fault," Dan wailed. "The ungrateful idiot. None of the research is his. It's all mine."

Bix and Alaan looked at each other, the pieces beginning to fall into place.

"The experiments, the studies, everything is all mine. Sidheon walked in one day and just took over. All he did was *not* kill me while taking all the credit. And because of my weakness, that nice Dr. Carinian is going to die."

"What?" Bix bellowed, shaking Dan like a rag doll until the smaller man put his hands up and begged for mercy.

"But she was always nice to me. I-I can't let her blood be on my hands. Please, please, God, give me the courage to do what's right," Dan prayed on a whimper. Tears streamed unchecked down his face and fogged up his glasses. "I arranged for you to receive the tip about this place. It was the only way to get you out here."

"Why?" Bix growled low in his throat.

"Because Sidheon wanted you out of the way for a few hours tonight," Dan whispered, then took in a gasping breath. "Because he...oh, I can't even say it."

"You'd better." Bix's voice was as hard and cold as dry ice. "This is your only chance to make this right, asshole."

Dan nodded, feet still dangling in the air, and plowed on. The words came out garbled and anxious, gagging him as he forced them out of his mouth. "Because he plans to take Dr. Carinian tonight. He's obsessed with her. The fact that she's probably uncovered his research by accident is the only excuse he needs to...to..."

"To what?" Now it was Alaan's turn to growl. His partner happened to like Carin.

"To rape her. Then he's going to kill her," Dan sobbed. "But she's such a nice lady. I can't let that happen to her."

The weasel tried to wipe the tears and snot from his face, but found his arm wrenched behind his back. Exactly where Bix wanted it.

"When?" the two Seekers shouted in unison.

"Tonight. Just after one o'clock."

Bix didn't need to look at his watch to know they had less than fifteen minutes to get all the way across town. He dropped Dan to the ground, not bothering to turn around when the man crumpled in a trembling heap.

Bix called back over his shoulder. "If you're lying and my woman dies, that's your ass."

Dan passed out cold as the sound of screeching tires echoed in his ears.

෮෬

She tossed and turned, unable to sleep. Bix. The man was on her mind in a really bad way. At this rate she'd never get to sleep without him. It didn't make sense to keep rolling all over the bed, so she rose and headed for the shower. Dressed in her favorite jeans and an "All Natural Girl" T-shirt, Carin packed a large duffel bag with enough clothes and other things to last a couple of days. She hoped Bix wouldn't mind if she stayed the weekend. But after what he'd laid on her tonight, she didn't think so.

After making love, the man made it clear he wanted her. Not just for the Sidheon case, but he wanted her, period. He hadn't used the vamp B-word—bond—but it was a start. If she didn't know better, she'd swear the big buzzard had developed a soft spot for her that went well beyond sex. He obviously trusted her and she had to admit she trusted him in return. If Bix weren't on the up-and-up, he wouldn't have exposed himself or his kind. If she'd been on the other side of things, there was no way between here and hell she would endanger her family by giving them up to someone who didn't mean a hill of beans to her.

And he'd gone a step further than telling her he was a vampire. He'd explained he was a Seeker. She'd never heard of such a thing, but he explained his job and who he worked for. In short, he was a bad-assed vamp that anyone with common sense would stay on the good side of. It also explained his honed body, quick reflexes and his need to be so damned bossy. Her man was a vamp warrior. In and out of bed. Oh goodness, she was making herself blush.

A black duffel sat at the front door, packed and ready. The full moon caught her eye and she studied it before closing the blinds in the living room. The bright silvery orb hung large and low in the sky, illuminating the clouds around it. A shiver moved through her body. The night felt eerie, odd. She cocked her head and tried to put her finger on the weird feeling, but it eluded her. She'd be glad when Bix started teaching her how to use her psychic talents. Maybe then she'd be able to sense this kind of stuff instead of being paranoid about what she didn't understand.

Carin's eyes filled with tears and a strange melancholy stole over her like she'd never be back here again. She missed her house already and she hadn't even gone anywhere yet. *Oh for goodness sake,* she grumbled to herself. Emotionally attached to a building? Yep, she definitely needed to get out more.

Shaking off the strange weight settling on her shoulders, Carin pulled on her sneakers and slipped her house key into her pants pocket. She grabbed the duffel, stuffed her purse inside it and snatched up the directions Bix had left for her on the coffee table. With one final look around, she stepped into the balmy night and shivered. It wasn't particularly cold out but the army of goose bumps marching over her arms wriggled under her skin and left a marked chill behind. Carin stepped back inside to grab a light down jacket anyway. It was time to go. Arms tucked into the sleeves of her coat, she slid the deadbolt home and didn't look back.

Clouds had drifted over the moon. A chill wind rose and sent a small torrent of dried leaves across the lawn. It felt like a storm was coming.

Her sneakers made no sound as she trotted down the steps and made a beeline for her car parked in the driveway. She clicked the unlock button on her car key fob, then looked warily up at the streetlamps illuminating her driveway and half of her block. Only...they weren't illuminating. Every single one of them was out and it was pitch black in front of her house. The hairs on the back of her neck danced wildly. Someone was out here. Her fingers had just tightened on the handle of the unlocked car door when a big hand shot out and struck her on the side of the head.

She went down in a heap and landed with a harsh thud flat on her stomach. It knocked the wind from her lungs but she wasn't out. Not by a long shot. Nobody got away with cold cocking her in the side of the head. She felt something both icy and hot rush across her back, but she ignored it and rolled over to face her assailant.

A strange face with a malevolent grin loomed over hers. A fanged grin? *What the hell?*

The stranger lowered his mouth to her neck. A gag caught in her throat from just a whiff of his rancid breath. Yuck! It reminded her of old rotting pork. She tried to use her arms to push him back and stretch away from him, but he was too strong. Fine, she might not be a vampire, but she was no weakling. She bent her knees and pulled her legs close to her chest, creating an effective barrier between her and fang boy. Kicking with all her might, her legs sent the man flying backward. He landed in the rose bushes lining the side of the driveway. Thankful she lifted heavy weights frequently, she rolled to her knees and was on her feet in a boxing stance, ready to get it on.

Three men approached out of the darkness. One of them she recognized.

"Aleth? What the hell is going on?"

"Hello, Dr. Carinian," Aleth Sidheon droned, sounding bored with the whole business. "These are some friends of mine. It appears you've been snooping into other people's research. We can't have that, now can we?"

Her back was on fire where something wet seeped through her jacket. Her knees trembled as she fought for consciousness, but she had to know what this was all about.

"Snooping into what?" she asked with much more gumption than she felt. The two men flanked her now, and the one she'd kicked into the rose bush made his way back to their little party with several thorns sticking out of his face. He didn't look happy at all. They were all armed with wicked-looking bowie knives, moving around her until they formed a perfect circle.

How the hell had Sidheon figured out she'd nicked some of his specimens? She cleared her mind and thoughts—Bix had told her she projected too much—and concentrated on finding a way out of this mess. Better yet, maybe if she screamed Bix's name loud enough in her head he would hear her somehow.

"We didn't mean to frighten you, Doctor. After all, death is nothing to be afraid of," Sidheon said with a chilling, long-toothed smile. So, her reasoning that Bix was after the good Dr. Aleth Sidheon because he was a vampire had been correct. So *not* good. "Besides, I have some fun planned for us first."

She laughed outright. Not a cute little chuckle, but a good belly buster of a laugh. As much as her vision began to swim, she just couldn't seem to stop. When she finally caught her breath, she gathered a fat wad of spit in her mouth and let it fly. Damn, he dodged it. And now he was pissed. She could feel the anger radiating off him.

With a signal from Sidheon, Fang Boy lunged in synch with the other two. She was grabbed from behind and felt the tender skin of her neck ripped open from her chin down to her collarbone. But that pain was nothing compared to the continual blows to her face and body, pummeling her, rocking her until she tasted her own coppery metallic blood as it pooled in her mouth. She tried to kick out at the man directly in front of her, tried to get away from at least one set of hands ravaging her body. But her arms were wrenched behind her back and pulled tight until she thought her elbows would meet. Silver blades flashed in the moonlight and a fresh agonizing burn radiated from her stomach and expanded out along her ribs.

It was too much. She was dying. One more hack or cut and her life was over. Then she saw it, the blade poised to deliver the final stroke headed towards the left side of her chest in a perfect, lethal arc. Following the knife with blurred vision, Carin made her peace with God.

A furious, agonized roar vibrated the air. Had she been screaming? Her burning, scratchy throat felt raw enough. Suddenly there were no more hands pulling her arms from the sockets. No more fists striking. No more blades ripping. Only the welcoming coolness of concrete under her body. No, the coolness wasn't welcome. She didn't want to die. That was the sole purpose of the last ten years of her life—to prevent the very thing that had come for her tonight. Damned son-of-a-bitch, death.

The last thing she saw was Bix's bare hands ripping Fang Boy's throat out while a blond giant gutted another of the creeps who'd been gutting her. God was so cool. He'd sent her two avenging angels—Bix, dark as sin and hard as stone, and the other was just as tall and powerful, but blond and so beautiful it almost hurt to look at him.

She wanted to shout to the bad guys, wanted to yell, "That's what you get, you punks." But the blackness came too swiftly, giving her no time to form the words.

ஐᏣ

Bix sat in the middle of Carin's driveway and hauled her gently into his lap. The air was thick with the scent of her blood. The knowledge of what those bastards had done almost sent Bix over the edge into uncontrollable rage. Any blood not

121

given freely was a crime in and of itself, but the blood of a mate went beyond a crime. The blood of a mate was sacred.

Her face was a bloody mess. The gouges and slashes on her neck and chest bled profusely. Her coat was shredded and the T-shirt underneath was soaked with her own blood. Bix's cry of anguish and utter hopelessness filled the night. Sidheon would have to wait. His woman needed him now.

Without a second thought, he bit the large vein at the juncture of his wrist and squeezed his hand into a fist several times until the blood flowed freely.

Bix forced her mouth open with his free hand. Her breathing was way too shallow, her pulse faint, and she wasn't responding. His blood poured down his hand and mingled with the hot red liquid soaking her top. His blood wouldn't do her any good if he couldn't get her to swallow it.

Alaan ran back to the SUV parked halfway on the sidewalk, opened the back door and then returned to Bix's side. He heard Alaan's footsteps but couldn't turn off the automatic snarl of warning, baring his fangs at his partner. He didn't want anyone else to touch Carin, not even his best friend.

"Bix, we don't have time for this. She's on the verge. Snap out of the prime shit and let me help you with your woman."

Alaan's words cut through his feral reaction. Carin. She was dying. If she left him, he didn't know how he would ever bear it.

"Alaan, help me. Open her mouth and hold it open."

Alaan did as Bix asked and carefully inserted his fingers into the corners of Carin's mouth, forcing her cooling lips apart. He held her mouth open while Bix shifted her weight, supporting her with one arm and flexing his bleeding arm. His blood trickled in and pooled in the back of her throat. She still didn't move. Didn't swallow.

Bix hauled back and slapped her hard in the face, wincing at the loud smack and the palm print etched into her swelling, bruised cheek. Her swift intake of breath, followed by a round of gagging as the pooled blood slid down her throat, told him she was conscious for the moment. She groaned and tried to turn her head away.

"Come on, sweetheart. Stay with me."

"Bix? Where are you?" Her voice was faint, weak, and his heart ached at the sound of the misery in her very thoughts.

"I'm here, Carin. Come on, baby, I need you to swallow for me. Stay with me just long enough to swallow."

"Head...hurts. Don't want to die... Owww."

"I know, baby, but I need you to do as I say. Now."

"Bossy."

"You have no idea. Now do it. Swallow."

He held her head still while Alaan forced her mouth open until she'd taken several large swallows. Bix sighed with relief when she lifted her head a fraction and turned into his embrace, seeking the source of the warmth flowing down her throat. He pressed his wound more firmly against her bruised lips, thankful when she latched onto it and suckled until she fell into blessed unconsciousness.

Alaan disappeared into the back of the SUV again and retrieved a small first-aid kit. Bix held out his arm just long enough for Alaan to wrap some good old-fashioned gauze around the puncture wounds and tape it securely.

With the power and grace born of a vampire, Bix was on his feet in a flash, cradling Carin's huddled form against his body. Settling into the backseat, he wrapped his big body around her to shield her from as much movement as possible.

Alaan shut the door, grabbed Carin's overnight bag off the front lawn and threw it into the front passenger seat. He returned to the driveway, tossed the dead vamp bodies into an inconspicuous corner of her backyard, then jumped into the driver's seat. He slammed the vehicle into reverse and stomped on the gas.

A quick glance over his shoulder and Alaan's heart broke. He watched his friend in anguish, stroking his mate's hair as his body sheltered her from the slightest bump or movement of their vehicle. Bix looked up at Alaan with haunted eyes full of despair and his heart wrenched for his friend. He flipped open his cell and hit the speed dial. A sultry purr filled the line.

"Natasha. It's Alaan. I need to speak with my mother right now."

"Sure, what's going on?"

Alaan glanced into the rear-view mirror. Bix was shaking his head resolutely. Nodding his understanding, Alaan spoke into the mouthpiece of the cell phone again.

"My mother, Natasha. While I speak with her, you will make arrangements for a plane to be readied at the private airstrip in San Diego. We also need a mop up of three dead vamps at 14362 La Jolla. Backyard. You have ten minutes."

Natasha jumped off the line. Alaan held back a sigh of relief when a familiar, soothing voice replaced Natasha's—the Matriarch, Alaana Serati, his mother. Alaan filled her in on as much detail as he could in the ten minutes it took to get to the private airstrip owned by the Council and the clans.

Carin was placed on the plane in a reclining seat with as many pillows as they could find to tuck up against her and around her head. In minutes they were headed towards V.C.O.E. North American headquarters in the mountains of Montana.

Chapter Eleven

God, she had a splitting headache, and a splitting everything else. But at least something pleasantly warm and hard was pressed close against her body. She longed to reach out and touch it, but that meant she'd have to wake up. No, never mind. The way the pain leached through her semi-conscious mind, she knew if she fought to reach the surface of lucidity she'd regret it terribly. She'd never been big on pain.

A quiet, deep voice rumbled through the hard warmth next to her. Was the warmth speaking to her? No, it spoke to someone else a bit farther away. Now there were two voices, one she thought she recognized. *Oh, please be quiet*, she thought, wishing the talking would stop so she could fade back to the calm and pain-free blackness.

As she listened to the voice, she remembered the concrete coming up to meet her face as her own blood soaked through her clothes. And Bix crashing onto the scene looking like a dark avenging angel with his black hair standing on end. It was the first time she'd seen his fangs bared in anger, but she hadn't been afraid of him. She knew he was there to take care of her. Then she'd floated in a weird sort of limbo, no voices, no sound, just a soothing calm. Until now.

"She's lucky, Bix. There's no way she should be alive."

"What's the extent of her injuries, Doc?"

"A couple of broken ribs, numerous lacerations on her neck, arms and across her chest, all stitched. We also stitched her up across her stomach and right shoulder where the knives penetrated. Most stomach wounds are fatal, but somehow her attackers missed her lungs and intestines."

Bix shook his head as he listened to the laundry list of injuries Carin had sustained. And all because he hadn't been where he was supposed to have been. With his mate. Would she ever forgive him?

"She's also got a nasty bruise on the back of her skull. No concussion, but the bone of her cranium is bruised a bit. And of course the black eyes and facial wounds."

"Damn," Bix muttered, kissing the top of Carin's head. He tightened his arms around her, determined she would never leave his bed again. She whimpered in her sleep and he loosened his hold.

"Is there anything I can do for her?" Hell, why was he asking that question. He'd already done, or rather *not* done, quite enough.

"She just needs rest and plenty of nutrients. She's on a liquid diet with plenty of sleep aid and pain meds mixed in. And if you don't mind, I'd like to put a little of your blood in with her meds. It'll speed up her metabolism. She can come off the IV in a few days if she continues to improve."

"What's the bottom line?"

"She'll heal. No scars. No problems. And..." The doctor paused, walking around to the other side of the bed to wrap a tourniquet around Bix's free arm. "I can smell you on her. You know both the blood and semen of a prime male have regenerative properties for humans. She was fatally wounded

126

and even the sex you'd had only hours before wouldn't have been nearly enough to save her. If you hadn't acted quickly and forced her to drink some of your blood, she never would have made it."

Bix watched the doctor finish drawing from his ropy vein and inject the rich, red blood directly into Carin's IV drip. He let out a pent-up breath and dropped yet another kiss into the riot of curls on top of Carin's dark head.

"Baby, I'm so sorry. I should have been there sooner. If you never forgive me, I'll understand. You mean so much to me, sweetheart. Thank you for not dying on me. Even if we're never together again, just knowing you're alive is enough for me."

But was it? Losing her would rip his heart out, but it no longer mattered what he wanted. The only thing important to him was her happiness and safety. If it meant she wanted a future without him in it, he would accept it.

Bix thought he felt an answering call from deep inside Carin's mind, but it faded to nothingness. He looked up and saw the doctor injecting pain medicine into her IV. If she had been close to consciousness, she wouldn't be in about six seconds. After all, vampire pharmaceuticals were the best.

He lay next to her wishing he could will her awake just to look into her soulful brown eyes, but she needed sleep to recover. Though they were both naked under the covers, he was reluctant to touch her again now that he understood the extent of her injuries. Easing away from her battered body, he carefully left the bed. He didn't want her out of his sight, but she'd be knocked out from the pain meds for several hours. If he was going to answer the Council's summons, now was as good a time as any.

He showered in record time, threw on a pair of jeans and a black T-shirt, padded into the living room in bare feet, and eased the bedroom door closed behind him. His boots, filthy with caked-on blood and dirt, were in the same corner he'd kicked them into in the dark hours of the morning while the surgeons had worked on Carin right there in his apartment. Passing up the boots for a pair of comfortable sneakers, he slipped a warm sweatshirt over his head and strode out of his apartment. Two steps into the hallway, he stopped short. Alaan was waiting. They clasped hands but said nothing. The two of them hit the end of the hallway with long strides and descended the wide, cedar-planked staircase, headed for the Council Chambers on the first floor of the sprawling rustic mansion.

"Jon, wait."

Damn it. "Natasha, I can't talk to you right now."

"But why did you bring that woman here?"

"I don't believe it's any of your business," Bix snapped impatiently. "But since you're are a Council's Liaison, I'll indulge you just this once. The woman is Dr. Carinian Derrickson."

"Your target?"

"The same. And she's mine."

"What? You're claiming your target? How dare you bring her here." Natasha's long black hair swung from side to side as she spewed bitter displeasure.

She jumped when Bix's hand shot out and grabbed Alaan's arm, holding him back. Fangs bared on a snarl, his partner promptly put the female in her place.

"You will not address a prime or a Seeker in that tone, woman," Alaan hissed.

Natasha took a step back, the shock on her face as easy to read as an open book. In fact, Bix was a bit surprised himself. He couldn't recall Alaan or himself this worked up over a woman. Any woman, except Sher. The sounds emanating from both their throats brought a picture to mind—feline males fighting to protect their territory and their females. The truth hit him square in the gut. In no time, Carin had them wrapped around her little finger. And Bix didn't want to be wrapped any other way.

Natasha lowered her head in deference to the prime males standing before her. She located an interesting spot on her shoe to study. But it wasn't good enough. He expected, and would have, her submission. Council Liaison or not, she was subordinate to him and every other elder prime's authority. Only the females of Clan Serati were immune, but even those warrior women showed proper respect to their males.

Bix crossed his arms over his chest and stared at her. Hard. She'd let her mouth get away from her, and now she had to eat crow for it.

"I am waiting, Natasha."

"I apologize, prime male Jon Bixler, prime male Alaan Serati," she mumbled the proper and formal apology.

Bix felt her anger pulse and grow like a psychic cancer as she turned and slunk away. He had a feeling he hadn't heard the end of this. Damned female.

෨෬

Several hours later, Carin hovered on the edge of consciousness. Muzzy brained, she was sure her body was mired under several layers of wet blankets. She didn't open her eyes, but knew something or someone was in the room with her. Something malevolent, evil. Something that wished she'd never wake up. Forcing the cotton from her mind, Carin willed the gears in her brain to start turning a bit faster. She had to wake up. She just had to.

Her eyes snapped open and she called out to Bix with all her mind's strength. A very tall, very mean-looking woman stood over her. The woman was striking, with fine European features and long straight black hair. But the hatred in her large green eyes lent her a savage quality. Especially since those green eyes flashed fire and anger down at her. Carin didn't remember ever meeting this woman. She felt like crap and didn't particularly feel like being threatened at the moment. Her mouth began to work before her mind could catch up with it.

"Who are you and what the hell are you doing in here?" she drawled groggily, pulling no punches.

"I'm Natasha Vanett and I belong here. Question is, what the hell are you doing here?"

"Well, forgive me if I don't quite feel like talking. But as you can tell from the bloody dressings, the bandages all over my body, and the tubes running in and out of my skin, I'm just not feeling all that great."

"By rights you should be dead, you bitch."

"Did I harm you in another life or something?"

"Jon was supposed to be mine, you stupid cow."

"Bitch, I'll stomp a mud hole in your ass." Stupid cow? She'd kick the shit out of the woman then see who was a stupid cow. Carin tried to sit up. Damn, that hurt. Pain slashed through her stomach and back and left her flat on the mattress panting. God, she wished her pain medicine hadn't worn off. Now she had two reasons to be mad. The vindictive Natasha woman standing next to her bed, and the pain she'd caused herself with her temper.

"Look, bitch, I don't know what's up with you and Bix, and I don't want to know. But don't be coming in here fucking with
130

me because you have a problem with him," Carin fumed. The effort it took to be angry made her head throb. "If you want Bix, you can have him."

"I think your mate will have something to say about that."

The soothing female voice floating to her from across the room was unfamiliar to Carin. She managed to lift her head enough to see who spoke, but the effort made the stitches in both the side of her neck and across her stomach pull and sting. Her head swam and the room began to move a bit sideways. Her stomach churned from the strange sensation. Bile rose up in her throat as she prayed for her stomach to settle. The last thing she wanted was to start heaving and tear loose anything temporarily held together with stitches.

The owner of the voice came into full view and stood next to her bed. The woman had a grace and quiet dignity Carin had only seen in much older women, yet this lady didn't look a day over forty. Petite, her short crop of platinum blonde curls framed a perfect pear-shaped face with eyes the color of Caribbean seas. Her skin was smooth and silky, like the cream she wished she could have on top of her latte in the mornings. In a word, the woman was stunning. Carin watched in awe as the woman measured out a pale yellow liquid into a mug with small manicured hands. The yellow stuff was mixed with little white sugar-looking crystals, and dumped into a larger steaming cup of something else.

"Hello, Carinian. I am Alaana Serati, Matriarch of Clan Serati. How are you feeling?"

"Like hammered shit," Carin muttered, then clamped her lips together as the salty precursor to vomit filled her mouth.

"Do you remember anything, or feel like talking?"

Hell no, she didn't feel like talking. Not about all the pain she'd felt when those vamps worked her over, nor did she want to discuss waking up to find a spiteful what's-her-name standing over her wishing her dead. Oh yes, she remembered just about everything, but didn't want to voice it. That would make it too real. Just the memories of those vamps' hands on her body made her skin crawl. The inside of her jaw twinged with the threat of the bitter fluid rising up her throat. God, she didn't have the energy to throw up right now.

"Ewww." She shuddered, taking as deep a breath as she could considering the snug binding wrapped around her chest. "I feel like I have to throw up."

Alaana stepped close, eased an arm around Carin's back and helped her sit up enough to drink. Carin's eyebrows would have flown upward but even *they* hurt like hell. She was a muscular, good-sized woman, but this petite blonde lifted her with a strength that belied her small frame. She held Carin with one arm and pressed the steaming mug to her lips. Sighing with comforted relief as the hot liquid, honey sweet with a hint of ginger and lemon, soothed her stomach straight away.

"Thank you. If there's anything I hate, it's throwing up. I actually hate it more than I hate doing laundry."

Alaana chuckled good-naturedly and said, "It must be the same for women everywhere." She then turned her stern eyes on a scowling Natasha. "Why are you here?"

"I just came to welcome our guest," Natasha said, backpedaling faster than a one-legged man on a tricycle.

"In her condition? She is covered with bandages and stitches and you came to meet her now?"

Carin watched Natasha's mouth work but nothing came out as she shrugged stupidly at Alaana's continued questioning.

"These are Bix's private apartments. Did he give you permission to bother his mate?"

Mate? There was that word again. Carin's eyebrows tried to rise once more, but they throbbed as much as the rest of her body. What was it with this mate business? Bix mentioned vampire bonding and mating, but he'd never gotten into the mechanics of how it worked. Nor had he asked her to be his mate.

Natasha backed down, but even an idiot couldn't have missed the cold glint in her emerald eyes as she lowered them to the carpet. And Carin was no idiot.

"You may leave now, Natasha," Alaana said with a dismissive wave of her hand, not bothering to look towards the chastised woman to see if she obeyed. "Now, Carin, I will help you finish this. It's tea mixed with some healing herbs and a dash of modern medicine."

"Huh?" Carin asked, genuinely unsure of what was just said to her.

"In short, it's tea with a powerful painkiller in it. Thankfully, Bix was able to get some of his blood into you. It will aid the healing process, but it doesn't do much for the pain. And by the way, welcome to both our retreat and our clans."

The older woman's words had a deeper meaning than their simplicity implied. Carin felt it all through her soul. Alaana's smile made her feel at ease and welcome. It was the first time in a long while she felt a part of something other than her own little one-some.

A few seconds later, Bix burst through the door at full speed with a tall, beautiful and equally blond tank right on his heels. Oh my God, he was real. She thought she'd dreamed him up when she lay bleeding on her driveway. So he *had* been there with Bix, fighting for her, trying to save her. But who was he?

"What is it? What's wrong?" Bix skidded to a halt next to the bed, almost knocking Alaana over in his haste. "I heard you calling me. What's happened?"

Alaana greeted the golden-haired hunk first. "Hello, Alaan. I'm happy you're home though I wish the circumstances had been different."

Carin ignored Bix for the moment, too entranced by the Alaan person stepping forward to take Alaana's dainty little hand in one of his huge ones. He leaned over and planted a kiss on her palm. Guess chivalry wasn't dead.

After doting on him a moment, Alaana turned to a wide-eyed Carin—or as wide as the swelling would allow—and introduced her.

"Carin, this is my son, Alaan. He and Bix brought you here."

So, one of her avenging angels was Bix's friend? And boy was this blond giant a good-looking devil, uh, angel. Woo, goodness, the man was fine. Dayum! Bix's grumbling snagged her attention away from Alaana's gorgeous son.

Finally addressing Bix's original question, the Matriarch answered for Carin. "There is nothing wrong now. However, Natasha was here pestering your mate."

"What?" His hand held Carin's tightly as he looked directly at Alaana.

"From the looks of it we've got a little warrior on our hands. Your mate was ready to skin Natasha alive, and in her condition, too," Alaana declared proudly.

"That woman said you and her have a thing going on," Carin slurred. Wow, that tea stuff sure worked fast. But she couldn't go to sleep yet. She had to know what was going on between Bix and the green-eyed bitch on wheels.

"Damn it, even in my own apartments I can't protect you," he seethed.

"Down't be ridilicus, uh, ridiculous, Bix. 'Course yulve patected me." Oh yes, she was fading fast along with the pain already gone from a flaming roar down to a muted purr.

"What the hell is Natasha's problem? I've never led her to believe I wanted her. Hell, I've never even slept with her," Bix growled.

That was all a semi-awake Carin needed to know. She gave up the fight to whatever anti-nausea pain reliever Ms. Alaana had given her. Besides, the drug had been winning for the past few moments anyway.

May as well throw in the towel. She really hoped she didn't snore.

◿☃

His attention on Carin's peaceful, but swollen, purple and black face, Bix felt a pang of guilt once more. He could have lost her that night. He'd been out there chasing phantoms and shadows while Sidheon tried to kill his woman. Damned rogue. Just wait, he'd get him soon enough.

Glad Carin was asleep, a furious Bix herded Alaana and Alaan out of the bedroom door and into the oversized living room. He'd been in the middle of laying down his strategy for capturing Sidheon to the Council when he'd heard Carin's panic in his head as clearly as if she'd been standing there. He'd run out of the Council Chambers without even excusing himself, spurred on by the fear pulsing through their newly forming bond. She'd been afraid of someone—Natasha. How dare the woman threaten his mate. Hell, he'd skin her himself.

Bix paced a hole in the thick carpet in front of the cold white brick fireplace. He yanked his fingers through his hair and blew out a breath laden with frustration. His jaw ticked double time as he tried to get his anger under wraps. He was a Seeker. He could do better than this. *Come on, Bix, get it together, man.*

After a moment, he dropped onto the couch next to Alaan. The Matriarch of Clan Serati sat facing them in a matching loveseat.

"Thanks for looking after Carin, Matriarch."

"My pleasure, but she was doing a pretty good job of looking after herself before I fed her the sedative." With a smile and a regal nod, Alaana rose and headed for the door. Alaan stood in respect to see her out. She stopped and turned a stern gaze on Bix. "I expect to receive a date for the joining ceremony, Bix. Alaan, keep him out of trouble in the meantime."

Bix's mouth fell open. When he'd burst through the door, he'd been so concerned about Carin he'd blown off and forgotten about the Matriarch calling Carin his mate. Well, he sure as hell remembered now. But how had the Matriarch known?

Alaana smiled at Bix's bemused expression.

"I am not a vampire Elder of Clan Serati for nothing, Bix. Very little gets by this old bird. The connection between you two is obvious."

Bix's expression didn't change. In fact, he was more amazed than ever.

Alaana chuckled. "Anyone can see she's your mate. It's all over you both," she said cheerily, and waltzed right out the door without a backward glance.

Bix turned and let his fist fly towards Alaan's gut. The cheeky bastard was laughing at him.

ೞಌ

"Good morning, sweetheart."

"Mmmm, owww. If you say so," Carin whimpered and tried to pull in a deep breath, wincing when her lungs and all the sore spots on her chest burned. The stitches pulled, but at least the pain was manageable at the moment.

"How are you feeling?"

"Same as when Alaana asked me last time, like hammered shit. Where exactly are we?" she mumbled, wishing she could raise her hand to scratch at her scalp. Before she could attempt to exercise the thought, Bix buried his fingers in her hair and took care of the itch for her. There was a lot to be said for this psychic boyfriend stuff.

"Psychic boyfriend, eh?" Bix chuckled. "And to answer your question, we're at V.C.O.E. North American headquarters in Montana. We have a huge estate in the Flathead Valley on about four hundred and fifty acres, just west of Kalispell."

"Is this your place?"

"I keep this apartment for when I'm here on Council business. I have my own spread about a half hour chopper ride north of here." He smoothed her wild tangle of hair away from her swollen face, and buried his fingers with gentle strokes as he spoke softly to her.

"Bix, kiss me. Very gently, please," she asked sleepily.

He complied, lightly pressing his full lips to hers. Each shallow breath brought with it his natural masculine scent. The overlay of clean musky soap tickled her nose. She inhaled again, appreciating the pleasant respite from the strong antiseptic smells clinging to her skin.

"Mmmm, thank you for that," she whispered.

"What do you remember, sweetheart?" Bix continued to scratch lovingly at her scalp.

"I was about to open my car door when I got cold cocked by a mean-assed vampire with big teeth," she finished on a contented sigh. "That feels really good. Does a bath come with it?"

"We'll eventually get to the bath, with bubbles if you like. I'll even wash your hair for you. But right now I need to know what happened. Where the hell were you going at that time of night?"

"I couldn't sleep. I was on my way to see you to tell you I'd decided to help with your little rogue problem."

"You were on your way to my house? In the fucking middle of the night? Damn it, Carin."

"I know, Bix, I know. It was stupid but it's a bit late for recriminations. Besides, it makes my head hurt." And that was all she had to say about it. Carin was grateful for the quiet knock on the apartment door.

Bix's grumpy, "Who the hell is it now?" made it clear he was reluctant to get up. Easing out from under the blankets, he left the bed and pulled on a comfy-looking pair of worn, black sweatpants. Carin watched his gloriously naked, oh-so-proportioned perfection move over to the dresser, grab a shirt and head towards the bedroom door. His powerful back muscles tensed and bunched as he slipped a white T-shirt over his head. The man was so sinfully handsome, and she felt swollen and bruised. Probably looked like a multi-colored Pillsbury Dough-girl. She sighed dejectedly. Even breathing hurt.

When Bix returned, a friendly faced older man in a light blue smock and clogs strode in behind him with a big medical bag. She was sure it was filled with goodies just for her.

"Hello, Carinian. I don't know if you remember me, but I'm Dr. Lyons. We've been taking care of you the past few days. How are we feeling today?"

"Hold it," she squawked, "I've been here how long?"

"Three days now. We kept you heavily sedated after the surgery," the doctor replied.

"Surgery? Three days? Three *whole* days?" At Dr. Lyons nod, she lost it. "I can't stay here. I need to go home. I've got to get back to work. I can't just play hooky from work."

She squirmed, trying to ease towards the edge of the bed. Her eyes tried to widen with a mix of panic and pain, but they were too swollen. What the hell was she thinking trying to get out of bed? Bix allowed the heat of his temper to flare up the link between them. She shouldn't be moving around unnecessarily. He wanted to keep her still but there wasn't one place on her body he could touch without causing her pain, except the top of her head. Grabbing a handful of the thick cottony locks, he held her gently against the pillows.

"Carin, you're not in any condition to go anywhere. You feel like hammered shit because you look like hammered shit. Now. Be. Still."

"Oh, that was just cold," she ground out. "Just full of compliments, aren't you, Bix?" *"Bastard."*

Bix grinned, hearing her sentiment loud and clear in his head, glad her spirit hadn't been diminished by her ordeal. He moved out of the way and let the doctor examine her. Dr. Lyons pulled the covers back and Bix's heart slammed up into his throat. God, she was a mess. Her bandages were bloodied through, and the flesh around her stitches was red, swollen and raw. The scent of her blood clung to the sheets and filled the air. He felt his temper escalate once again.

"Bix, cut it out," Dr. Lyons said with a stern look.

Solely focused on Carin, Bix looked up at the edge in the doctor's voice, unsure of what the man was talking about. Cut it out? Cut out what?

Carin's thoughts pounded into his head. *"You're growling at the doctor, Bix."*

Bix felt her discomfort and knew if she opened her mouth, she'd start screaming as the doctor poked at her wounds and changed the dressings. His control stretched to the limit, hearing her thoughts and feeling every ounce of her distress. If only he could take her place, spare her every sharp pull, every deep ache. Unable to keep his fists from flexing in agitation, he clamped down on his bottom lip, uncaring that his fangs were in the way. Blood trickled from the puncture wound.

"Bix, it hurts but he's got to change the bandages, so don't be upset with Dr. Lyons. All that growling is making me edgy. And tell your teeth to go away. I'm not in the mood to see them right now."

His gut clenched with one particularly ragged cry. She was trying so hard to be brave and was doing a better job at it than he was. Finally Bix couldn't stand her suppressed screams.

"Dr. Lyons, give her something for the pain and then continue the exam."

"Can't I go without the meds today? I feel well enough." She pushed each word through gritted teeth. But Bix hadn't missed the way she bit down on her tongue. Hell, if she clamped down on it any harder he was sure she'd sever the thing clean off. Her chest rose and fell with her panting, but why she believed she could get anything past him, he would never know. He knew her stitches were on fire, her head throbbed, and she had constant nausea. Dr. Lyons had only checked the stitches on her neck and irrigated the knife wound on her shoulder, and she was a quaking wreck.

And the crazy woman thought she was going without meds today? Hell no. But before Bix could say anything, Dr. Lyons calmly removed his blood-smeared examination gloves, tossed them into a biohazard bag and marched back to the side of the bed to call her bluff. Good man.

"Well, Carinian..."

"Carin," she croaked, her trembling voice thick with stifled sobs.

"Okay, Carin. We can see if you'll go without meds today. How about I check the stitches across your stomach? If we can do that with relative comfort we can remove your catheter and lay off the pain meds. Of course, if the catheter comes out you'll have to get up to go to the bathroom. If you can't walk to the bathroom by yourself we'll have to send someone in to help you..."

"Oh, hell no. Touch my stitches and I swear when I get better I'll hunt you down and give you a rhino-sized enema. Give me the damn meds and get the hell away from me."

Dr. Lyons laughed outright.

Carin clapped a hand over her mouth, eyes wide with mortification. "Oh God, please tell me I didn't say that out loud."

"No, you didn't, but you're projecting loud enough for the whole mansion to have heard you." The doctor chuckled.

"Oh Lord, I'm so sorry, Dr. Lyons," Carin mumbled as her skin blushed an alarming shade of purple.

"No problem, young lady. I'll just add the meds to your IV and leave you alone for awhile."

As soon as Carin's eyes drooped, Dr. Lyons finished his examination and pulled the covers back over her naked body. "By the way, she's healing nicely, Bix. The IV can come out tomorrow and she can eat real food again. Your blood is speeding up her healing. If we could get a little bit more into her, I'd give her another three or four days and she can get up."

"And without my blood?"

"It'll be a couple of weeks, maybe three before she can get up or start to move around."

"Give it to her."

"We can wait until she wakes."

Bix sat in a chair across from the bed, held out his arm and said, "I said give it to her. I'm a prime male of Clan Vanett, Head Seeker for the Council and this is my mate. You will give her some of my blood, Doctor. Right now."

With a deferential nod, Lyons attached Bix to a portable transfusion unit. After delivering a pint of rich red blood to their patient, he turned to leave.

"I'll be back to check on her this evening. I'll see myself out."

Never once taking his eyes off Carin's peacefully sleeping face, he called a detached, "Thanks, Doc," from the chair. Beautifully brilliant and all-out feisty, she'd come awfully close to leaving this world. Yet she trusted him? Even in her drug-induced stupor, he'd felt her...love?

Alaan ducked his head into the bedroom as the doctor was leaving. "The Council wants to see you again, Bix. I can stay with Carin, if you want."

"No, she'll be all right. The doc just gave her some pain meds. She'll be out for awhile."

"Good, then I'll go with you to the Council chambers. Afterward, want to spar a bit? Work off some pent-up energy?"

"You've got it. I'm aching to kick somebody's ass." Bix smirked as he rose and followed Alaan out of the bedroom.

Alaan laughed heartily and smacked him in the middle of his back. "Think you're aching now? Wait until I'm done with your sorry ass."

Chapter Twelve

After only a week back at headquarters it felt like the millionth time Bix had stood in the middle of this damned round room. This estate was one of many huge properties owned by the V.C.O.E. And as they all were, it was a splendid mix of old-world charm and contemporary comfort. But today he didn't feel like admiring it as he usually did.

He waited, Alaan at his side, at the bottom of the large platform taking up one side of the room. At the top stood a gigantic solid wood, half-circle table with intricate carvings of vampire history across the top and sides. A depiction of the formation of V.C.O.E., how the ten clans came to be and details on vampire life as far back as could be remembered. For vampires, that was a very long time. Each headquarters facility on every continent boasted one of these works of art.

Finally, the Council filed in through a side door. Nine of the ten clan Elders and their mates walked up the carpeted steps to the high dais and sat down at the table. It looked like they were up on a stage big enough for a Broadway production. Matriarch Alaana Serati and her mate, Ralen, were Elders representing both Clan Serati and the U.S. Mountain region and were responsible for these proceedings. After all the other Council members were seated, Alaan's parents remained standing and motioned the two Seekers standing calmly in front of the dais forward.

Bix and Alaan climbed the stairs and stood before the Council, hands clasped behind their backs, legs braced apart, at ease.

"Bix, Carin seems to be coming along. Dr. Lyons tells us she's doing just fine," Alaana stated as she took her seat, her mate at her side.

Bix, following protocol, nodded to Alaana Serati, but didn't say a word. And he wouldn't until he was asked a direct question or invited to speak freely.

"Any news on Sidheon's whereabouts?" Ralen Serati asked.

"Sidheon took off when Alaan and I interrupted his attack on Dr. Derrickson. The Seekers in San Diego have been looking for him on my orders, but they've seen neither hide nor hair of him. He and his assistant, a man named Dan who told us about his plan to kill Carin, cleaned out their lab and just up and disappeared. A number of vamps who worked on the biotech campus are missing as well."

"What about you going back to San Diego to help the Seekers there?" the Matriarch suggested.

"I won't leave Carin under any circumstance. Especially not while she's recovering," Bix replied firmly, but calmly.

"Is she willing to help us with the Sidheon problem?" This from a medium height vamp with dark hair and slanted eyes. The Elder of Clan Li.

"Yes, she'd already decided to help us before she was attacked," Bix replied, stoically.

"Some have expressed concern over bringing her here and exposing our world."

"With all due respect, Elder Li, Carin is our best chance of uncovering what the rogue is up to. And even if she hadn't been willing to help us I wasn't going to let the son of a bitch kill her. It was bring her here, or let her die. Death didn't seem like a viable option, sir," Bix said, not bothering to keep the sneer off his face or out of his voice.

The Elder's eyebrows rose, but Bix wasn't moved. This was his woman they were talking about. Stupid vampire politics. Somebody didn't like the fact that he'd brought her here? Too damned bad. Probably Natasha. As Council Liaison for the U.S. Western region, her opinion would be taken into consideration, even if she was just being a spiteful bitch. Bix ground his back teeth, took a deep breath and held Elder Li's gaze. Back down? Not fucking likely.

"Relax, Seeker. We, and I mean the whole Council, agree your decision to bring Carin here was a good one," Alaana interjected, casting a warning glance towards Elder Li.

"Is there a reason you feel so strongly about this human?" The very direct question came from Standing Rock, Elder of Clan Akicit. The golden-skinned, dark-haired, sharp-featured vamp projected the true nature of a warrior by his very presence alone—strength, loyalty to what was right, and most important, a balance between nature and spirit.

"She is mine." Bix's stance was stiff as he snarled the words.

"Has she accepted a mating, or a bonding?" challenged Standing Rock, unmoved by Bix's outburst.

"Not yet, sir." Bix tensed, ready to take on the entire Council if need be. "She was on her way to me when the rogue tried to gut her. Trust me, the woman is mine."

Alaan stepped forward, put a firm hand on Bix's shoulder and gave him a telepathic push. "Stand down, Seeker. What the hell is wrong with you, going primal in front of the Council?"

It was a good question to which he had no answer. Bix backed off and waited for the reprimand he knew he'd earned.

"No one is challenging you for her, prime male. Every one of us, being mated, has experienced what you're going through right now. Some of us have even bonded with our mates. It is normal to want to protect your woman. For that, we will grant you a bit of leniency. This time."

"Thank you, Elder Standing Rock, sir." Bix gave a slight nod, but otherwise he didn't express a bit of remorse. He didn't feel any because he'd spoken the truth when he said Carin was his. As soon as she was well enough she would accept the mating and the bond. Period.

"Now if we can get back to the business at hand," came a bored melodic voice from the far end of the table. The Elder of Clan Sewelle, a tall, dark-skinned man with light gray eyes and flawless skin, reclined in his chair. His mate, an equally striking woman with skin almost the color of semi-dark chocolate stroked long, lovely fingers up and down his arm. He looked like he'd rather be doing something else, like spending time with his woman in a horizontal position. Bix didn't blame him.

Alaana spoke up from her seat at the center of the table. "I have a feeling whatever Sidheon is doing affects all of us. Including our less reputable cousins of Clan Hatsept. They will be invited to join us to discuss how we will proceed."

"Aw hell, not them. They're the scum of the vampire world," Alaan spoke plainly.

"They may be, but they are not rogues nor have they been excommunicated by our governors for any crime against us or humanity. They may be a bit unconventional, but they keep to their own, they do not expose our world and they don't hunt humans."

"Yeah, but they keep harems, Elder Serati. Harems, for shit's sake." Alaan scowled at his mother.

"You will watch your tongue, young Serati," Alaana snapped. Softening her tone, she said, "And while it may be true, last I heard every woman in their harems wishes to be there."

"What's wrong, Alaan. Jealous?" Natasha purred from below the dais. She sat cross-legged in a chair off to the side after slinking into the briefing late.

"Hold your tongue, Liaison," Alaan spat back at her, and then dismissed her as if she were less important than the carpet underneath his black combat boots. None of the Elders stood up for her. It was within Alaan's right as a Seeker and a prime male to dress her down for her impertinence.

"All of the clans have agreed to come and meet with us about this, and some of them will join us in the hunt. They will start arriving next week."

"How many Hatsepts are coming?" Alaan asked the Matriarch.

"All of them."

Both Seekers painted on their game faces when all they really wanted to do was protest. Loudly. Neither of them minded the representatives of the other nine clans, but *all* of the Hatsept Clan? Damn.

"We'll meet to plan and strategize. At the end of the meetings, we'll celebrate our alliance with a grand gathering. We're long overdue for a good party anyway. Bix, Alaan, gather your Seekers. You have all the rest of this week to prepare."

Great, just great. Clan Hatsept playboys on the same estate with my woman. Bloody-fuckin-fabulous, Bix snarled to himself.

૪૦ ૡ

"Any progress?" Sidheon was already bored with the conversation and he'd only been on the phone for a few seconds.

"Actually, yes. I've managed to end up on the same estate with Dr. Carinian Derrickson. Your incompetence landed her practically in my palm."

The voice was somewhat snide, but if this person could get him what he wanted, Sidheon was willing to deal with the insolence. For now. But later, they'd settle up good and proper.

"Can you arrange an abduction?" Sidheon anticipated the answer with glee.

"Of course, but why bother? It would be easier to kill her than to get her off the property. She's being watched closely."

"If I wanted her dead I wouldn't have bothered to contact you."

"You mean if you wanted her dead you would have taken care of it correctly the first time?"

Sidheon rolled his eyes towards the ceiling of the quaint little villa he was renting in Marin. This relationship was getting old fast. He let out an exasperated sigh, pushed the speakerphone button and continued feeding.

"You know," Sidheon sighed, relishing the rush from the blood he ingested while nearing the limit of his patience, "I think you and I are going to have a serious disagreement sometime soon. Keep up the sniping and I'll simply expose your connection to me and let the V.C.O.E. have you. It would be quite convenient considering you happen to be right there at headquarters. Clear enough?" Just then, the man attached to the throat Sidheon ripped open let out a bloodcurdling scream. Perfect timing.

The line was silent for a moment, but he heard the deep, even breathing of the vampire on the other end as options were weighed and considered. Of course there were no true options, but he wouldn't say anything. He'd wait until he had his hands on the disrespectful imp.

Finally, the voice replied, a lot less flippant, "I understand. I apologize for any disrespect. Since you want Dr. Derrickson alive, I'll arrange something after her healing cycle is completed. And for your information, she seems to have gotten under the skin of one of the Seekers. Actually, *the* Seeker. Name's Jon Bixler and he's a mean bastard, not to mention their commander. Just want you to know what you're up against."

"I'm not concerned in the least. Just make sure you take the proper precautions before putting anything in motion. I don't want to have a Seeker on my tail while I'm trying to get a piece of Dr. Carin's."

"All this intrigue to fuck one human female?" The voice was incredulous. Sidheon couldn't have cared less.

"And I need to explain this to you because?" Sidheon drawled. Every word purposely dripped with condescension. Yes, he wanted more from Carin than her sexy body, but why explain his motivations to the hired help?

"Never mind. I'll see to things on my end and let you know as far in advance as I can."

"Now that's a good little disgruntled vampire," Sidheon crooned. He knew it annoyed the one who was supposed to be helping him. Good.

"Fuck you, Aleth. You'd just better make this worth my while."

"But of course." The line went dead, but not before another piercing scream reached the ear of his accomplice—the "little disgruntled vampire". Sidheon made sure of it.

≿∂උ

The sun had just begun its rise over the eastern mountains when Bix tiptoed into their bedroom, bundled Carin up and carried her outside.

The entire place was a winter wonderland sitting on endless acres of gently sloped, snow-covered hills with a nice mix of trees and open space overlooking Smith Lake. In the distance, white peaks of the Rocky Mountains could be seen. Carin felt like a kid at Christmas. Having grown up in San Francisco, gone to college and started her career in the same city, she'd never seen snow. And San Diego certainly wasn't a place known for the fluffy cold stuff. As they walked, Bix pointed out the estate's private golf course down the hill and off in the distance, promising to teach her to play if they were still in residence here come spring. She kind of hoped not, preferring to learn to ride horses on his estate rather than trudging across the greens playing golf. She just couldn't get over it—vampires played golf and rode horses. Real country-clubbers.

The only sound was the soft crunch of Bix's boots in the snow as he moved at a leisurely pace in consideration of her sore bones and achy, but healing, body. The main house was at a good distance but visible when he stopped at an open-topped gazebo surrounded by towering evergreens. Bix set her on her feet, and Carin stepped inside and surveyed their haven in awe. Instead of wood flooring, the inside of the shelter was all snow-covered grass covered by a tarp and piles of thick, soft blankets. Her mouth watered at the delicious aroma wafting up from a large breakfast basket perched on one of the sturdy benches built into the wall of the gazebo. Her man had been plenty busy this morning.

The clear, jewel-blue sky was visible through the top of the structure. She'd have to come out here at night with a telescope and view the stars, well once Bix let her out of his sight. In a word, the spot was perfect, beautifully secluded, and an ideal place to enjoy a bit of privacy.

She removed her shoes and Bix shooed her into the middle of the very comfortable, extremely thick pallet. After tossing her an even thicker blanket to cover herself, he set the breakfast basket within arm's reach and lit a blazing fire in an oversized sunken pit smack in the middle of the shelter. She smiled behind his back. The man had thought of everything. Food, warmth and a ton of soft down pillows made it nice to be outside in spite of the bone-chilling cold. Her insides went all fuzzy when he tossed a huge chunk of cured wood into the pit and looked over his shoulder with a mix of care and naughtiness in his one-sided grin.

"You comfy, sweetheart?" Bix inquired as he toed off his boots and joined her under the covers. She nodded but kept her eyes on the flicker of building flames blasting waves of welcome heat to where she reclined buried under the blankets. Her thoughts were surprisingly quiet. This was the first time she'd been out of bed in more than a week, and given her scrape with death she couldn't believe how calm she felt. Death scared her more than anything, yet here she was, stitched wounds and all, just as happy and content as you please. Bix kept the companionable silence. Retrieving a large thermos from the basket, he poured her a mug of steaming hot chocolate.

Scooting back to lean against one of the little benches, she sipped the steaming brew with a contented sigh. Bix passed her a flaky raspberry pastry made especially for her as a get-well-soon gift from the resident chefs. A fresh banana and another cup of hot chocolate finished her off. Mmm, she couldn't remember the last time something this simple tasted so yummy.

"Aren't you going to eat?" she asked, concerned when he didn't have anything but whatever he was drinking.

"I'm a vampire, sweetheart, I *am* having breakfast," he said in salute, holding up a mug of something. He answered her question before she could form the words. "It's warm cranberry juice laced with cinnamon and blood. Probably sounds disgusting to you?"

She shrugged and shook her head, not grossed out at all. Then again, she'd had plenty of time to think about the need for blood while trying to find a way to turn herself. Her logical mind couldn't make sense of being weirded out over him sitting here swilling what he needed to survive.

"I also eat regular food, but don't require it for anything more than calories and protein to keep my muscles going. I'll have a huge lunch with lots of meat and greens, maybe some bread, then a moderate dinner. That's about it."

Always the scientist, she mumbled to herself as her mind worked a mile a minute. "It seems the only flaw in the vampire make-up is the need for added protein in order to sustain sufficient amounts of hemoglobin. Hmm." Finally she looked up at him and asked, "So, there's no Vitamin D problem?"

"Only one we create for ourselves," Bix answered.

Carin's brows drew down into a frown as she tried to puzzle it out.

"The best source of Vitamin D is sunlight," he continued. "If vamps don't spend much time in the sun, we simply have to supplement the nutrient another way."

A rush of curiosity of all things vampire filled her mind until she changed subjects so fast, her own head spun. Finally she popped the question she'd been purposely holding onto.

"So, Bix, are you finally ready to tell me what's up with this mind zing thing that's going on between us?"

Bix's head tilted in surprise. His mind ran to catch up with her line of thinking but deep down, he wondered what had taken her so long to ask him about this. Bottom line was he had to have her, but Carin was no pushover. Bracing himself, prepared to make her see his way of things, he plunged right in with plain words and a set expression.

"Carin, we're mates." He sat a moment, looking her directly in the eye, almost challenging her to gainsay him. She didn't say a word. Okay, where was the explosion or at least a bit of resistance at being told she was his mate, rather than asked? The woman was a puzzle. Stubborn and unmovable one minute, compliant and accepting the next. Surely he must be crazy for liking it.

"I've heard that word *mates* tossed around quite a bit since we met. You explained it to me before in San Diego. How 'bout some more details, handsome?"

Handsome? He'd been told plenty of times he was good looking, but from Carin it carried a little more weight. Okay, a lot more weight.

"Being my bondmate means you call to me on every level. My mind, body, even my blood craves you. Mating and bonding aren't the same. I could mate with anyone I want, preferably a female vampire, but you're one of very few human women I can truly mate *and* bond with."

"But what forms this bond?"

"Nobody really knows. It's just something that's always been part of our heritage, and it's been developing between us for a little while now. Your natural empathic abilities allow you to feel others' emotions, but between you and me, it's more acute because of the bond. It's also why you can hear my thoughts, but no one else's. As a vampire my psychic abilities are more developed than yours. With some skill a vamp can pick up just about anyone's thoughts. With you I not only hear you clearly in my mind, but I feel what you feel, see any image you want to send me, and vice versa. I can teach you to shield your mind from others, either vamp or human. Teach you not to project your thoughts. But none of it will work against me. And only me, Carin."

Setting her empty cup aside, she burrowed back down into the blankets on her back. Bix joined her, easing her into his arms until her head settled into the crook of his shoulder. He pressed a lemon petit four that tasted like cheesecake against her lips.

She'd been jonesing for sweets since Dr. Lyons gave her permission to eat regular food. He smiled when an emotion that could only be described as ultimate satisfaction hummed along the bond.

"Oh, now that was good."

"Glad you enjoyed it," he replied aloud as she chewed, tilted her head back to look up at the sky, and watched a thick fluffy cloud float by. He chuckled—she thought it looked like a fat white rabbit that'd gorged itself on her late grandma's cooking.

"So, why didn't you tell me all this before, Bix?"

Offended at her question, he pressed, "Damn it, Carin, I wanted to win you on my own, not pressure you with being my bondmate."

So that's what he'd meant the many times he'd told her she was his? He was sort of telling her without coming flat out with the information. Such a typical male. But she couldn't risk entering into a relationship with anyone, not if he was going to die on her like all her family had. Wait, this wasn't an issue anymore—Bix wasn't going to die anytime soon. But if she mated with him would it be an issue for her? Would she still die young? She couldn't quite pin down, let alone voice, what she felt about any of this just yet, so she kept her mouth shut and her mind quiet.

Bix tensed at her silence. Time to change the subject again. No hard task, she had plenty of questions. "How am I healing so fast? Except for the really deep wounds across my back and stomach, everything else is almost good as new, like it never happened."

Every bruise and cut on her face was gone, no scars or scabs to be seen. Dr. Lyons had taken all of her stitches out a couple of days ago and the skin was baby soft and brand new in spots. The deeper cuts were still a bit swollen and tender, but other than that, she was almost pain free.

"With both my blood and semen in your body, you'll notice quite a few changes. The more you have, the quicker the transformation."

"Okaaay? And that means...?"

"Basically, what you were trying to accomplish with your serum can be accomplished by mating with me. The properties of my blood and semen are regenerative to humans. Over time your DNA will be enhanced. You won't get sick. Your endurance, strength and senses will all heighten."

"In short, I'll be stronger, faster. We can rebuild her. We have the technology to build the world's first bionic woman."

He nudged her in the side and she was more than glad she was healed enough to giggle while taking a bit of playful touching. He continued, "But the bond isn't complete until I take some of your blood, just a little bit. From that point on, your life will be tied to my life, but only if we've agreed in our hearts to be mated and bonded."

Carin blinked. "Huh?"

"Think about it. It's not like I've never taken blood from a woman, or given my blood to a female vamp. But there was no urgent or innate need to bond with any of them. They didn't call to me like you do. The bond didn't form."

"Sounds like some kind of paranormal biological instinct?"

"I guess you could say that. Since I'm long-lived, the psychic and blood bond between us will make you long-lived, too. You won't turn or need blood like I do, but you won't age like a normal human either. And, baby, sharing blood between mates is beyond anything you've ever experienced. Think our lovemaking was good before? Wait until I take your blood while we're stroking." He waggled his eyebrows with a lascivious grin and she giggled again. An instant later, he sobered. "But I won't take your blood unless you ask me. Ever."

Well, she'd get around to it, but not today. Her questions about whether she'd die of cancer or some other funky disease were answered. She would live a good long time...if she accepted the bond. And there were a few other things she wanted to think through, like did he love her? Besides, the idea of being courted was appealing. To have a big, strong, do-what-I-say real man's man like Bix chasing her? Hmm. The thought had merit. Yep, let him pursue her for a while. As crazy as she was about the man, she wasn't sure why she felt like playing hard to get. She snuggled closer, her head on his chest as they lay under the gem blue sky.

His heat seeped through his clothes, warming her from the inside out as a deep awareness of his wants and needs meshed with hers and sank underneath her skin. Within minutes her body wasn't satisfied with snuggling and started to thrum just from having him close. She tried to resist...for about ten seconds, then climbed up on his chest and stretched to reach his oh-so-tempting mouth. The kiss was gentle and sweet but it got old quick. Soon she panted against his lips with the typical response he evoked in her—wild, savage hunger. But he pulled back, keeping the kiss just on the surface as if he were afraid to let her taste him deeply.

"Bix, kiss me damn it."

"You're still healing. Let's take it easy, baby. I don't want to hurt you."

"I'm hurting right now. Right here," she said in a clipped voice as she took his hand, slid it boldly between her legs and watched his eyes cross when her hips rolled and humped his palm.

He tucked her underneath his body and pulled the blankets up to her chin. Before she could protest, his head disappeared under the blankets.

She tensed then relaxed when she felt her sweatshirt journey up her chest and bunch up above her breasts. She hadn't bothered with a bra this morning. Boy was she glad about it now. Bix's large hands closed over one of the sensitive peaks while his hot mouth closed over the other. She lifted the covers just enough to breathe in the scent of his hair and skin that wafted out from underneath. Gasping from a pleasure so acute and overwhelming, she couldn't form a word, a moan, or even a thought. Her breath froze in her throat, and not because of the frigid winter air.

Her skin felt singed, as if she were too close to the fire. Bix's mouth worked magic over her stiff nipples and her breasts swelled until she was sure the skin would burst wide open on a flood of pleasure. Liquid need snaked down her body and pooled between her thighs in a rush of moisture.

Suddenly, Carin wanted nothing more than to be naked out here under the sky, surrounded by trees and snow like some sort of wood elf.

"Naked you want, naked you get," came a quiet, hungry thought. Ooh, Bix.

He kept her completely covered while carefully removing her sweatshirt. His warm, wet tongue traced over the healing scars across her stomach, then followed her sweatpants down and off. The new skin was ultra sensitive, his kisses alone were almost enough to make her come. He knew she liked that little nibbling thing he did in the center of her navel and in no time flat she quivered like a bowl of somebody's jam. Correction, *his* jam.

Bix spread her wide, settling between her legs with her bottom in his hands as he dove headlong into her pussy. She marveled at how hungry he was for her but could totally relate to the swirl of hot emotion emanating from him. He ate her like a starving man, tracing the folds of her creaming slit with urgent, sure strokes of his tongue, humming his pleasure against her clit. God, it felt so good. All of her senses seemed to home in on the points of pleasure where hot mouth met even hotter cunt. The scent of her sex floated up into the morning air. Her skin was so sensitive the slightest change in the pressure of his tongue and fingers seemed magnified. Even the silky softness of his raven black hair seemed more acute as her fingers tightened in it, holding on for dear life.

Carin's tongue began to numb where she bit down, trying to keep from screaming out her pleasure. A single, long finger slipped into her tight pussy and stroked her from the inside while Bix's tongue stroked her from without. His deep moans quivered up through her wet flesh, streaked along her nerve endings until her very scalp tingled.

"Oh Lord. Oh God," she wailed.

"Quiet, woman. We're outside, not in the privacy of our apartments."

Her spine jerked spasmodically when he sucked her clit into his mouth, pulling it almost all the way out of its little hood and swirling his tongue around the sensitive tip in torturous circles.

Close your mouth, she told herself on a loud moan. *Anyone could walk up or hear you...*

His incisors nipped the throbbing bud.

Aw hell, screw it.

Her orgasm slammed through her and, on a chest full of air, Carin yelled at the top of her lungs.

Chapter Thirteen

After enjoying the morning with Bix outdoors, Carin felt wonderful. Before he left to meet with the Council, he settled her into a plush suede recliner, and adamantly explained that his concern for her health and well-being came before anything and anyone else, including the Council's wishes. Dr. Lyons had given her permission to do whatever she liked, but after Bix's long speech about her health, she'd promised to rest one more day. The Council wanted to speak to her, but since he wasn't letting her get up, they would just have to come to her.

Her dozing was interrupted by a knock on the apartment door. How did Bix ever get any sleep? It seemed like someone was always banging on his door needing one thing or another. Well, they could just bang away because she didn't feel like getting up.

She yelled, "Come in," and closed her eyes again.

Bix strolled in followed by all ten Elders with their mates and bondmates. The party silently filled up the living room. Carin was thankful her man had a huge apartment.

A tall, extremely good-looking older gentleman with salt-and-pepper hair stepped forward and offered his hand.

"Dr. Carinian Derrickson, I'm Jarred, Elder of Clan Vanett. Thank you and your mate for seeing us. How are you feeling?" His voice was smooth and friendly. He'd also identified himself as a Vanett. That was Bix's clan. His father, maybe?

"No, my uncle," Bix answered, his hand resting gently on her shoulder as he stood behind her reclining chair.

"I'm much better, thank you for asking, Elder Vanett," Carin replied politely.

"Bix has informed us you intend to help us understand and eliminate the rogue, Sidheon. Is this true?" This question came from Alaana. She already knew the answer but was currently wearing her political, formal Elder hat. Carin understood the need to publicly affirm what she'd already promised the woman in private.

"I do intend to help. Actually, I think I know what Sidheon is doing but without a decent lab I can't prove it."

"Do you know how he plans to use whatever weapon he's developing?" This from a redheaded older vamp. Actually, all the vampire Elders appeared just a bit older than everyone else she'd met so far. Must be the same in every society—Elders rule.

"I don't know how he plans to use his research, at least not for sure. I'd be willing to take a pretty good guess, but I do need to run some tests," Carin assured.

"Are you sure you want to help us, human? Your kind are typically weak-kneed, hardly steadfast enough for a task like this."

Carin's neck cocked a hard left at the insolent tone in this particular vamp's voice, but he sure as hell looked like he had every right to use any tone he wished. His eyes were such a pale blue they were almost white with hair to match. A beautiful mass of uniform white locs hung past his shoulders. Would Bix get mad if she asked to play in them? Probably. Perfectly proportioned body, ruggedly handsome and much younger than the other Elders. And he had no mate with him. Interesting.

Bix moved from behind her chair and stood in front of Carin, fangs bared at the encroacher. "I'll peel the scalp from your pasty head if you continue to disrespect my woman."

"Prime male Jon Bixler and prime male Shale Krulm, you will cease this nonsense immediately." The order from Alaana caused both men to snap their mouths shut.

Carin's eyebrows rose in admiration. She'd never seen Alaana pissed off, but the little woman could be a veritable dragon when she wanted to. And right now, she wanted to. Marvelous example of womanhood, Alaana. Then her mate spoke up. This was Ralen Serati, Alaan's father? Wow, was there any such thing as an ugly vampire? If so, she had yet to see one. Dayum!

"Krulm, you represent your clan until your Elders arrive. I suggest you rein in your poor manners so we may give them a good report." Ralen sighed each word with an exasperated drawl. Obviously this ground had been covered before. He turned to Carin with a friendly smile. "Now, Carinian..."

"Carin, sir."

"Of course, Carin. How can we help you with your research?"

"One moment." She motioned Bix to lean down so she could whisper in his ear. He threw back his head and laughed heartily. After a loud wet smack on her mouth, he disappeared into the bedroom, grinning like a loon. He returned with the same black duffel she'd packed the night of her attack.

Bix laid the heavy bag across her legs. Clothes and underwear went flying as she tossed them over her shoulder to the floor behind the recliner. Finally, she pulled out an inflatable cube with a little battery pack attached. Inside were several samples of blood, skin and various viscous liquids, all still cold. Her documentation, notebooks and tests, along with everything she'd nicked from Sidheon, were in the very bottom of the duffel.

"Now," she said, smiling broadly, "all I need is a decent lab and we can get started."

Pandemonium broke out as everyone started speaking at once. What was in the vials? Could she get started right away? Amazing how it had been right under Sidheon's nose when he'd attacked her. And on it went. Never one to bask in the limelight, Carin finally raised her voice above the racket.

"Get me into a decent lab and I can start working tomorrow. On one condition." When she had everyone's attention, she voiced her request.

"I want to join the team that hunts Sidheon."

"*No*," Bix roared. Damn, that shout seemed to come from every corner of the room at once.

"What do you mean, no? That son of a bitch tried to kill me, Bix."

"Sweetheart, I..."

"Don't you sweetheart me, damn it. That bastard's ass is mine and don't you dare start in on the I-don't-want-you-to-get-hurt crap, either. I've already been hurt." She wanted to bite off her tongue when Bix flinched as if he'd been struck. When he threw up his hands and headed for the door, she felt like a total heel.

"Bix, it wasn't your fault he attacked me. You saved my life, and I want to repay you by taking that asshole out, that's all."

He turned around, his fingers flexing convulsively. The man was mad as hell, but what could he say? She wasn't going to take no for an answer. Alaana's husband wore a sympathetic look, but said nothing. After all, the Clan Serati women were known as ferocious fighters, but not because their males wanted them to be.

"Carinian Derrickson, we of the Council agree that you have the blood right to assist in the hunt for Sidheon. However," Alaana continued kindly, "that does not mean you must physically fight the rogue. You can defeat him by helping us on the scientific front. Leave the muscle work to the Seekers, hmm?"

"I understand, Matriarch," Carin spoke firmly, bowing her head in respect. "But if I can't go on the hunt, then I ask something else." Her gaze moved from one vampire to another, silently daring them to gainsay her next words. "I want to learn how to fight, vampire style."

Nobody seemed to think it was a strange request, so she continued, "I want to fight dirty. No holds barred."

Alaana spoke up again. "Bix, you are the Seeker's expert in hand-to-hand tactics. Even if this woman were not your mate, you are the best one to teach her what she wishes to learn."

Yeah, but did he want to teach her? She knew the Council could have overruled his stand on her blood right to hunt, but none of them could overrule him on matters of her safety. No doubt this situation fell under that purview. But before Bix could speak, Carin boldly stated her case.

"Look, Bix. I'm strong and in great shape," she stated flatly, holding up her arm to show off her rock-hard biceps. "With a little training I know I can master the ability to fight. I refuse to be a victim ever again."

Brows pulled down into a deep frown, he practically growled at her. "Are you saying I'm not capable of protecting you?"

"Don't be silly. If it weren't for you, I wouldn't be here. But I won't have you trying to fight a sneaky-assed vamp like Sidheon while you're worrying about me. I'm your mate. Let me prove I'm worthy of it. Teach me how to fight."

"Unless you have a reason not to do this, the Council agrees that you teach her what she needs to know. If it's the price we have to pay for her cooperation, then so be it."

With that, the Council left the apartment leaving Carin to face a glowering Bix.

The second the Council was out the door, he stalked over to her, straddled the recliner with his long legs and grabbed each armrest in a brutal grip. He leaned down until they were almost nose-to-nose.

"Damn it, Carin, of all the things to be stubborn about."

She drew her neck back and started to snap his head off, but bit her tongue instead. She didn't know vamps could flush until Bix's face turned an alarming shade of red as the veins in his neck pulsed furiously. The thick ridges of bulging muscle on his arms tensed to the point of threatening to rip the armrests right off the chair. Anger and anxiety bubbled up and out of his very pores and rolled over her in smothering waves. It was disconcerting to feel the emotions roiling through him, twisting every measurable inch of his gut like a tangible thing. His anger was genuine, his fear of losing her, true and deep. Her anger and stubbornness melted. She reached out a hand and stroked his face.

"Bix, honey, I-I didn't realize how you felt about this."

His concern and care for her, imprinted clearly in her mind now, were potent and encompassing. Overwhelmed and humbled by the depth of his panic, she couldn't even finish the thought. Bix loved her. Deeply. He hadn't told her in those words but she felt it in her bones, in her heart.

"Baby, I can't handle the thought of you being in danger," he bellowed, then snapped his mouth shut and looked away. Breathing through his teeth with fangs fully extended, he remained quiet a moment longer.

Carin waited to see what color he would turn next. She didn't have long to wait. He snapped his gaze back to hers, eyes blazing silver fire and raging anger. "It's not something I can allow. Ever," Bix rumbled like a roll of thunder off in the distance.

"Bix..."

"It would kill me if anything ever happened to you. Hell, I don't know how I kept from going crazy when you were attacked the first time."

"Bix, sweetheart..."

"Shit, there's no way, no fucking way you're...Mmmph..."

Bix found himself silenced by Carin's mouth as she reached up, grabbed him by the collar and plunged her tongue deep, tasting him, taking him. She'd been drinking spiced mulled wine. Cinnamon and honey, damned yummy. What had he been saying? Hell, he didn't have a clue. The woman robbed him of his senses, and when she sat up to massage the growing bulge between his legs he went up in flames.

"Oh God, Carin. Woman, you drive me nuts."

She didn't answer, nor did she look smug. Her expression was, well, he couldn't quite put a label on it. Her big brown eyes held a mix of caring, deep desire and...love? But no, he had to make her understand that she would not, under any circumstances, put herself in danger. He fought for a small measure of sanity and had almost grasped it when a small gust of cool air surrounded his cock. But when it was replaced with the swipe of her tongue there wasn't anything he could do but stand there and let her have her way with him. Powerless to stop her, his brain had shut down and his body taken over. And when had she unbuttoned his pants?

She let the recliner down, pushed him back a step and sat on the end of the chair, gobbling him up like she hadn't had a meal in months. The sensitive, wide head of his cock bumped the back of her throat and sent a rush of molten sensation down every nerve ending in his engorged rod until he fairly hummed with need. Warm slender fingers reached down to cup his balls, sliding up and over the sensitive spot underneath his full sac until his ass tingled.

"Oh, yes. Damn, woman."

She moaned her approval of his pleasure and his balls tightened unmercifully. Bix sank his fingers in her thick, curly hair, trying to hold a measure of sanity against the intensity of the sensation. And still she pushed him, pumped up and down his shaft with her sweet mouth following her hand along the way. Lips wrapped around the head as her tongue swirled over and under it, then plunged back down again. Oh, was he ever going to blow. But not without her.

Bix swept her out of the chair, stripped her bare and carried her to the bedroom. The reflection in the mirrored headboard held his attention. His midnight hair was all over his head, his jaw tight with unleashed passion. Eyes, dark gray and glittering with gold, expressed an urgency he'd never felt with any other woman. He licked his fangs and let his mind fall wide open. His body jerked in response to the shiver of anticipation dipping into every vertebrae of Carin's spine, clear down to her luscious ass.

In one smooth move, he had her laid out on the bed and impaled on his ready length. He tried to pull back, tried to go easy on her, but the need to brand her, to once more stake his claim in her willing body rode him hard. Grasping her by the hip, he plowed into the depths of her soaked heat. Almost immediately, the honey-dipped walls of her pussy fluttered tight and milked him with a carnal ferocity bordering on exquisite pain. He sent the hot, delicious sensation of her pussy wrapped around his cock into her mind, wanting her to experience everything he did with the same intensity that assailed him. Three strokes and he was out. And so was she. They came together in a thunderous storm of steamy come and collapsed chest-to-chest, sated and sapped of strength.

When he could breathe again, he tried to lift himself from Carin's prone body. Every muscle was exhausted and heavy. He knew he was crushing her, but when he tried to roll away, she tightened her strong arms around his wide back and refused to let him up.

His sweetheart slept deeply, dead to the world, but still held him tight in her slumber.

"Carin," he whispered with a soft kiss to her forehead. "Carin, baby, wake up."

"Nooo, don't wanna," she whined. She was so cute. He smiled and peppered her with kisses until her eyes fluttered open. "Come on, baby, let me up. I know I'm smashing you into the mattress."

He rolled over, taking her with him, and tucked her underneath his chin where she fit so perfectly.

"You awake?"

"Mmm hmm." She eased deeper into the hollow of his neck.

"As you know, the clans are gathering here to collaborate on the Sidheon problem, right?"

She huffed, obviously not the least bit interested in this conversation. "Yes, Alaana mentioned it earlier. I remember."

"There are going to be a lot of strange vamps on the estate. Promise me you'll be careful."

"Fine, I promise," Carin purred distractedly, and then stretched like a sleek cat. A cat filled with his cream. Curling her legs around his, she yawned and snuggled closer, reaching for sleep.

Bix pushed up on his elbow and glowered down at her. "Damn it, I mean it, Carin. Be careful. Not every clan is known for their good deeds."

"Yeah? Like who?" Another yawn.

"Like those asshole Hatsepts. They're real bad boys, baby. If I'm not around, or Alaan or Elder Serati, then a friend of mine will keep you company. Her name is Tameth. She's a Seeker."

Wide awake now, Carin fairly crackled with excitement. "A female Seeker? Hey, that means she can kick vampire ass, right?"

"Right, sweetheart. In fact, she's the only female Seeker stationed in the Western territories."

"Are there other lady warriors?"

"Yeah, all Serati Clan females, and all overseas, thankfully. They're a fucking handful, unlike anyone else I know," he drawled sarcastically.

"I am not a handful...well maybe just a small one." She giggled as he nipped at her ear. "So what about this Tameth chick?"

"She's going to teach you to fight instead of me."

"What? Why?" Carin sat straight up, her expression clearly alarmed and hurt. She thought he didn't want to help her learn to defend herself.

"First of all, you're projecting again. You've got to learn to keep a rein on your thoughts, sweetheart. Second, Tameth won't go easy on you, while all I'd be thinking about is not hurting you."

"Okay, well that makes sense."

Her grin split her face as he explained. In a couple of days, Tameth would begin Carin's self-defense training along with psychic and telepathic exercises to help her control the habit of projecting her thoughts. She would also show Carin some lower body defense moves to give her upper body injuries a little more time to heal.

"Then it'll be on to kick-butt city," Carin squealed, showering Bix's sweaty face with kisses. He rolled his eyes and gave up the fight. Well at least one of them was happy about it. Damned woman.

Chapter Fourteen

Carin dropped into a solid horse stance and balled her fists, ready to box. Her sweat covered T-shirt stuck to her back. Even her bare feet stuck to the workout mat as she shifted her weight from one foot to another. "Don't go easy on me, damn it. I can take it. Besides, it'll never become instinct if you don't make me work for it."

"I won't risk Bix's wrath by thrashing his mate," Jaidyn said calmly, bobbing from side to side as Carin aimed for the targets on his hands. He was Alaana's personal guard on loan to Carin today while Tameth was in yet another meeting with Bix, Alaan and the V.C.O.E. security forces to prepare for the arrival of the clans.

"First of all, we're not bonded yet. And second," she grunted, aiming for his head with her left foot, "mate or not, what Bix don't know"—a perfect back spin off her weak foot— "won't hurt him." The last was said with a loud yell as she pounded into Jaidyn with a closed backhand to the head followed by a left hook.

Carin grinned. Obviously Jaidyn needed no more incentive to protect himself from her thrashing. He wouldn't hurt her, but she knew the perfect roundhouse kick to the center of her target, mainly anywhere on Jaidyn's upper body, was the end of her freebies.

So far she liked being a vampire's woman. The injuries from the attack by Sidheon and his goons should have landed her in the hospital for months. Yet thanks to the DNA of Bix's blood, and making love to him, of course, she'd healed at an incredible rate. Dr. Lyons assured her that she was almost as good as new, and all in just a few weeks. Amazing. Already her eyesight was sharper, her speed and reflexes quicker.

And she was completely pain free...until Jaidyn tossed her over his hip, and she landed with a deep thud flat on her back.

"Owww, that hurt. Damn." The fading scar from the knife wounds across her back throbbed.

"Dr. Carinian?"

Oh now what? She rolled over on her stomach, looked up and stifled a groan.

"Matriarch Serati sent me to inform you that you are ten minutes late for your breakfast appointment." The voice was cold and flat. The face it belonged to was pretty, but just as emotionless.

"Thanks, Natasha. I'll head up right away." Carin gave the woman a small, tight smile, bounced up off the floor and wiped her face with the hand towel Jaidyn offered. Lord knows she was sore and likely had a nice bruise on her back from the little trip over his hip. But bruised or not, she wasn't stupid. There was no way she'd let Natasha see she still had some healing to do. She turned to Jaidyn and bowed. "I'll see you this afternoon for our follow-up session."

Jaidyn took his towel from her fingers and motioned towards the door. "I will escort you to Mistress Serati's suites."

"I'm perfectly capable of going by myself. Geez, what is it with you guys and all the escorting? I can barely take a pee by myself," Carin complained, straightening her workout clothes and wishing her battered tailbone belonged to somebody else.

"It's called being the mate of Jon Bixler, ma'am," Jaidyn replied, pointing to the middle of her chest with a wry grin.

At the deliberate reminder of Carin's new station in vampire society, Natasha turned and stomped out the door, her face an out-and-out storm cloud. Her heels click-clicked on the polished hardwood floor of the sparring room and Carin wondered if the woman could fight.

A conspiratorial grin appeared on her sweaty face and spread wide when the twin to her smile stretched across Jaidyn's face. "You did that on purpose, didn't you?"

"Of course I did. I am loyal to Bix. He has saved my ass more times than I can count. I would not be worth my salt as a Seeker if I passed up an opportunity to bedevil that woman for her cattiness when you were barely conscious, and her petty whining to the Council. The wench is in need of a spanking. And not the pleasurable kind."

"Did you say wench?" Carin chuckled.

"I am a bit old-fashioned," he said, motioning her out the door, showing more teeth, if that were possible.

"How old-fashioned are we talking?"

"Born 1620 in Gascony, France."

"Wow, have you ever seen a Musketeer?"

"Sweet Carin, I trained the Musketeers."

"Really? No way! Say, how much longer do you think you'll live?"

"Probably a couple hundred more years. I am getting up in age even by our standards," he chided.

Once upstairs, Jaidyn knocked on the door to his Matriarch's apartments and entered. Ralen greeted them at the door and left the apartment with Jaidyn. Carin automatically headed for the small table out on Alaana's covered terrace as she'd done every morning since Bix had let her out of bed. A small fireplace built into the stone wall kept the area warm and allowed them to enjoy the snow-covered mountain valley over breakfast. In the mood for a hot, sesame seed bagel, cream cheese and orange slices, Carin filled her plate as Alaana poured her a steaming cup of hot chocolate. Now this was a great reason to mate with a vampire. She'd been lactose intolerant for years before Bix came along. Now, she could eat anything she wanted. And right now she wanted loads of cream cheese mixed with strawberry preserves and chocolate made with real steamed milk. Oh baby, this was the life.

After a sip of her hot bit of heaven, she sat back with a sigh. "Ms. Alaana, you should really try some of this. It is to die for," Carin crooned, rolling her eyes up to the sky in sated delight. Alaana lifted a beautiful ceramic snifter in salute, then took a sip. Carin was sure it was some kind of beverage laced with blood. She curled her lip, not the least bit interested in trying any. Sorry, nothing but a taste of Bix could beat out hot chocolate in her book.

"Have you made any progress in the lab, my dear?"

"Of course," Carin replied, slathering more whipped cream cheese on her bagel. "But why don't we kill two birds with one stone. After breakfast, let's do my psychic training thing up in the lab while I fill you in on what I've discovered. It would be easier to show you what I've found than to tell you."

They talked about typical girl stuff over breakfast and once the dishes were cleared, the two headed for the door of the Matriarch's suites. Carin opened the door and took a quick step back when Jaidyn appeared as if the very hounds of hell were on his heels. They obviously weren't going anywhere without him.

Gesturing back and forth between Jaidyn and Alaana as they moved towards the wide curving staircase, Carin asked in wonder, "Where'd he come from? Did you...?"

"Yes, child, I called him telepathically. Pretty soon you'll be able to do the same with Bix at any distance, any time without letting everyone else hear you. You're already pretty good at controlling your psychic shields."

"But I thought only bonded couples could do that," Carin asked in wonder.

"Jaidyn and I are bonded."

"Huh? You mean Ralen shared you with..."

"Something like that, dear. The Serati women have always bonded those who are called to protect us. I am bonded to both Ralen and Jaidyn, meaning we've shared blood and the 'zing thing', as you call it, is there between the three of us. However, I am married only to Ralen."

"Well, this just gets better and better," Carin muttered.

"Well, don't get any ideas. Bix may be like a son to me and an adopted Serati, but he will not share you with anyone for any reason. Not even Alaan."

"Between Bix and my job I don't think I'd have time to dally. Besides, nothing beats my lab," Carin exclaimed on the way through the laboratory door. She'd given Bix a list of what she needed the day she told the Council she would help them. By the end of the week they'd procured everything she asked for, and then some. Everything was set up in a state-of-the-art sterile environment up on the fourth floor. The first time she'd seen the huge all-white room her breath caught in her throat at how closely it resembled the space at her job. Well, her soon-to-be former job. She'd agreed to stay on with V.C.O.E. and help with their research. In fact, she was going to be a project coordinator, a consultant for the pharma and biotech facilities owned by the Clans around the world.

"Now," Carin explained as she readied slides, documents and examples to show Alaana. "Vampire strength comes from a naturally occurring extra chromosome passed from vamp parents to their children. There are no genetic anomalies in the vampire DNA sequence, hence no disease in vampires or their children. I'm not a vamp child, but when Bix's blood and semen was introduced to my human cells in a large enough quantity, my cell walls broke down long enough for the DNA to be altered. The vamp DNA then instructed my cells to repair themselves immediately to keep from being damaged. As a result, the cells were changed and I began to exhibit natural vampire traits, with the exception of the need for blood. Vampire cells divide fifty times faster than a normal human. Your metabolism is also faster. Now, because the vamp DNA altered mine, my cells act just like yours. So, healing occurs faster and I also have an increased need for protein to keep up with my new metabolism."

"But the vampire DNA does not become your DNA. How is it that human mates not only exhibit vampire traits, but do not get sick or age as they normally would?"

"Good question. The vamp DNA actually seeks out and repairs defective human cells. The DNA is not replaced with yours, but modified and in many cases, perfected."

"But what does all this have to do with Sidheon?"

"When I took vampire cells and introduced Sidheon's serum to them, it was obvious the cell was destroyed, but I didn't know why. In a nutshell, Sidheon has found a way to somewhat undo the coding of vampire DNA."

"What exactly are you saying, Carin?" Alaana asked. Her face was pale and her mouth pinched tight. The woman knew bad news was coming and Carin didn't particularly want to deliver it.

"I'm saying Sidheon has found a way to destroy vampirism. Notice, I said destroy, not reverse or for lack of better words, cure. His serum doesn't turn vampires into humans sans vampire traits. He basically damages the vampire DNA, but instead of the cell remaining intact, it is totally destroyed."

Carin saw understanding dawn in the Matriarch's eyes, but the woman's brow was tightly knit as if she had trouble fathoming what was being said. "Okay," Carin continued, "it's like this. A real vampire unused to walking in the daylight might develop a bad rash or a burn from bright, direct sun exposure until he can control the allergy, right? No blowing up, no death or frying to a crisp. Well, picture one of the recent vampire movies where the vampire is exposed to the sun and literally disintegrates into a pile of ash. Then take a look at what Sidheon's serum does."

She put a skin sample taken from Bix's arm on a slide, introduced the rogue's serum, and placed it under the microscope. She motioned Alaana forward to take a look, then stepped back.

What the Elder saw made her draw back, her mouth tilted down and drawn into a tight line. When she spoke, her voice was full of fury. "That son of a bitch. I hope my sons kick his ass into a million pieces."

When Carin removed the slide from the microscope, the tiny skin sample was black as charcoal. The cloth she used to clean the slide held nothing but ash.

ᘓᘗ

Armed to the teeth and on high alert, every Full Seeker, Beta Seeker, and Iudex Judge on the property streamed into the command and surveillance center in the middle of the estate. Those still en route were conferenced in and the security plans for the duration of the Elders and clan members' stay were laid out in detail.

The perimeter defenses, security and alarms were all controlled from this building. In the central communications hub, huge screens imbedded in the walls showed every angle of both the inside and outside of the property, except for the Council Chambers and the private apartments of the residents. Complete with state-of-the-art, military grade computing systems and satellite imaging capability, vampire law enforcement could survey almost anyone and anything from this facility. The estate could also be transformed into a stronghold if they were to ever be discovered and subsequently hunted.

Deep in the middle of the command center was the Seeker's private domain—several conference rooms surrounded by floor to ceiling glass. For today's gathering, the glass walls became solid white and soundproof at the click of a button.

As Alaan pointed out strategic points for emergency protocol on one of the large screens, Bix's thoughts turned to his woman, as seemed to be the norm these days. It had taken Carin a whole hour to get him to donate some of his skin and blood to use as test samples when what he'd really wanted was some early morning pussy. But her eagerness to get to her martial arts and weapons training, and work up in her new labs all but spilled out of her. He'd finally relented so they could both begin their day.

Everyone was in place when the first clan members arrived. Bix made his way down to the main house and waited just off the huge half-circle driveway on the sprawling front porch with the Council, scores of Elders and Liaisons who'd landed ahead of their clan members. They represented every territory and country where vampires lived all over the world.

Bix and Alaan looked at each other and groaned out loud when a convoy of bright silver Hummer H3s stopped at the double iron gates to request entry. Glad Carin was up in her labs, Bix radioed down to the gate and granted entrance to the Clan Hatsept members.

The two Seekers growled in unison, "Damned pimps."

Chapter Fifteen

The Council, Elders and clan members were briefed by Bix, Alaan and Carin in a series of meetings. Each night, Carin fell into bed exhausted, asleep as soon as her head hit the pillow. Bix was thoroughly frustrated. The only thing that should have her too tired to move was making love with him.

By the end of the week all talks were concluded and a strategy for flushing out Sidheon was decided on. The next evening the Council chambers were cleared out and transformed into a tropical paradise. Quite a feat in the middle of winter in Montana's Rocky Mountains.

A thick red carpet graced the center of the floor, creating a plush pathway to the steps of the Council's dais. The large half-moon table, covered with a luxurious dark gray jacquard tablecloth, held the Council's feast. Tables set up against just about every inch of the walls were covered with wines, punches, roasted and grilled beef and buffalo steaks, all kinds of fowl, and even lamb. A host of fresh salads, greens and fruit were sliced, diced and displayed to perfection. Even strawberries and honey melons, which were out of season, had been flown in for the event. The spread was quite impressive. Even if vampires had been incapable of eating food, the decadent chocolate silk mousse, kiwi tarts, rum cakes and sugared fruits were tempting enough to make anyone eat his fill anyway and deal with the consequences later.

A slew of sensuously dressed women from every Clan descended the curved double staircases for the festivities. But Bix only had eyes for one.

He spotted Carin the moment she appeared at the top of the left staircase. After his mouth stopped watering, he would have to remember to thank Alaana and her Serati Clan sisters for helping Carin find something to wear.

The spaghetti straps of the beaded royal blue A-line dress set off Carin's cinnamon skin and showed off her strong physique. A single sparkling blue sapphire pendant hung around her neck and teased the top of the vee of the lush valley between her breasts. Matching studs sparkled on her dainty earlobes. Her hair was down tonight and fell in a riot of soft curls and twists that teased her shoulders. Accentuating her flat stomach and the flare of her curvy hips, the dress floated to her knees in a wisp of chiffon silk. But what did him in were her shoes. Strappy high-heeled sandals tied up her ankles with royal blue ribbon highlighted sexy, shapely, strong legs. And held him there. Dayum!

Tameth walked by her side in a sophisticated black and silver affair. Cut low in the back, it allowed her exotic olive skin to peek through a thick fall of jet-black hair. Alaan watched intently while everyone close by watched Alaan watching Tameth. Once at the bottom of the stairs, Tameth eyed him boldly from head to toe. Bix grinned when his friend's brow knit in a fierce scowl. When Alaan stalked away grumbling about women showing too much skin, Bix almost laughed outright. Then Carin was there.

His hackles rose when he noticed his eyes weren't the only ones following his dark-skinned beauty down those damned steps. Every unmated male vamp eyeballed his woman. He met her at the bottom of the staircase along with a dozen other males, all holding out a hand to help her down the last step.

Shouldering the poachers out of the way, Bix snaked an arm around her waist and hauled her up against his side. He snarled from one vamp to the next, fangs bared. A direct challenge to any who dared dispute his claim.

"Bix, cut it out," she hissed. The woman tried to suppress a smile at his possessiveness but did a piss-poor job of it.

"You're supposed to be good tonight, Bix, so stop scaring the straights."

Was that a chuckle he heard trickling down the bond?

"Mine," he growled into her thoughts.

"Yours? Well, maybe. Maybe not," she teased. Easing away, Carin looked back at him over her shoulder, eyes sparkling with mischief. The woman left him standing there and slipped away to the high dais to greet Alaana. Her hips swayed sensuously and her delicious ass winked at him as she went.

"Damned woman," he muttered to himself.

"Amen," Alaan grumbled, returning silently to Bix's side.

೮つՇ୪

Carin was amused at her current conversation. These boys were fine as hell with some serious pick-up lines. All of them looked related to the vamp who'd pissed Bix off when the Council had come to see her. Every one of their heads was stark white, some straight, some curly, some loc'd. The thick burgundy drapes were pulled back to allow the moonlight to glow through the crystal floor-to-ceiling windows along one whole wall of the ballroom. The lunar beams cast a bluish sheen on their gorgeous heads, surrounding them with the illusion of faerie dust. Too self-assured by half, their athletic, muscular bodies and devilish good looks ran the gamut from ruggedly handsome to male model chic. All were dressed to the nines in classic black. None of them bothered to sheathe their fangs. Of course she wasn't interested, but any woman worth her salt would flirt at least a little bit under such yummy circumstances.

"You are a beautiful woman with a body made for hot, sweaty sex. If you're good, perhaps I'll take you to mate," said one Armani-clad Hatsept.

"Or perhaps you will partner me. My cock is much more decadent than my cousin here. Besides, he already has three mates." This from a vamp with such a thick head of hair she was almost jealous. Damn, a woman would kill for hair like that.

"Yes, but my tongue is more talented," said yet another gorgeous white-loc'd vamp, "so may I have this dance?"

Before Carin could open her mouth to turn them down tactfully, her arm was wrapped around a tense, bulging forearm. She didn't have to turn around to know who it was. She'd recognize that soul-stirring growl anywhere.

"This woman is taken, Hatsept."

"Says who?" challenged all three b-e-a-utiful vamps.

"Says me. Keep fucking with my woman and I'll stomp a mud hole in your pasty-faced ass."

"Bix, don't you dare start a fight," Carin demanded with an exasperated, there's-too-much-testosterone-in-the-room sigh. But Bix didn't seem to be listening. When his and the bad boys' fangs extended to movie-like proportions, she pinched him hard on the inside of his biceps and scowled for all she was worth.

"Damn it, Bix, I mean it. You start a fight and I'm outta here. Now let's dance." In the end, she had to grab a good chunk of his ass to get his attention. He turned on her with a snarl. Did she care? Not bloody likely.

"You snarling at me? Don't make me kick your ass up in here, Jon Bixler." She was royally bluffing and inwardly relieved when a thoroughly amused smile spread across his face.

"Damn, boys, my woman has more balls than all three of you." He laughed, took her by the waist and led her onto the dance floor.

The music was hip and loud, just the way she liked it. And tonight was for getting her groove on. Carin hadn't had this much fun in ages, but she was a new woman—energized, sexy, full of passion. A new zest for life, rather than fear of death, expressed itself in her movements to the funky beat. She placed her hand on Bix's chest and traced a line about his body as she danced around him. Finally, she settled with her back to his, bent her knees, and slid her body up and down and back and forth against his. She danced with Bix until a light sheen of sweat covered her arms and put a shine on the skin underneath her sapphire jewels at the vee of her breasts, tempting her lover's eyes to stray to the tease of cleavage.

Oh, this was soooo much fun. Then the lights dimmed and a slow song began. The words were sensual, the beat sultry. Bix moved in close. She looked up into his beautiful gray eyes and gulped. A heady combination of love and lust stared back at her. The pit of her belly danced wildly. Oh goodness. She was in trouble.

It started tame enough when Bix pulled her close and placed a chaste kiss on the side of her temple, which barely reached his shoulder. But then he dipped his head again, this time blatantly inhaling the scent of her hair. His arms tightened around her body and one strong hand dipped low to graze the globe of her left cheek, sending a sizzle down her ass. The other hand discreetly played with the side of her breast. She couldn't keep her breathing even.

"Kiss me, Bix," she whispered fiercely, tilting her head up with eyes closed. She knew he'd give her what she asked for. No need to look. Just feel. Bix would take care of her. She felt his mouth move towards her, but he didn't meet her lips. Instead he tipped her chin up more and licked the side of her neck, from her pulse point up to her ear.

The intense answering ripple in her womb almost made her forget to erect a psychic shield.

"Oh damn, that was nasty. Do it again."

Bix gave her another hot swipe of his wet tongue along her sensitive skin. She shivered as her head fell back. Her skin felt much too tight and her body grew hotter by the second. She barely registered the crooning of the music in the background as she reached into his tailored jacket, grabbed two fists full of his shirt and held on under a sensual assault that almost bent her over backward. Moisture gathered at the entrance of her channel and even *she* could smell her arousal waft up from between her thighs. Finally, he captured her lips. Bix started growling again, but for a whole new set of reasons, all of which she agreed with wholeheartedly.

"I can smell you, baby. Makes me want to go down on my knees and bury my head under your dress right here in the middle of this dance floor."

Lord knows she wanted nothing more than to find a dark corner, flip up her skirt and let him have at it. A primal need rose up in her, a need for him to take her. To make her his in every way. Forever. Her kneecaps quivered and she spoke to them. *Don't you dare dump me on my ass. Stand firm, girl, stand firm.*

"*Firm? I've got something firm for you, baby,*" Bix whispered into her head and pressed his long, swollen ridge of flesh firmly against her belly.

Her shield dropped like a stone. Bix, along with a horde of other horny vamps, heard her telepathic scream. "*Oh, Bix, I'm yours, baby. Please... Oh God, bite me.*"

He looked directly into her eyes, fangs clearly visible. "Are you sure, Carin? There's no going back if we do this."

She rubbed feverishly against him, trying to do her best to look like she was still dancing rather than humping against his leg. "Yes, I'm sure, Bix. I'm yours, and you're mine. I can't imagine being with anyone else or sharing you with anyone else. Ever."

"The mating is to bind you to me, not the other way around," Bix said firmly, all smug Seeker confidence.

Alpha to the bone, arrogant and self-assured. And right now, she didn't give a rat's ass. "So you say, damn it. You're mine."

She knew she could be a stubborn bitch on wheels, but this man was going to be wholly and completely hers and love it. Even if she had to kill him. Her breathing hitched with anticipation as he lowered his head to the sweet pulse on her neck. She could feel his fangs aching fiercely, his need to bite so strong, *her* gums tingled. So powerful it burned from where his mouth touched her down to the little hairs on her toes. He rubbed his incisors against her tender skin.

A sharp voice cut through the fog of lust and need.

"Bix and Carin, please join me on the dais." Alaana Serati stood there, calling to them. "And no necking on the dance floor for you two. We will do this according to tradition." Then she smiled at Bix's grimace at having his love play interrupted.

"Damn, her timing sucks," Carin growled into his chest.

Bix unwrapped his arms from around Carin's lush, ready body and chuckled. He didn't bother mentioning there hadn't been a formal, traditional mating in front of the whole V.C.O.E. and all the Clans in...hell, he couldn't remember how long.

Hand in hand, they followed the Matriarch to the raised dais and up the steps onto the platform, leaving the throng of bodies, some dancing, some necking, below. The second the Council rose from their seats the music stopped. Bix bowed low and Carin curtseyed to show their respect to the Elders, then turned to face the crowd as the lights came up to reveal a number of vamps in various stages of undress.

Alaana's voice rang clear over the hushed mass. "Jon Bixler, Seeker of the Vampire Council of Ethics, son of Clan Vanett, and adopted son of Clan Serati. While this gathering is to show the clan's solidarity in eliminating the threat to our species by the rogue Aleth Sidheon, we also wish to acknowledge the finding of your mate and bondmate, Dr. Carinian Derrickson."

After a short round of applause, whistles and well wishes, Alaana continued. "Do the Elders of Clans Serati, Vigee, Li and Sewelle recognize the mating of Seeker Bixler and Carinian?" Each Elder named called out in the affirmative with a vocal "We do" as did each Elder for Clans Akicit, Hatsept, Rolle, Vanett, Bourek and Kraig. All ten clan Elders agreed, which was a miracle in and of itself.

Bix smiled down at Carin's radiant face as the crowd clapped and hooted again. All except the bad boys of Clan Hatsept. It took those white-haired players a minute to clap along with the rest of the clan body since it was apparent that Carin wasn't available for ravishing.

"Seeker Jon Bixler, Dr. Carinian Derrickson, we the Elders of the vampire clans recognize not only your mating, but your bonding as well. We wish you goodly success. Bix, you may now take your bondmate."

His fangs lengthened and gleamed under the bright lights. Carin already had some of his blood in her, but to complete the bond he needed to feed from her. To take care of her part of the ancient ceremony, he bit into the fleshy part of his forearm and held it up to her. He smiled when she didn't hesitate to take his blood. He could feel the pull of her lips down to his throbbing cock, which he didn't bother trying to hide.

Turned on by taking his blood, she slid her tongue over her lips to capture every precious drop when she was through. His gaze followed the little pink organ from one side of her beautiful mouth to the other. Her expression was downright dreamy when she looked up at him, deliberately projecting her love—not just to him, but to everyone within psychic hearing distance. She let her head fall sideways and gave him as much room as he needed to lay it on her.

He gathered her close and positioned her so every vampire on the ballroom floor below could see what he was about. When the first drop of her sweet blood touched his tongue, his knees almost buckled from the concentration of energy flashing through his body. It was like drinking fire laced with lightning. Addicting. Arousing. When she moaned and clawed at his arms, he pulled back, thinking she was in pain.

"Oh Lord, don't stop. More," she cried, trying to pull him back to the column of her throat.

Instead he licked the wound to capture the slowly oozing trail of blood, swung her up into his arms and strode out of the ballroom. He didn't stop until they were in his apartments.

He stormed over the threshold and kicked the door shut behind them. They made it as far as the living room.

Carin landed in the middle of the plush cushions with a bounce. Her thighs fell open to reveal a slip of a thong. The little piece of enticement was his favorite color and his favorite flavor lay just underneath it. Carin. She raised one leg and let it drape over the back of the couch. Her hands traveled over sheer thigh-high stockings, over the soft chiffon bunched at her waist and up to silk-covered breasts.

The heady scent of her arousal filled the room. Bix licked his lips, stepped away from her luscious body and stripped faster than even he thought possible. His jaw tightened along with the rest of his body, as he avidly tracked the movement of his woman's fingers as she stroked swollen, heavy breasts with one hand. She lifted the other hand and her firm, full lips wrapped around a finger, then two.

Bix's skin felt stretched too tight over muscle and bone when her pink tongue came out to play. No tentative display of just the tip, but the entire length of Carin's hot, wet tongue stroked up and down her fingers as if she were trying to swallow them.

He encircled his erection and stroked it in rhythm with her fierce sucking. He closed his eyes a moment and let his head fall back on a groan, imagining her taking him just like that, deep in her mouth until he touched the back of her throat.

When he looked at her again, her eyes were hard and hungry. But she wasn't watching his face. Her focus was riveted on his hand stroking the length of his cock, up and down, then smoothing up and over the deep purple head, down along the pulsing shaft, and back again.

She moaned his name and his feet moved as if the very strings of her sultry voice wrapped around and pulled him, spirit, soul and body.

He approached slowly, all sinewy grace, muscles rippling and tensing as they rolled underneath his skin. God, would she ever get used to seeing this magnificent man in all his naked glory? Her pussy wept at the sight of his proud cock bobbing, reaching for her with every step. The heat in her veins skyrocketed until her skin sizzled and melted like caramel syrup tossed into a hot pan. Just the sight of him made her mouth water, her breath heave in and out of her chest. She wanted, needed to taste him so badly, she trembled. Even her lips quivered as her tongue snaked out and left a wet trail over them. She sat up and waited. Waited for him to bring her what she desperately needed.

He stood in front of her now, his delicious cock mere inches from her face. Just as she opened her mouth to take him deep, out of nowhere defiance rose up. While she wanted him to take her, it was the "taking" part that called to her blood, the need to make him prove he was strong enough to handle her. Instinctively, she went with it. She snapped her mouth closed, looked up and waited.

"You. Naked. Now." Bix's voice was raspy and his speech halting, as if he had trouble stringing the words together. Carin knew exactly how he felt.

Tearing her gaze away from his rock-hard length, she rose from the couch and stared up at his towering, tense frame. "No, don't think so," she purred, then turned away from him. A low, menacing snarl sounded behind her. It was all the warning she received.

Strong hands grabbed her by both arms and whirled her around. Her womb throbbed in cadence with her heart and sent a gush of silky need trailing down her thighs.

"Wrong answer, Carin."

She looked up into the eyes of the deadly predator Bix always kept under such tight control. Yes, this was what she wanted—his control in shreds, just like hers. The tick in his jaw said his passion was barely leashed. He wanted her desperately. Did she dare push him any further? A half-smile quirked up at the edges of her lips. Of course she dared.

"I've changed my mind." Surprised her voice was somewhat steady, she braced herself for what would come next. She'd always gone to him willingly, but something about this, about their bonding, made her want to be taken, won and subdued.

His head tilted to the side and a single raven-black brow winged its way upward. "I don't think so, baby."

Bix's large hand held both of hers over her head. She was strong, but he was stronger and her struggles gained her nothing. The fingers of his free hand wrapped around the spaghetti straps of her dress and in a single yank, they landed across the room. Sequins and beads flew everywhere as the lovely royal blue silk was torn from her body in shreds. A delicious tremor snaked down her sides as her bra, thong and stockings followed, leaving her with only ankle-strap high heels and the sparkle of beautiful sapphires and gold against her skin.

The heated skin of his powerful chest scorched her breasts as he pulled her roughly to him, grinding his engorged cock against her trembling belly and the smooth mound of her pussy.

Opening his mouth wide as if he were going to bite her sent a new rush of wetness glazing down the inside of her thighs, and she knew he could smell it when he let out a deep, hungry groan. His fangs, and the cock pressed into her stomach, grew and stretched beyond anything she would have thought possible.

Her knees threatened to buckle when he lowered his head and played with her like a lion toying with his prey. The tips of his incisors trailed along the sensitive skin of her neck, around the front of her collarbone. By the time he nipped her just above her right breast, the shivers racing along her nerve endings blazed through her pores, peppering her body with glowing sparks, burning every inch of her body. It was exactly what she wanted.

He released his grip and her hands fell uselessly to his shoulders. Bix filled his hands with her breasts, wrapped his lips around the crown and pulled roughly. Her very soul vibrated as if a dozen bungee cords wove a path from her aching nipple to her navel, and tied off at the base of her spine. The urgent draw of his demanding mouth and the scrape of his fangs strummed over the connection, and each cord vibrated endlessly. He worked her breasts, from one to the other, until she whimpered helplessly, her body a wanting, restless knot of tense muscles.

He picked her up, dumped her on the couch again. When she scrambled to her knees, his honeyed gray gaze glittered dangerously while his fingers sank into the coils of her hair. Hairpins flew in a wide arc as her face was brought to a level with his cock.

"Now suck." The words were pushed through clenched teeth and came out a rough order she had no intention or desire to challenge.

She instantly obeyed, taking him into her mouth so suddenly his breath left his chest on a whoosh.

"Oh yeah, that's it, baby. Suck it."

She glanced up to see his head thrown back and the cords of his neck straining against the flushed skin. Damn, he turned her on. She hummed and licked and sucked until his hips pumped furiously against her lips. And she wanted more of him. Wanted to milk him with her tongue. She let all her thoughts and emotions swirl out from her mind in a fierce storm cloud of lust.

"Mmm, you taste so good, Bix. I want to suck you dry."

"Tempting, but not tonight. Tonight I'm going to show you how a vampire really fucks his mate."

Oh, Lord, what did he mean, exactly? Their loving had always been wild and explosive. What would be different this time? And could she handle it?

"Trust me, Carin, you can take it. You will take it."

In a blur she was turned around on the couch on her knees, her body bent forward over the low back, and her ass in the air. Bix pulled her towards him, rocking against her cunt, coating his cock with her slick juices. Long, rough fingers slipped up and around her clit, rimming the folds of her swollen, wet pussy until she felt the throbbing of her blood in every cell of her body. Her belly fluttered with every breath as passion flared and consumed her like a fire fanned by a hot desert wind.

And still he teased her mercilessly, pushed her to mindlessness. Every muscle quaked and flexed with need.

"Bix, please..."

"Please what, baby?"

"Please, take me. Fill me. I-I..."

He positioned himself at her welcoming entrance and pressed slowly into her. When the crown of the thick head popped through her tight opening, he leaned forward, the muscles of his pecs jumping and twitching against her back. Bix whispered in her ear as his cock continued to torture her.

"Is this what you need?"

"Oh God, yes." She squirmed and wiggled against him, trying to get more of him inside her thirsty heat. His fingers dug into her hips and held her still as he pulled back, giving her just the tip.

"Then tell me you need it. That you want it," he growled, sucking a sensitive lobe into his warm mouth.

"I need it. Oh God, Bix, I need you, baby. Please."

"Whose pussy is this?"

"Yours!"

"And what do you want me to do with my pussy, Carin?"

She knew what he wanted, and was more than ready to give it to him. Anything to put out the raging fire in her blood.

"I want you to take it. Take it all."

He slammed into her then, so deep she felt it behind her eyeballs. His glorious cock stretched, filled, speared into her wetness with amazing speed. Vampire speed. In—tormented every nerve ending deep in her slick heat. Out—tantalized the sleek flesh of her cunt in a blur of wicked movement. In seconds a devastating orgasm thundered through her very soul.

He gave her no time to recover from the blistering climax. Instead, he threw her into another one, and then another until she was excessively sensitive. Each stroke triggered a scream, and every thrust made a sloshing noise as he moved within her drenched sex.

When her knees buckled under the onslaught, Bix, still planted deeply, picked her up and carried her into the massive bedroom. Rearranging her body so she lay on her back with her thighs over his shoulders, he rode her into sensual oblivion.

His roared release sounded in her ears but faded quickly as Carin, crossed eyes and all, drifted into blessed, sated unconsciousness with a silly grin on her face. Talk about a wedding night. Damn, the man had fucked her blind.

ഇ‍ൽ

"Your lack of progress is trying my patience, my dear."

"Look, timing is everything. Until you've taken care of your own business, stop riding my ass," she said matter-of-factly.

"Believe me, my dear, I'm not riding your ass. Yet. But I do look forward to it. As soon as I find a suitable place for you to bring my visitor, I'll make sure you're ridden well."

Sidheon's sinister, sexy chuckle filled the phone line and a deep ripple spread across her womb. The man was so good at being bad it made her insides quiver, reminding her of the first time they'd met in person while on one of her supposed vacations.

He personally patted her down for weapons and listening devices.

"These days a wire could be worn anywhere, even in your bra, or in your hair," he said, stripping her down to her underwear and motioning her towards a chair in the middle of the room. His henchmen glared murderously at her as they filed out. She recognized a couple of them. Hell, she'd provided the intelligence for the missions that had run them to ground, provided evidence resulting in their prison terms, and later

arranged their parole. And with the V.C.O.E., justice was dealt harshly to a rogue.

Once they were alone, Sidheon bombarded her with questions about why she wanted to help him bring down the Council.

"You told me Dr. Carinian was the target of the Head Seeker. Now you tell me he claims her as mate. Why?"

"Because you needed to know what you were up against if you chose to continue pursuing her," she said, far from afraid but still eager for the little interrogation to be over.

"Why? Because you care whether I get hurt?" he drawled sarcastically.

She laughed and shot a retort back at him just as cynically. "Hardly. You're no good to me dead."

"Why would the Liaison for the Western territories betray the V.C.O.E.?" he queried. Beautiful jewel blue eyes bored into hers, reaching for her secrets even as they moved over her practically naked body. She shivered from the very ends of her raven black hair down to her toes at the transformation of those eyes from stark hard coldness to blazing hot lust.

"I want revenge against a certain Seeker."

"Because...?"

"I don't see how that's any of your business," she snapped, trying to ignore the heat gathering behind her knees, snaking up towards the vee between her legs.

A gifted psychic, her shields hadn't been strong enough to keep him out of her head. The vamp sensed and exposed half-truths and her rising desire until he had more than just the answers to all his questions. In the end, they both got what they wanted—Bix in exchange for Carin. The rest of their meeting was spent on her hands and knees, on her back, on the table, on the floor, screaming her promise to do anything he wanted as long as he kept her full of his lovely cock while sinking his fangs into her willing body. All the while she'd imagined Bix's handsome face so close to hers, his lips on hers, and his strong hand spanking her.

Pushing the memories away to concentrate on the current conversation, she decided to avoid a fight with this dangerous vamp. Especially since she would see him again soon.

"Listen, lover, things are getting hot around here. Let me know the minute you have things settled on your end, and I'll do the same, all right?"

"But of course," he said calmly.

"Miss me, lover?" she asked playfully.

"Miss your lovely round ass. Perhaps I'll let you wrap my dick in that tight hole? Depends on how good a girl you are." Sidheon laughed.

She blushed, glad he couldn't see the mix of heat and contempt in her eyes. Disconnecting the secure cell phone, she slammed it down on the desk even as her mind filled with thoughts of what a talented tool Sidheon had. Too bad he was going to lose his balls by going up against Bix. The head Seeker was a formidable fighter who believed the only fair fight was a won fight. Sidheon didn't stand a chance. But no matter, once Sidheon killed Carin, Bix would be bereft and alone. And she would be there to comfort him, just as she planned.

೮೦೦೪

Content and purring, Carin lay in her favorite position—sprawled across her husband's chest with her head pillowed on one of Bix's large shoulders. They'd spent the past week shut away in Bix's apartments. Since it was bigger than her whole house in San Diego, complete with all the amenities, they hadn't even come out for meals in the main hall.

He'd surprised her with the knowledge he could cook. In fact, her stomach was still rejoicing from the dinner they'd shared earlier this evening. A meal even her grandma would have appreciated—fried chicken, hot water cornbread, fresh greens and strawberry shortcake complete with gobs of whipped cream.

While thoughtful, kind and his usual bossy self when it came to her well being, he wouldn't tell her a damned thing about the upcoming hunt.

"So," she said sweetly, "do you know when you're leaving to hunt Sidheon?"

"Natasha's still gathering and coordinating the intel for the mission. These things take time. She'll let me know when it's time."

"Why can't someone else be Liaison? Why does Natasha have to call the shots?"

The answer was a wide, very rude yawn. Damned man.

"Who's going to work with me on my fighting skills while you're away, sweetie?"

"Who do you want?"

"Maybe Jaidyn again? Or one of the Hatsepts who stayed behind?" Carin crooned, listening to Bix's strong heartbeat. He stiffened at the mention of the "H" boys. She bit her lip to keep from grinning as she stroked a lone finger up and down the middle of her husband's nicely chiseled pecs. Her fingertips pinched and tugged a tight male nipple. When the muscles jerked under her touch, followed by a low hiss of air between his teeth, her wicked juices started to bubble.

There was nothing she loved more than turning Bix on. Since all the hoopla of the gathering was over and almost everyone who didn't live at headquarters had gone home, there was plenty of time to do just that.

"Are you going to answer my question, Bix?"

"You keep sliding your hand towards my dick like that and you'll have more answers than you can handle, baby."

The man gritted his teeth like he was in pain as his chest rose and fell, breath quickening with each caress of her fingers. Times like this made her feel both powerful and humble. Powerful that a mere human woman could bring such a strong vampire to his knees, and humbled by the fact he trusted her enough to let her.

"Answers like what?" Carin purred, smiling big like the cat that swallowed the canary. The next thing she knew she was flat on her back, her mind full of Bix's thoughts.

"Answers to questions like, how do I always manage to be full of Bix's cock?" He spread her legs wide, one over each of his shoulders. *"And will my pussy ever stop creaming?"* Ass cheeks clenched as a soft breath wafted over her moist, puffy lips. *"Will my husband ever get tired of eating my pussy?"* A fang scraped over her unhooded clit, followed by a talented, wet tongue. She gasped, burying her fingers in the sheets. *"And can I possibly come any harder than I already have?"* His pink tongue pierced her hole and slid deep, lapping at the hot insides of her creaming channel, eagerly devouring the steaming flesh like she was his favorite flavor of ice cream cone on a hot summer day.

"I have all the answers, Carin. Do you like those questions, baby?" The words resonated in her brain with a maddening hum.

"Oh God, yes." She squirmed against his questing mouth, seeking release. She was so close. Bix sent his emotions streaming into her mind. The depth of his love pushed her closer to the edge. But when the clench of his gut, the ache of his cock, and how much he needed to be inside of her flowed through their bond, she squashed down her own need and concentrated on Bix.

In that moment, giving him what he needed was more important than breathing. Up on her elbows now, she pushed away from his tormenting mouth and flipped over onto her stomach. Ass up in the air, chest writhing against the bed, Carin gasped as her hard, tight nipples and swollen breasts sizzled against the sheets. But Bix was still as stone.

Reaching back, a single finger slipped into her soaked cunt, teasing and enticing her husband to fill her with his massive cock. Bix's enchanting gray eyes were riveted on that finger, and she knew the prime male inside of him itched to break loose and take her wildly.

Unable to stop the swivel of her hips, she wriggled and squirmed seeking the fat head of his dick pushing up against her dewy lips from behind. His hands tightened on her hips and held her still. But she wanted, needed to move. Wanted him inside, as raw and untamed as she felt. Fuck control. She didn't want him to have any.

"Fuck me, Bix. Take what you need, baby."

The plum of his engorged rod popped inside. She moaned loud and long, encouraging him with a shower of emotions and images. She showed him their mating night, the first time he'd taken her blood, bonding them forever. The first time he'd fucked her with a speed and depth possible only for a fully mature vampire prime.

And he hadn't done it since. Even after assuring him she'd loved it, he'd expressed concern of taking too much of her blood, and sexing her too roughly. After all, she had passed out.

But tonight she needed it. More important, he needed it—hard, hot, sweaty vampire sex. Blurring, mind-numbing sex. And she would make sure he got it.

Besides, what man could resist his mate begging for his cock?

"Mmm, Bix, it feels so good. Take me like a vampire takes his mate."

"Carin, I-I don't think..."

"I need it. I'm begging for it. I'm so hot my pussy is on fire. Please, Bix. Oh God, harder. Please, please, please..." Each word was a little more frantic, each breath a little more harsh. Then she said something she'd never said before to any man, and meant every word with all her heart.

"I love you, Jon Bixler."

The dam burst and the shafting began. He plunged forward, one stroke, two strokes, going deeper each time until he was seated firmly. Pulling out until only the head of his wide cock stretched her entrance, Bix pummeled forward, fast, then faster, until the movement of his hips was a blur.

Oh yes, that's what she wanted. What he, as a vamp, needed. To let go with his mate. And it felt so good, almost overwhelming. The solid expanse of his chest pressed hot against her back as he leaned over her, supporting his weight with one arm, and holding her tightly to him with the other. His balls slapped against her clit as he took her hard and deep. It sent her careening towards orgasmic bliss.

"Bix," she shouted as her womb spasmed and tightened. "Bite me. Send me out of this world."

Fuel powered fire flashed through her body the second his fangs pierced the sensitive skin on her neck. With a final thrust forward, he growled against her throat, taking the sustenance she freely offered as spurt after spurt of hot come splashed against her womb.

This time, they slipped into unconsciousness together.

Chapter Sixteen

Thump! Thump! Thump!

Bix rolled over, glanced at the bedside clock and groaned. Six o'clock. Who in their right mind would bother a newly mated couple this early in the morning? He untangled Carin's arms and legs from around his, rose from the bed and stretched with a deep, satisfied groan. His whole body ached from the night of wild passion he'd shared with his woman. His bondmate. In short, Carin had kept him up all night and laid it on him like no female, human or vampire, ever had. He couldn't recall ever being so feral and out of control with a woman. And she loved him.

He took a moment to examine the already healing scratches, bruises and bite marks marring his chest, neck and even the inside of his thigh. He'd brought the freak out of her, all right. The woman had been insatiable. He reached down and patted his dick. Damn, even *it* was sore, and his lips quirked up in a satisfied grin.

Thump! Thump! Thump!

Bix cursed all the way to the living room, yanking a pair of sweats up his legs on the way. Snatching open the door, he managed to twist his face into a fierce, though exhausted, scowl.

"Hey, buddy, sorry to wake you." Alaan didn't sound the least bit remorseful. Bix wanted to both preen and smack him when his best friend grinned boldly at all the marks on his chest. Instead, he moved aside and let him in. Alaan's smile disappeared as he said, "We've been summoned to the Council Chambers."

"Again? Hell, I've spent more time in that room with those fucking Elders than I have with my own woman."

"I think I have an idea of what's going on. Grab a shower. I'll wait for you." Alaan sunk down into what was now Carin's favorite cream suede recliner, then called over his shoulder, "By the way, you may want to dress in Seeking gear and pack a bag."

Bix looked at him inquiringly. When Alaan held his hands up and motioned towards the closed bedroom door, Bix didn't bother pressing. Even a Seeker's mate wasn't privy to all the details of their covert assignments and the man wouldn't say another word until they were on their way to the Council Chambers.

In ten minutes Bix was showered, packed and dressed in black tactical pants, a black Under Armour formfitting tee, black silent-soled SWAT boots and the flowing black leather trench of a Seeker. Carin called it his *Matrix* coat. Underneath, a shoulder harness held his 9mm Glock, the cartridges loaded with silver hollow point bullets filled with silver nitrate. His two-edged katana blade rested in its scabbard hidden in a sheath down his back.

With his hair brushed back and covered with a black baseball cap, he approached the sleeping form of his wife and leaned over to caress the soft skin of Carin's cheek. Casting a final look at her beautiful face, relaxed and youthful in slumber, he dropped a gentle kiss on her forehead and left the room without a sound.

On the way to the Council Chambers, Tameth, their pilot, Randall, and three young Seekers met Bix and Alaan on the stairs. Slade from Clan Li, and Alex from Clan Akicit, they'd worked with on a case in Denver last year. The third was Kenoe, one of the ballsy Hatsepts who'd talked trash to Carin the night of their official joining.

To Bix's surprise, as they walked to the Council Chamber doors the white-haired Seeker held out his hand. "It's an honor to serve with you, sir. We Hatsepts talk a lot of shit but your exploits are beyond legendary. You, your crew and your woman have our respect."

Bix shook the man's hand, nodded his acceptance and signaled Tameth to push open the Chamber door.

All ten Elders, minus their mates, were already seated. And every face was much too stern for this early in the morning.

"Well, looks like the gang's all here," Bix yawned grumpily, ignoring the buzzing undercurrent in the air.

Before Bix's team could even reach the foot of the dais, Alaana began the briefing.

"Natasha, present the information."

The Liaison gave each Seeker a sealed manila envelope and began the briefing without delay. "We have movement on Sidheon. He was spotted in New York just last night. Here is the information you need along with secure vid-cell phones programmed especially for this mission." At their surprised expressions, she said, "No one, and I mean no one, will have the frequency to which these phones are coded. We believe there is a mole right here at headquarters."

The whole room went quiet as they all weighed the ramifications of a spy at V.C.O.E. headquarters.

"I suggest you get a quick bite, a cup of coffee and prepare to head out." She curled her lip up in a snarl and glared at Bix. "Say goodbye to your mates." Sneering at Alaan, she snarled, "If you have one, that is. You depart in twenty minutes on Stealth One."

The Council filed out, except for Alaana and Ralen. Both descended the dais steps and made a beeline for their son and Bix. After hugs, kisses and slaps on the back for each of them, they too, departed.

Bix dragged himself up the stairs to deliver the news to Carin. They both knew the hunt would begin, but even he hadn't anticipated having to leave already. Mated barely a week and he was off to who-knows-where for God-knows-when? The woman was not going to be happy.

ജ൚ഗ്ദ

Bix hadn't been able to resist calling out to Carin between destinations. He thought back to that first night, how with a gentle push against her mind they'd reached another level of intimacy. After her initial surprise, she'd relaxed into the gifting with ease, as if it had always been a part of her. All because she trusted him.

"You're in New York? I can't believe we can speak from this distance," Carin crowed happily into his head. He'd smiled, glad he could make her happy with such a simple thing. Then the scientist came out and she'd pummeled him with questions.

"So how does this work? Why can't I talk to Alaana even though she's in the same building I am?"

"We're more than mated, we're bonded, remember? All vamps have some psychic skill, but it still takes a measure of

concentration, is difficult when not in the person's presence, and almost impossible from long distances. Unless you're bonded to your mate."

"Ooooh, how cool. So I can call you whenever I want while you're away?"

Bix smiled, she'd sounded so pleased.

"You could, but I'm asking you not to. It wouldn't be a good idea to get a summons from you in the middle of a fight with a mean-assed rogue. Just the sound of your sexy voice would distract me. I can't have a wimp like Sidheon kicking my ass because I'm thinking about my woman."

She'd giggled, said good night and promised to behave. He'd snorted at that one. Carin? Behave? Riiight. She was always up to something in that damned lab of hers, and now with Alaana Serati as her close friend and confidante, the brat got away with murder. And he loved it. Loved her.

They'd spoken thought-to-thought every night at exactly midnight, Montana time. And after three weeks Bix was sick and tired of being away from his mate.

Bix made his way to the rear of the jet. At a glimpse of Alaan's face he stopped short and surveyed the crew. Tameth sat on an oversized bench seat talking and smiling with Kenoe Hatsept. Alaan watched them with murder in his eyes. Shaking his head at his friend's strange behavior, Bix called the crew together.

"Okay, guys, it's been exactly twenty-one days and I'm fed up with running all over creation chasing this bastard. I want your opinion on what you think is really going on here."

Kenoe spoke, his words quiet and thoughtful as his fingers idly stroked the thick fall of Tameth's midnight hair. "His scent is in each place we go, but it doesn't smell quite right."

Alaan's blond brows knit together, eyes blazing and glued to Kenoe's hands. His jaw was set so tight it ticked and jerked. Bix tilted his head, wondering what was up with that. Alaan simply looked away with narrowed eyes and avoided his gaze. The man was decidedly uncomfortable, almost fidgety, but Bix let it go. They had more pressing things to tackle.

"You know," Tameth spoke, "this Sidheon always seems to be one step ahead of us, as if someone is feeding him information. I agree with Kenoe about Sid's scent. It smells...old."

Alex asked, "Isn't Sidheon a scientist? If his scent is off perhaps he's found a way to counterfeit it? You said some of the vamps that worked at the biotech facility disappeared right along with him. What if they're running ahead of us, spraying his scent all over the place and..."

"...And someone's feeding them info on our movements? Your Liaison did mention a mole, right?" Kenoe added speculatively, his expression thoughtful, troubled.

Bix and Alaan looked at each other, eyes wide as the implications of such a plot took root. As Carin would say, "Talk about a real a-ha moment."

Slade spoke up. "You think this whole undertaking was a set-up?"

"Yeah," Alex said, "perhaps the whole mission was a wild goose chase?"

"Goddamn it. Who the hell would have the nerve?" Bix bellowed.

Tameth's dark eyes searched Alaan's vivid blue ones. "Alaan, what do you think, handsome?" She seemed to love teasing him, and rolled her eyes when the big blond giant wouldn't return her gaze. "Come on, Alaan, say something.

You've got a good brain. Besides, you know I love your voice. It reminds me of Barry White."

Kenoe chuckled when Alaan grumbled something about throwing cheeky women over his shoulder for a spanking before he headed to the cockpit to keep Randall company. Bix called after him, "Have Randall turn off the transponder. I don't want to be tracked." Alaan nodded but didn't break stride.

Bix flipped open his phone and hit the speed dial. "Natasha, we're on the way back."

"What's going on? Have you got him?" she squealed with excitement.

"No, we don't have him. He's managed to elude us in every city we've tracked him to."

"Well, if you haven't managed to catch him why are you coming back early?"

"To see who set us up."

"What? No one would dare."

"Well, someone did. We're just outside of Tokyo. We've got at least eighteen hours in the air. We'll be there by late tomorrow afternoon."

"All right. The clans have gone home but all the members of the Council are still here. It's only ten o'clock in the evening here. I can call a quick briefing to let them know…"

"No. Don't tell anyone we're coming in early. If we're being shafted, I don't want anyone to know we're on to it."

"You've got it. I won't say a word. I'll double check the intel I've been receiving for clues. I should have something for you by the time you get here tomorrow afternoon. See you in eighteen hours."

"Fine. Bix out."

ಬಿಂಬ

Sidheon snatched his cell off the nightstand and flipped it open. He hated being disturbed in the middle of an experiment. He glanced at the phone number on the display and sighed. *Not again,* he thought wearily as he answered the call, not bothering with a hello.

"I am beginning to regret this arrangement. What is it now? And why are you calling me at this hour?" The bitch was either addicted or obsessed, he wasn't sure which. But either way, he was beginning to wish he'd never gifted her with a taste of his cock.

"There's been a change of plans. If you're not ready, and I mean right now, we'll have to call the whole thing off." The tone was impatient, laced with anger, determination and a good dose of fear. Sidheon didn't give a rat's ass. Oh well, there was no help for it—hired help must occasionally be reminded of their status. And their expendability.

"Really," he drawled. "I don't recall you being in charge of this little escapade. I understand you're taking a risk with a very small window of time in which to retrieve my guest. My world won't end if things must be, shall we say, delayed. However, your situation is a bit different, don't you think?"

"Don't threaten me, lover. I've done everything you asked, and enjoyed the occasional tryst as much as you, but I won't be declared rogue or killed for anyone. Not even for a vamp with a cock as nice as yours. So"—she blew a frustrated huff—"I need you to move your ass or I'm bailing, Sidheon."

Females. They could be so dramatic. But he hadn't gotten this far by giving in to female hysterics, even if they were warranted. But he couldn't allow the woman's panic to get *him* caught in the same net. If his little traitor went down, it would be all by her lonesome and he would simply disappear. End of story.

She was understandably terrified at the possibility of landing in the hands of the Seekers. And if Iudex judges got involved...hell, he didn't even want to think about what would happen with those ruthless bastards. But as long as it didn't happen to him, Sidheon didn't care one way or the other. Besides, the mole was history the second he got his hands on Carin anyway.

"You're bailing? I think not, my dear." With a yawn, he said, "Perhaps I should make a phone call to Alaana Serati? I'm sure she'd be interested in our special relationship, don't you?"

After a moment of silence, he continued. "I didn't think so. Now, you just get her here. I'll take care of the rest. If all goes according to plan, it will be days before the Seekers chasing my trail even figure it out. Actually, I'm a bit surprised they haven't figured it out yet."

"For your information, the Seekers will be back in less than twenty-four hours."

"No matter. I've already secured a nice little property where we can relax for awhile. Sending the coordinates now."

"I have them. I've got transportation. I'll have our guest there in less than four hours."

"Excellent, and my dear?"

"Yes?"

"Use the chemical I provided to subdue her. Other than that, she's not to be touched. Any touching will be done by me, understand?"

Dead silence.

Sidheon squeezed the bridge of his nose with two fingers and took a deep breath. Dealing with this vamp had been trying at best. Perhaps he'd just feed the impertinent skank to the Seekers and be done with it? If she hadn't been such an excellent source of information and a damned good lay, he would have seriously considered it.

"I said, do you understand? If you can't manage to answer me now, then perhaps in four hours I can get you to say the words I want to hear with a bit of sharp persuasion."

On an unsteady intake of breath, she whispered, "I understand. I'll do as you ask. No problem."

"Thank you, my dear. See you in four hours. By the way, I'm famished. I have plenty of blood, but not near enough pussy. Be ready."

Disconnecting the line, he rolled over onto his back. Now he could get back to his experiment—counting how many times he could come before Carin arrived. Dragging a voluptuous blonde female vamp onto his engorged cock, he felt the freeing sensation of his lengthening incisors clear down to his balls. A petite curly-haired brunette bared a slender neck for him on a sigh. Yes, this was the kind of research he could really take good notes on.

ஐௐ

"Carin, wake up."

"What? What?" Carin shot up in the big bed, jumped to the floor and looked around for danger. Her training was coming in handy—her fingers wrapped securely around a nasty-looking curved silver dagger, ready to fight before she was even fully awake.

This must be a dream. There was no other way Natasha would be standing in her bedroom shaking the hell out of her.

"Bix called the secure line," Natasha said frantically, already moving towards the door. "There's been trouble, Carin. He asked me to bring you to him."

The dagger clattered to the carpet with a dull thud.

"Bix? What? Where?"

"He's been injured. It doesn't look good."

Natasha's words hung in the air, then twisted and tightened around Carin's gut. Fear far more paralyzing than what she'd experienced when her mother and grandmother died wrapped around her lungs. No, this couldn't be happening. Not with Bix. He was a damned vampire. He wasn't supposed to die on her. But maybe there was something she could do? There had to be a way. Hope and panic mobilized her limbs. She snatched a sweat suit out of the dresser drawer while peppering Natasha with questions.

"Where is he? What happened? Should I get Dr. Lyons? Oh, my God. Move it woman, hurry up." She threw a few articles into a bag, pulled on her coat and was ready to go. On the way down the stairs she remembered something.

"Hold on a second. I need to tell Alaana I'm going."

"She already knows. Now let's go or we won't make it in time."

Carin fidgeted and wrung her hands as she moved down the staircase. Her throat tight with unshed tears, she pushed down the terror gnawing at her belly and asked more questions.

"Where is he, Natasha? What kind of injury has he sustained?" She cringed as Natasha ignored the first question and bowled her over with the answer to the second.

"It's a fatal wound. He's unconscious and losing blood rapidly, but holding on because he knows you're on the way."

Oh God, this can't be happening, Carin screeched to herself as their car flew towards the private airport on the south side of the vast estate.

"I'm really sorry, Carin. I know we haven't been on the best of terms, but I certainly didn't want anything to happen to Bix."

Running up the steps of the small jet, Carin dropped her bag at her feet, strapped herself in with trembling fingers and told Natasha to have the pilot move faster.

Carin kicked her bag under her seat and winced when her toe came in contact with something. No telling what she'd stubbed her toe on, but truthfully, she didn't care. All she wanted was to get this plane in the air and get to her husband. The bag wasn't cooperating with her nudging. She bent down and forcefully pushed it into place. When she sat up, Natasha stood over her.

The nasty sneer Carin had become so familiar with was back.

"Just a little something to help you sleep on the plane ride."

"But I don't have any trouble fly..." A prick in her neck was followed by a dull, freezing sensation. The last thing she saw was the face of a smug Natasha. *Oh, just great,* she thought as a strange gray haze settled over her eyes before darkness enveloped all.

Chapter Seventeen

It was almost six in the morning and his mistress hadn't risen yet. Jaidyn knocked on the door again, but Alaana still didn't answer. He sent out a psychic call to her and encountered nothing but an empty void. Even if she were blocking, he would have at least run into the block. He couldn't remember ever encountering no psychic signature at all. Something was wrong.

Jaidyn put all his strength behind the hard kicks against the door. When it finally gave, his insides tilted with alarm. Alaana was sprawled out on her front room floor. A nasty, but healing bruise covered her right cheek. Ralen lay next to her. Both of them were unconscious.

He tapped her lovely face while bellowing into her ear. "Matriarch!" No response. What the hell was going on here? The bruise on her face shouldn't have knocked her out like this. He leaned close and buried his nose at the base of her neck. A drug. He could smell it, but had no idea what it was.

Jaidyn eased her onto the couch and settled Ralen on the loveseat before dialing Dr. Lyons' extension. Ten very tense minutes later, the doctor monitored the Serati's vital signs just as the Council and Bix's team walked in.

The moment Alaan spotted his mother's pale face and limp body lying prone with doctors and assistants all around her, he hurried to her side and gently pulled her into his arms.

"Mother, what happened? Are you all right?" He looked up at Dr. Lyons as he swabbed an antiseptic wipe over the Matriarch's neck. "Doc, what happened?"

"It appears your parents were hit at the base of the skull, then drugged. I've given them something to revive them but it takes a few minutes to break through the grogginess."

Just then, the Seratis became fully lucid. Dr. Lyons checked them over and confirmed their overall excellent health. Other than a pair of fading headaches and matching bruises on the back of their heads, they were fine.

"Stop fussing over me," the Matriarch snapped, shooing away all the hands trying to help her off the couch. "Jaidyn, I'll have my breakfast now. Make sure Cook remembers that ghastly latte thing Carin sighs over every morning. In fact, I'll just go on out to the terrace."

"Yes, ma'am, I'll head downstairs and take care of it personally." Jaidyn kissed her palm. A glance past her shoulder to the table and chairs on the terrace sent a streak of alarm through him, but he couldn't put his finger on it. He turned on his heel. Bix was two steps behind him.

"Matriarch," Bix called, "I'm glad you're all right. I'll go to my apartment and change, then accompany Carin back here for breakfast. Feel up to briefing me on what happened while the two of you eat?"

"Same for me," Alaan insisted.

Alaana nodded her agreement and slipped a warm robe over her lounging set.

All of them were on the way out when something Jaidyn had forgotten snapped clearly into his mind and made him want to kick himself. He glanced at his watch, stopped dead at the threshold of the door and turned back towards his mistress. Even his concern for the Matriarch was no excuse for overlooking such an important point.

"Mistress, I am so ashamed." Jaidyn lowered his head in shame. "I forgot that..."

Her face pale and pinched, Alaana stalled just short of the terrace. "What is it, Jaidyn?"

"It's Dr. Carin. She should have been here twenty minutes ago."

Bix flew out the door with Jaidyn, Alaan and their entire team on his heels until the Matriarch pushed them all out of the way and darted past.

In Bix's apartment, Carin's fading scent and one look at the rumpled sheets, open dresser drawers and closet doors said she'd left in a hurry several hours before.

Jaidyn eased Alaana into his arms and cradled her head against his shoulder. For the first time in centuries the Matriarch of Clan Serati cried in front of someone other than her mates while Bix howled his loss to the rafters.

ଛାଓଷ

Bix's strangled roar ricocheted around the inside of his head followed by a deafening silence during the past hour he, Alaan and internal security spent tearing Natasha's private apartments apart.

Since neither of the Serati Elders had seen the perpetrators, there were no leads on who'd taken Carin, except one. Natasha, and one of the Council's small jets, was missing, too.

Bix had called telepathically to Carin the moment he learned she was gone, but like Jaidyn when he'd tried to rouse the Seratis, all he touched was a blank wall. As if she'd disappeared off the face of the earth leaving only a gray murky void where her thoughts should be. It left him more empty and alone than he'd ever been in all his long years.

"Well, old friend," Alaan said, jaw tight with agitation, "at least we know who the mole is."

"But why drop the hint if she was the mole all along?" Bix questioned hotly, barely containing the volatile mix of rage and uncertainty coursing through his being. His woman was missing and all he had was a barrage of questions. There was nothing a Seeker hated more than unanswered questions, and right now he had a sea full.

"Think about it, Bix. Natasha dropped the info about a mole, and what did we all do? We immediately assumed it *wasn't* her. The goal was to draw suspicion away from herself, and I'm sorry to say, it worked."

"Fuck!" His bellow echoed through the valley with intent so deadly, it chilled the already chilly air of what should have been a typical peaceful mountain morning.

"Why can't I feel her?" a livid Bix ground between clenched teeth, worry snaking its way through his gut.

"She may be unconscious," Alaan reasoned. Bix's spine went ramrod straight as he teetered on the verge of madness at the thought of Carin being knocked out, the possibility of someone touching her, hurting her. Again. No, he refused to accept it. He would find her and she would be fine. She just had to be.

"Listen, Bix, they probably gave her the same stuff they gave my parents. If they went to all this trouble to get to her, it wasn't to kill her. Natasha could have done that anytime."

Gripping tight enough to buckle the steel, Bix's fingers dug into the balcony railing as he looked out over the rolling hills in the distance. The hollow pit of his stomach constricted when instead of snow-capped mountains and frozen streams, Carin's lovely face and feisty spirit filled his thoughts.

"Why the hell would Natasha do this, Alaan? Forget her obsession with me. How could she do this to our people? She's betrayed every one of us."

"Some things just can't be explained. And to be honest, I don't care why she did it, only that she pays for it. Over and over again."

Bix whipped away from the terrace railing and stormed back into Natasha's apartment just as his cell phone rang. Tameth's calm, quiet voice was on the other end of the line.

"Bix, I've found something. I'm in the communications center."

"We're on our way," he snapped as he and Alaan took off out of the ransacked apartment at vamp speed. The comm center in the middle of the compound was crawling with Seekers and Iudex judges. Tameth sat in the midst of them, coolly confident, the only one in the huge room not stalking around with nervous energy or snarling mad. The only thing giving away her anger was the stiff set of her shoulders and the hard glint of her dark eyes.

When Bix reached her side, she showed him something they couldn't believe they'd missed in the first place. Natasha's personal electronic calendar and intelligence files had been wiped from her personal computer, but were backed up on a secure part of the V.C.O.E. network. All it took to expose them was the encrypted password, which Tameth guessed right away—JonBix1822. Bix's name and birth year.

There were phone records, names of contacts, dates the contacts were made and how, notes of exchanged information and what data was sent where. All of it.

Natasha had been gathering intelligence on Sidheon for months. She knew he worked in one of the biotech companies owned by V.C.O.E. The rogue had somehow garnered management support for his projects and gotten several of his cohorts hired into the facility. From the documents Tameth found, it was apparent Natasha kept the info to herself. When the Council decided it was time to eliminate Sidheon, she planned to deliver the data that would bring him down and secure a place for herself on Bix's team on a more permanent basis.

"Then why the issue with Carin?" Bix asked, still unsure what the bitch was up to.

Tameth hit a few buttons on the keyboard and the screens filled with more data. "According to these notes, Carin was a complication."

"Why?"

"Because the Council didn't want you to go kill Sidheon. They wanted you to infiltrate the facility and uncover his experiments. That introduced Carin to the equation."

"What the hell does she have to do with any of this? She didn't work on any of Sidheon's projects. She was only supposed to get me close to him, or at least that's what Natasha claimed."

"Yes," Tameth answered, "but she was assigned as your target because the Council had done a little research of their own. They knew Carin was not only the brightest mind in biotech science today, but she happened to be in the same facility as Sidheon. By sending Carin's boss out of the country and putting you in play, you could either give her authority to provide you with info on what Sidheon was doing, or the means to figure out for herself what he was up to."

Alaan asked, "And Natasha knew all this?"

"It's all here in her notes. There's even a picture of Carin here."

Bix's eyes narrowed dangerously as he said, "So that explains why Carin was my target, but..."

"There's more, Bix. Natasha was playing both sides. By sending you leads on Sidheon, then contacting Sidheon to tell him where *not* to be, she kept the Council's trust and Sidheon's. Basically, with Carin in play, all Natasha's plans to save the day and make herself the hero were ruined. Then when you mated and bonded Carin, Natasha had to improvise, change her plans."

"Plans for what?" Bix bellowed.

Tameth turned from the computer screen and looked Bix square in the eye. "To turn Carin over to Sidheon. If you hadn't mated her, it would have been a piece of cake. But since Natasha had always planned to make herself indispensable to you, Carin put a fly in her mix."

"Shit," Bix raged. All this because a woman he never wanted planned to remove the only woman he ever needed?

With all the files open now, the data Tameth managed to hack filled in all the pieces. There was only one question left.

Fists clenched at his sides, and his lips tight against bared fangs, "Where?" was the only word Bix could manage to form.

Tameth answered without hesitation. "I have no idea. There's a lot of information here, Bix. Even a vampire can't read at super speed. But don't worry, we'll find her."

Bix raked a hand through his hair and pulled. All this waiting and wading through shit irked him to no end. And the betrayal of someone of Natasha's caliber cut, and cut deep. The woman had been a Council Liaison for the Western territories, for fuck sake. Had held one of the most trusted offices for the care of their people and the enforcement of Council law. In all the years she'd served, she'd never been reprimanded, never stepped out of line—other than the occasional ill-timed remark regarding his or Alaan's love life. But her work ethic—flawless. Until now.

"How did she get a fucking plane out of here?" But even as the words left his mouth, Bix knew the answer.

"Well, we know she didn't do it alone. She didn't have to, not with her security clearance. Bix, she could have signed anybody in or out of here." Tameth clicked a few buttons and opened another file. "Wait a second, here's something. Looks like she requested clearance for a small jetcraft for a medical emergency last night. The request was active for about two hours, between ten o'clock and midnight. No flight plan is listed. Huh. Wonder how she pulled that off. It's got to be somewhere."

"I want to know where the hell Natasha took my woman. Grab one of the Beta Seekers and have them work with you. I want to know the second you get a breakthrough."

Tameth copied the files to a shared folder on the system, swirled her chair around and pinned him with a hard stare. "Bix, we just got here this morning and you haven't rested or eaten. Do both, or you won't be any good to Carin or any of the rest of us."

"I'll sleep later. We have work to do and I want out of here as soon as possible." His vid-cell emitted a low vibration. He flipped it open and stared into the bluish-white eyes of Kenoe Hatsept.

"We've found something in your woman's lab. You'd better get over here."

"This better be good," Bix snarled, snapping the phone shut. Tameth was on his heels all the way back to the main house and up to Carin's labs. Kenoe met them at the door, his movements urgent.

"Check this out," he said, pushing a strange-looking round of ammunition into Bix's hand.

Bix's brow furrowed, followed by wide-eyed understanding as he took in what he was seeing.

"It's all documented in her notes," Kenoe explained. "Your woman has amazing foresight. She's been working on a weapon. A weapon for you, Bix."

With Dr. Lyons and the help of the V.C.O.E. weapons masters, his Carin had replicated Sidheon's destructive serum and used it to create poisoned rounds for them to use in the hunt. And thanks to Carin, they had hundreds of them.

ଔଔ

The closer Carin got to wakefulness, the more nauseated she became. The feeling was much too familiar, reminding her of the effort it took to fight the pain meds pumped into her body after Sidheon's brutal attack. An attack requiring major surgery and Bix's blood the very same night if she was going to live.

She took a tentative breath, sure with her enhanced vamp senses any strong scent would make her hurl on the spot. The air was a bit dusty, but breathable and cool. Not wanting to alert her captors she was awake, she kept her breathing even, eyes closed and quietly inventoried her body. She didn't feel any pain anywhere, but she was stiff as all get out. Cracking an eye open, she looked around as well as she was able and breathed a sigh of relief. She was alone on a very comfortable bed in a nicely appointed room. But where? Couldn't possibly be a hotel. Surely someone would have asked a few questions about an unconscious woman being hauled into the building.

Brilliant hues of orange and pink shone through the sheer curtains of a large square window near the bed. Wherever she was, the sun had been up for at least several hours. Her keen hearing picked up the sound of roaring waves. The ocean.

Carin bit down on her tongue to keep from cursing a blue streak. She wanted to yell, rant and slap herself in the head for being so damned gullible. Trusting Natasha was tantamount to deserving the Darwin Award. The first thing she should have done when the woman claimed Bix was injured was reach out to him along their bond. She'd have probably discovered he was just fine, relaxing after a day of searching for Sidheon in whatever city he was in tonight, or rather, last night.

Not once had Bix forgotten to contact her since he'd been gone. If he'd been hurt wouldn't he have called her, either by phone or telepathically, instead of Natasha? How could she have been such a dolt? Now here she was, God-knows-where, with Natasha and no telling who else. And did Bix even know she'd been taken? Geez, what a mess.

Her throat was parched and there was a nasty taste on her tongue. Must be the side effect of whatever drug Natasha had given her.

Oh, just wait until I get my hands on that damned woman, she thought, struggling to sit up so she could scratch. Such a simple action shouldn't have given her so much trouble. What the...?

Well no wonder—her hands and feet were tied and her neck itched furiously where Natasha's very long, but thankfully thin, needle had pierced her flesh. Hunching her shoulders trying to get to the irritated skin made her head whirl and her stomach roil from a bit of vertigo. And now she had to pee. Double damn.

And what about Bix? Where was he? Quieting her mind in hopes it would also quiet her stomach, Carin reached inside herself and called out to Bix. The little corner of her mind where she could always feel the faint hum of her husband's presence was...empty. The strong, bright silvery thread of consciousness that connected her to Bix seemed clouded over as if it had no substance. With every reach, every touch, it slipped out of her fingers. He simply wasn't there. The knowledge that she was truly alone sent her churning stomach into overdrive.

The sound of muffled footsteps caught her attention. The door eased open and the room flooded with a scent with way too much rose in it for her tastes. Natasha.

"Hello, Carin. Glad you're awake." She walked over to Carin's bed, sat on the side and checked the bindings. "Comfy, I hope," she said snidely.

Carin felt her temper rise but smashed it down ruthlessly. She would have to keep her head if she was going to get through this. *Scientist to the forefront, woman. Get some damned answers.*

"Natasha, what are you up to?" Carin asked, deliberately slurring her words. Let the woman believe she was still loopy from the sedative. "Why did you take me from headquarters? And where's Bix?"

"Bix?" She looked down at her watch, mumbled something about eighteen hours, and said, "When we spoke last, your darling Bix was on his way back to the U.S. He should have walked into V.C.O.E. headquarters sometime yesterday evening. Only he won't find you there."

"Yesterday evening? How long have I been here?"

"About thirty-six hours," she answered acidly.

"Thirty-six hours? What the hell did you give me to knock me out? A horse tranquilizer?" Hell, no wonder she had to go to the bathroom. Thirty-six whole fucking hours. Well, damn.

"A little bit of vamp pharmaceuticals at work."

Oh, so now she was a guinea pig, too? This just got better and better.

"It's a neuro-inhibitor mixed with a strong sedative. Keeps you from being able to engage your psychic abilities and makes you more...compliant. You'll feel kind of funny for a little while longer yet."

At Carin's look of wonder, she continued, "The night of your bonding, the Matriarch said Bix had found his bondmate. Many of the younger vampires probably had no idea what she was talking about. But I understood perfectly, and if I know Bix, he's taught you how to use that bond. We can't have you calling in the cavalry, now can we?"

Well that explained why she felt fuzzy in the head and couldn't hold her psychic bond with Bix long enough to call out to him.

"Look, woman, I've never done anything to you. Why take me?"

"Because I want to hurt Bix as deeply as possible."

"Now what the hell kind of sense does that make? You once claimed he was your mate. Why would you want to hurt him?"

"Because he took you, a puny human woman, instead of me. Because he's scorned me for years. I've saved myself for him, and for what? For him to push me aside?" Bounding from the bed, the woman paced the room ranting. Half of what she said made sense but if she was trying to play on Carin's sympathy, she was coming up awfully short.

"But everything is fine now," Natasha purred. "I've found a new lover, one eager to take me. And take me often."

"So you want to hurt my man because he didn't want you," Carin snorted incredulously, shaking her head. "You know, you're awfully pathetic for a vampire female. You sure you're not some other species or something?"

Carin refused to flinch when Natasha raised her hand threateningly.

"Shut. Up." Fist in the air, she hissed, "I want nothing more than to smash your face in, you bitch. But my lover wants you unharmed. What for, I'll never know. After he's done with you, and I do mean done, Bix will be in need of, uh, shall we say, comfort? And I'm more than prepared to give it to him."

"And what does your lover think about your obsession with another man?" Carin asked hotly.

"Don't be so naive. Oh, I forgot, you can't help it. And everyone seems to believe you're so smart."

Carin cocked her head at such venomous condescension. It was as if Natasha took Carin and Bix's relationship as a personal affront.

"The answer should be obvious. I'm a means to an end for him, and he's a means to an end for me. And the end will be Bix and me. Period."

"Well, who is this idiot who would endanger his life for you?" Carin asked pointedly.

Carin's eyes went beyond large when the bedroom door opened again. She looked back and forth between Natasha and the new occupant, rolled her eyes and laughed.

"Oh, you've got to be kidding me."

Sidheon sidled up behind Natasha, reached under her arms and stroked her large breasts. The woman hummed as his pale fingers moved over her body. After what felt like endless moments, the creep stepped back from Natasha, gave a nipple one last flick with his thumb and looked down at Carin as if she were a piece of meat cooked to order. She wanted nothing more than to sink into the floor and disappear, but forced herself to meet his gaze boldly.

"Hello, Carin. How nice to see you again."

"Kiss my ass, Aleth." She wanted to take the words back when his gaze slid down her legs and raked over her butt.

"Tempting offer, I may just take you up on it. And if you're a good girl, I'll make sure you get your breakfast."

Just before the words "fuck" and "you" slipped out of her mouth, her stomach grumbled embarrassingly loud. Carin clamped her lips shut. Besides, from the menace she felt emanating from him, and what Bix told her, Sidheon was as ruthless as they came. And with her hands and feet tied, she couldn't run or protect herself. There was no choice but to bluff through this, scared shitless or not.

"I think I can manage to be good, at least until my husband gets here. Then we're going to spend some time kicking the vampire shit out of you." Carin grinned shamelessly as Natasha's mouth flew open in an outraged "Oh." Sidheon's glinting blue eyes filled with heat of the amorous kind. His predatory grin tipped up into a true smile when she said, "And by the way, I take my eggs over hard and my bacon crisp, but not burnt, thank you."

"Natasha." Sidheon's words held an unspoken command.

With a huff the woman stepped over to the door and opened it just enough to call for someone. A figure Carin couldn't make out from her position on the bed shadowed the other side of the door. When Natasha was finished speaking with whoever it was, she slammed the door closed with a huff.

Sidheon moved to Carin's side, leaned over her prone body and pressed his cold nose against her neck. Inhaling her scent, he groaned as he licked a small patch of skin on her collarbone. Closing her eyes, she suppressed a shudder when his incisors came into play and the pressure of his fangs slowly began to give way to a sharp prick.

Aw hell no! She might be down, but she sure as hell wasn't out.

"Don't you dare take my blood without my permission," Carin said quietly but forcefully. Sidheon jerked back, eyes wide, his expression full of surprise.

"I see your mate has taught you some of the rules of blood taking. Not that I usually play by the rules, but I promise you, you will come to me willingly, Carin." With that, the sting left behind from his fangs was replaced by the prick of cold steel. A needle.

"Just the neuro-inhibitor. We'll leave off the sedative. For now."

A pale and sickly looking fellow shuffled into the room with a breakfast tray. Cowering, the man set it on the nightstand, untied her and scurried towards the door, followed by a glowering Natasha and a smirking Sidheon. Left alone to eat, she cursed as the deadbolt slid home.

Later, the same frail, pale man with tissue-like skin and lank hair ambled in to remove her dishes. It had been exactly what she'd asked for—eggs over hard with crispy bacon. Toast and coffee thrown in for good measure, which she sniffed first to make sure there was nothing in it to knock her out again.

She still didn't know if her husband was well or not. With nothing in the room to occupy her mind, she warmed up by running in place and went through her martial arts exercises.

One thing was for sure—if Natasha walked into this room alone, she'd get a royal ass kicking.

ଈଠ୦ଔଌ

Rest was impossible. Everything smelled like his wife. Every corner of their apartments made him think of something she'd said or done. Tired of tossing around in their bed, Bix showered, packed a bag and left the apartment for the communications center. He would sleep in his office there and be ready the moment Tameth had something.

He walked into the huge high-tech building and all conversation stopped. Every eye turned towards him. He knew he looked like hell because that's what he felt like.

Without a word, Alaan walked to the nearest phone, called down to the main building and had the cooks bring Bix food and blood.

He felt useless. Everyone was hard at work, either in Carin's labs loading the modified ammo into cartridges under Kenoe's direction, or here in the comm center trying to help Tameth wade through Natasha's endless electronic files, looking for any sign of where she'd fled. Carin had been missing for more than thirty-six hours, yet all he could do was wait.

Stalking around the comm center like a caged animal, Bix had never felt so close to losing it. They just had to uncover something and fast. The more time it took for them to get to Carin, the more time Sidheon had to harm her.

When he'd walked into Carin's life, he'd had no idea the rogue had been keeping a quiet eye on the woman, coveting her all this time. And Natasha, the jealous bitch, had taken her to every loyal vampire's worst enemy.

His head snapped around at the urgent call of his name.

"Bix, we've got something," Tameth yelled over the din of male voices filling the room.

"Where?"

"Northern California. Stinson Beach, to be exact."

"Alaan..."

"Already done, buddy, already done." And he was out the door, a trail of vamps right behind him, fully aware of what needed to be done. In seconds, the room emptied of everyone but Tameth and Bix.

"Tameth, send the data to Stealth One and Two."

"Yes, sir." Her fingers flew over the keyboard. "Hey, you all right?" Tameth asked.

Bix didn't answer, couldn't form the words. He had to concentrate on what he thought he felt. He had to be sure because it would simply kill him to be mistaken. Just out of reach was a flutter in his mind, an awareness he hadn't realized he would miss until it was gone. The bond with Carin. Faint, but there just the same.

He couldn't have a conversation with her yet, but she was alive. Whatever they'd given her must be wearing off.

"Tameth, how long is the flight to California?" he asked, already moving towards his office to grab his bag.

"In our stealths, about two and a half hours."

"How soon can we be off the ground?"

"The planes were readied the moment we learned Carin was missing. Ten minutes to get the pilots in the cockpits and we're out of here."

"Make it happen."

"Done."

ಬಂಗ

Sidheon hadn't come to see her all day, but the same pasty-faced man brought her dinner. When he approached with a syringe loaded with a pale yellow liquid, Carin cringed.

The man didn't seem to want to be there any more than she did. Perhaps he'd cut her a break?

"Hi," she said, keeping her voice quiet so as not to frighten the frail-looking man. "What's your name?"

"Chase, ma'am," he replied, just as quietly.

"Chase, do you have to give me that damned neuro drug?" she pleaded, allowing tears to fill her wide eyes. And it was no act. She was afraid for her husband, afraid for herself, but unwilling to simply give up without a fight.

"I-I'm sorry, ma'am. I don't have a choice. Sidheon wouldn't hesitate to kill me if he found out."

"Well, thanks anyway." She bawled outright and the tears ran unchecked down her cheeks.

"Please don't cry. I know who you are," Chase whispered.

Carin tilted her head to the side, her eyes narrowed in question.

"You're the mate of a Seeker. *The* Seeker."

"How do you know that?"

"Sidheon doesn't pay much attention to what his servants hear," he said. Regret and anger laced each word.

"Sidheon is in for it. My husband will find me, and when he does, Sidheon is toast."

"I was one of the vamps who worked at Idac and stupidly accompanied Sidheon when he took off running from your mate."

"You're a vampire? B-but Chase, what happened...?" Carin couldn't believe it. Had he always looked like this?

"I had no idea what the bastard intended to do to me."

What the hell was he talking about? What had Sidheon done to this man? This vampire? But before Carin could answer the question, the man moved with more speed than he seemed capable, stabbed the needle into her bedding and discharged the drug through the blankets and into the mattress. With a sad wink, he disappeared out the door and locked it behind him.

After the strange encounter with Chase, she didn't feel much like eating, but knew she had to keep up her strength and be ready for God-knows-what.

A mere fifteen minutes later she felt the neuro-inhibitor wearing off and her mind began to release the cotton-like muted fuzz wrapped around it.

Idiot. Sidheon had probably tested the drug on vamps. While she had vamp-like abilities now, she wasn't a vampire and he'd obviously miscalculated how long the stuff would work on a human. Instinctively pushing her psychic shields into place to make sure Sidheon would remain unaware of her rapidly increasing lucidity, Carin breathed a sigh of relief when no one came barging into her room to stick her with any needles.

By dinnertime, she was just beginning to feel halfway right again when her mind tilted sideways.

Bix charged into her head, filled it to the brim with concern and boiling rage. Assuring her husband she was fine, Carin smiled when he cursed a blue streak, spitting mad and promising all kinds of nasty things in store for Natasha.

"Bix, Natasha's working with Sidheon." She stiffened when his blue streak turned black. The man used some curse words she'd never even heard before. Was that old Latin? Boy, he was pissed, and he was coming for her. And Sidheon. But when he told her what he wanted her to do, she almost lost her dinner.

Chapter Eighteen

Carin watched the rolling surf through the bolted window of her bedroom. At least it had a private bathroom and she wouldn't have to be held captive and smell like one, too. A small knock sounded at the door. Carin snorted. Like she could walk over and just open it. The damned thing was locked, so why the hell were they knocking?

She crossed her arms over her chest and stood, toe tapping with annoyance as it slid silently open. Chase, head lowered to the carpet, ambled in.

"Hi, Chase. What's wrong?" she asked kindly.

"Dr. Sidheon says you will dine in an hour downstairs. He sent this for you to wear." He kept his gaze on the floor as he held out what was supposed to be clothes.

Carin's lip curled up on one side when the man produced something fit for the best Los Angeles hooker. A short leather skirt, a cap-sleeved leather bodice and high-heeled leather ankle boots, all black. All in her size. There was no way in hell she was going to wear this. Had never worn anything remotely close. Ever. Only Bix had managed to get her the slightest bit out of her conservative bent, and she hadn't gotten up the nerve to sport an outfit like this even for him.

"Look, you tell Aleth I said he can take this outfit and stuff it up his ass." She made to toss him out when the sickly man's raspy words brought her up short.

"I—He said. Well, D-Dr. Sidheon said if you, if you refused...he would p-personally re-tie your hands and feet and...and," Chase stuttered.

"And what," she asked hotly.

"F-Feed you by hand."

"What the hell does feeding me by hand have to do with these clothes?" she screeched, her temper as hot as San Diego in July.

"He said you would be, um, be naked, ma'am." If she didn't know better, both she and Chase blushed but the man remained so deathly pale she couldn't tell. Carin snatched the leather outfit from the man's hands, shoved him out the door and slammed it shut.

In exactly one hour, she walked into a large dining room, escorted by a very uncomfortable Chase who saw her in and ducked out as fast as his shuffling skinny legs could carry him. The room was shaped like a large rectangle and reminded her more of a conservatory than a dining room. The lengths of both sides of the room were all glass. Skylights made up most of the ceiling and beveled panes filled an entire wall looking out to the darkened beach. Comfy-looking couches and chairs surrounded a man-sized fireplace. Huge pillows done in burgundy and black brocade took up the rear of the room. The place would be lovely if Sidheon weren't in it.

The scent of roast pork and fresh bread assailed her senses as she sat at the head of the table. Sidheon smiled at her from the other end with a pouting Natasha at his side. Her steps faltered but a second later she snapped her backbone into place and shook off her fear and surprise. Besides, her two known enemies weren't the cause of her discomfort. It was...the others. The dining table seated twenty-two, and every seat was occupied by both male and female vampires who all looked like they'd rather eat her than the spread Sid had laid before them.

Keeping her mind quiet, Carin concentrated on the sumptuous feast and stuffed herself with honey-baked turkey, rosemary bread stuffing, fresh asparagus in some kind of butter sauce and hot yeast rolls. The meal was finished off with baked caramel apples and, for Carin, a cup of steaming hot black coffee. The vamps indulged in blood-laced champagne.

She sat back in her L.A. 'Ho costume, pushed back her chair just a bit, crossed her booted feet and put them up on the table. Sipping the strong brew, she was more than aware the short leather skirt gave Sidheon an eyeful of almost the whole length of her bare legs. So, he'd thought to tie her up and hand feed her if she misbehaved? Nasty bastard. Only her promise to do as Bix asked made her tamp down her anger and put on a sweet-as-apple-pie face.

Several other pale and unhealthy-looking folks cleared the dishes. She thanked a particularly skinny female for a refill of her coffee. Her wan, weak smile made Carin wince. The girl looked like a strong northerly wind would blow her away. Carin looked closer at the wait staff and immediately knew the truth. Chase wasn't the only ill vampire here. Every one of these frail-looking so-called servants were vampires.

What the hell had happened to them? Why did every vampire around the table appear healthy while all the staff looked sick? Fuming, Carin slammed her cup down, ignoring the hot coffee sloshing onto her skirt and tablecloth. She shot to her feet with her hands fisted on her hips, glared at Sidheon down the long length of the table and roared.

"Aleth, what the hell is going on? What have you done to these vamps?"

"Oh, not much, my dear. Why don't you take a closer look, good doctor?"

With a flick of his wrist, the same young woman who'd smiled so happily at Carin's compliment now approached her with trepidation, dropped to her knees and cowered on the floor.

"There, there, I'm not going to hurt you. I promise," Carin crooned to the female as she took her seat once more. As the girl relaxed, Carin gently touched the cool skin of her face and neck, and then quickly examined her teeth and the whites of her eyes.

Sucking her breath in on a sigh, Carin couldn't keep the heartfelt sadness out of her voice. She was so sorry for this female it was all she could do to keep the tears in check.

"Aleth, how could you do this? You've altered them. This girl's skin feels like tissue paper. There's no way a vampire female should be this frail and weak." Carin looked down at the miserable face and whispered for her ears only. "I'm sorry. We'll fix it, okay? I promise. Now go on before you get in trouble."

As the girl scampered away, Sidheon rose, tugged Natasha out of her seat next to him and stalked around the table towards Carin. With one arm around his consort, he leaned lazily against the table, much too close for comfort. Carin's eyes never left his.

On an exasperated sigh, she asked, "Aleth, what do you want with me?"

A lone finger snaked out to wrap around a loose strand of her hair. "You know, Carin," he said, his voice smooth as silk, "I'd hoped to woo you, perhaps even make you my mate. I've always been fond of you. Your beauty, and of course, your genius."

Natasha flinched as if Sidheon's words physically cut her. With fury in her eyes, she yanked away from him but remained by his side.

Sidheon grabbed Natasha by the hair, yanked her back against his body and pressed his groin flush against her butt. A hand slipped under the traitor's blouse while he conversed with Carin as if they were all out for an afternoon stroll. Ewww, now this was just nasty, and not in a good way.

She wanted nothing more than to storm out, but remained in her seat instead, reminding herself that she'd promised to keep Sidheon in that damned dining room as long as possible. Carin picked up her coffee again and tried to ignore the mad scientist and his even madder Liaison. But boy was he making it hard.

Carin gulped a fortifying swallow of the strong brew and said, "You've always been fond of me, Aleth? Really? You could have fooled me, especially when you tried to gut me in front of my own house."

"Just a misunderstanding really. I was quite relieved when I heard you'd taken a sabbatical from Idac." He tweaked Natasha's nipples through her bra and the female vamp gasped and moaned desperately as if someone were cutting off her air supply. Yet Sidheon's gaze remained glued on Carin. "Before my partner here confirmed anything, I knew no one but V.C.O.E. could have pulled off something like that on such short notice, and only if you were alive."

"But why try to take me out at all?"

"Because, my sweet Carinian," he purred into Natasha's ear, "I knew you were at least aware, if not sure, of what I was doing. I couldn't risk allowing the V.C.O.E. to get to you."

"Yeah, this is all good and fine, but you still haven't answered my question. Why hold me here? I'm no threat to you, even if I did know what you were up to. And where the hell is *here* anyway?" She tried to block out the sound of Natasha's ragged moans as Sidheon played with her breasts and slid his hands up under the front of her barely there skirt.

"Well, since nobody knows where you are, I see no reason not to tell you. You're in a quaint little manor on a beach in Northern California. And while you're here, you're going to tell me exactly what you think of my research."

He wanted to talk about his research? Shit. Not good. It got worse when he explained his plans for V.C.O.E. The bastard planned to use his biological weapon to blackmail the Council. If they refused to make him the leader of a rogue vampire state he would use the serum he'd developed. And since it only affected those with pure, unaltered vampire DNA, he could put it into a main water or food supply and no one would be affected except his kind. Every vamp in the area would be toast, literally, in a matter of hours.

"Let me get this straight. You want every vampire declared a rogue by the Council to be placed under your guidance so you can create a rogue state and live happily ever after?" Carin couldn't believe what she was hearing. The man was definitely crazy. What made him think he could control a whole horde of lunatics with fangs? She was amazed at what she was hearing and forgot to put her psychic shields in place. Watching Natasha writhe and moan against Sidheon as he kneaded her breasts like bread dough wasn't making it any easier.

She screwed up her face in disgust. Sidheon chuckled and flicked one of Natasha's nipples into a hard, stabbing point.

"But you're right," Sidheon continued, "the Elders would want to know how I planned to control them. The same way I'll control the Council. Cross me, and they die. Give me what I want or they die. Finance my projects, or they die. Simple, yes? As for you, I don't actually need you. I do, however, want you."

Carin's skin crawled when Natasha's blouse slid down her arms to the floor, a black lacy bra following close behind. Carin felt her lip curl as she watched the woman raise her arms behind her, wrap them around Sidheon's neck and pant like a dog in heat. All the other vampires seated around the table pushed back their chairs and headed for the comfortable love seats and mounds of pillows in front of the huge fireplace. Watching Sid and Natasha make out must have given them ideas of their own. Soon the whole room was full of moans, groans and all-out lust.

"You don't need me, Aleth, and judging by the handful of tits you're juggling, you don't want me either. I want to go home. Right now."

"Now, now, my sweet Carinian. You aren't in a position to make any demands, except one."

"And what's that?" she sneered, swinging her feet off the table and pushing out of her chair to glare at him.

"You can demand me to fuck you. I'll definitely comply. In the meantime," Sidheon growled into Natasha's ear, his attention still on Carin, "I'll just have to amuse myself with...other things."

He turned sideways and pushed Natasha to her knees. She didn't hesitate in unbuckling the rogue's belt, undoing his trousers and sliding them to his ankles. A pair of forest green boxers followed and Carin saw more of Sidheon than she'd ever hoped to in her lifetime. She might have been impressed with the size and weight of his cock if he hadn't been a repulsive bastard. And Natasha was gobbling the man up as if her daily protein intake was in Sidheon's cock.

Every couch and pillow in front of the roaring fire was filled with writhing vampire bodies, the male and females paired off. A few were in threes, and all of them naked.

Sidheon grabbed a handful of Natasha's hair and snatched her up off her knees, hiked her skirt up and bent her forward over the table.

Carin almost gagged when he pushed into the woman's willing body and hissed about how tight the fit was. Eyes closed, she tried to block out Natasha's groans and moans. But when the woman began screaming bloody murder, Carin's eyes snapped open. Her dark brown eyes clashed with Sidheon's azure blue ones. The man hungrily watched her while he fucked Natasha into such a screaming orgasm the woman clawed at the fine finish of the table.

Gross. Carin stilled, concentrated to keep a shield in place, then reached frantically across the bond calling Bix's name in her head as loud and strong as she could.

"Easy, sweetheart. Easy. I'm almost there. Time for you to go."

She stiffened as Bix's thoughts rushed through her brain. She closed her eyes and sent him a mental picture of what she was seeing. *"Take it easy? Are you shitting me? There's a damned vampire orgy going on and you want me to be easy? Damned man. Why, I ought to..."*

"Carin, move it."

"Fine, already," she hissed, easing towards the door. She grabbed her stomach like she was going to throw up and ran for it.

Just as she reached the dining-room entrance, every pane of the wall of glass was blown inward. In swarmed a score of pissed off Seekers and Iudex judges with one thing on their minds. Kicking some Sidheon ass.

૪૦૭

While her husband was taking them out in the dining room, the best thing Carin could do was stay clear of the fighting to keep him from worrying about her. She had to get out of there and the beach was calling her name. She looked behind her and gasped, praying some new energy into her legs as she flew through the foyer and towards the front door. A naked and angry Natasha was close on her heels, and Sidheon right behind with his semi-hard cock hanging out of his pants.

Her fingers wrapped around the doorknob when she was jerked backward by her hair.

She grimaced as rough fingers tightened all the way to her scalp and yanked. Hard. On a pain-filled gasp, she yelled, "So did you tell him, Natasha? Tell Sid how you really want my husband, and not him."

"Shut up, bitch." Natasha's hand snaked out to land a nasty blow against Carin's left temple while the other tangled deeper in her hair. Carin's scalp burned and she just knew she was bleeding where the hair was being pulled out.

"You know, I'm getting tired of you yanking me around. I told my husband I'd let him handle this, but keep it up and I'm gonna have to kick your ass."

"What's this about her husband, Natasha?" Sidheon crooned, Natasha's jet black locks wrapped around his hand. If she hadn't been pissed off, she would have smiled at Natasha's frown as *her* hair was being pulled. Maybe she'd appreciate what it felt like to have someone constantly yanking on her scalp.

"You idiot, Aleth," Carin yelled, then grunted as Natasha pulled harder. "All Natasha wanted was to get back at Bix for rejecting her. But after you killed me, she planned to get him to mate her."

"I see," he drawled. "Tired of my cock already, Natasha?"

"Sidheon, she's lying. I-I swear."

"She never wanted your tired old cock in the first place." Carin knew he took it for the insult it was. After all, Natasha was a mere seventy-six years old, while Sidheon, who didn't look a day over forty, was at least one hundred and fifty.

A primal, beyond angry roar shook the building. All three of them looked back towards the dining room to see Bix tearing into every rogue stupid enough to challenge him.

"Wow, would you look at him," Carin said in awe. Bix was every bit the bad ass she thought he was. Every blow was dealt with deadly precision. His face full of fury, he ripped out a throat here, snapped a neck there. Then when his katana cleared the scabbard on his back, he was a hurricane in action.

Natasha's mouth was wide open as she watched Bix in battle. Carin understood because she couldn't take her eyes off him either. He looked like death itself come to take someone to hell. His handsome face was set in tight lines as his sword and knives flashed in the light cast by the fireplace. He turned, swirled, slashed and punched. Big and powerful, he dwarfed everyone in the room except for her blond avenging angel, Alaan. Power rippled through his arms and back as he lifted a full-grown vamp off the floor and threw him out of one of the ruined windows. Rogue after rogue fell before him. Blades sheathed, his gun cleared the holster and silent shots took down several more while he made his way towards them.

Holy shit. They ashed over.

Then her husband turned and saw her being harassed by Sidheon and Natasha. Lips curled back in a nasty snarl, fangs fully bared, Bix started towards them with singular intent, slowly, as if he had all the time in the world.

Sidheon untangled his hand and backed away with a wry grin as he tucked himself back in his pants. "Well, I'll just leave you two ladies to settle your differences, eh?" Then he shot out the front door and into the night. The sound of crashing waves filled the foyer in his wake.

Bix reached her side, took one look at her outfit and licked his lips. "Wear that for me when we get home?" He winked and took off after Sidheon, but not before he called over his shoulder. "Take care of Natasha, sweetheart."

Just the words Carin wanted to hear.

Natasha circled Carin, stalked her like a starving wolf with its prey within its sight. Sweat dripped off her face as she managed a sadistic grin.

"I'm going to enjoy your man after I kill you. After all, Bix wanted me first. He'll welcome me back with open arms after you're dead."

Just thinking of the possibility of the woman touching Bix made Carin stark raving mad. And like her grandma used to say, a pissed off sistah was a dangerous thing indeed. Holding up her hand in the universal one-finger salute, Carin met the challenge.

"Come get some, bitch."

Natasha lunged, missing by mere inches as Carin brought her elbow down in the middle of her back. Air whooshed from Natasha's lungs as she hit the floor. In a blur, she rolled over onto her back, sat up and scooted away so fast her head slammed into the wall behind her. Carin closed in. Every dirty maneuver Tameth and Jaidyn taught her streamed through her mind as she punched, kicked and gouged like she would never have another chance. The woman was not walking out of here unbruised or conscious. Grabbing a handful of tangled hair, Carin flung her into the middle of the foyer floor, and pounced like a lioness on the hunt.

On her feet in a flash, Natasha ran full speed at her, fangs bared and fists clenched for damage. Carin laced her fingers together, waited for the perfect moment, and when Natasha was close enough she swung her arms like a baseball bat. She heard at least a few of the fine bones of Natasha's face crack under the blow of her double fists. She decided she rather liked baseball and didn't stop the raining blows until Natasha lay limp and still on the cold tiled floor.

God bless vampire DNA. With her enhanced speed and strength, she'd held her own against Natasha in a fair fight, and beat the shit out of her until the female vamp was nothing but a pile of unconscious sore bones.

A quick trip into the dining room revealed the fighting was almost done. After a swift rip at the tablecloth, Carin and several sturdy strips of cloth were back in the foyer securing her quarry on the floor with a series of good solid knots.

Chapter Nineteen

Bix was right behind Sidheon as he streaked across the beach. Thankfully there was no traffic or bright lights on this part of the beach behind the house.

"Stop, Sidheon. I'd rather not kill you if I don't have to."

When Sidheon showed no signs of stopping, Bix turned on the steam, pumping his legs and arms with blinding speed. Sidheon was almost within arm's reach. Bix stretched out his hands, his fingers mere inches from the back of Sidheon's neck, when his world exploded.

Sidheon turned and fired a weapon hidden on his body. Blinding pain radiated through Bix's chest and down his left arm. His katana landed with a soft huff in the sand as he fell face down like a fallen tree.

In all his years he'd never felt anything this excruciating. He rolled to his back in agony. The starry night sky wavered, the stars fading as his vision blurred at the edges. The pain flared and burned through his very blood. Any moment now his skin would lay in smoldering strips in the sand, melted from his bones.

"You idiot. They don't call me brilliant for nothing," Sidheon crowed, standing over Bix now with a triumphant grin. "Dr. Carinian isn't the only one smart enough to make poisoned rounds. Too bad you've more brawn than brains."

Sidheon raised a piece of driftwood as large as a small log at the exact moment the blistering pain across Bix's chest begin to ease.

Moving as fast as he was able, he avoided the driftwood. It landed with a thud, throwing a plume of wet sand into the air in the exact spot his head had been. Shit, Sid wasn't fooling around. If Bix could just stay clear of the rogue's blows long enough to get the feeling back in his sword hand.

He rolled to the right towards the waterline. But he wasn't fast enough. The driftwood connected with his shoulder. Damn, that hurt. Managing to raise his right arm enough to keep another blow from connecting with his forehead, Bix felt his fingers again.

His right arm stung from the contact of the wood. The next instant, his gun was in his hand and a large black hole began to spread from the center of Sidheon's chest where a modified bullet penetrated with a near-silent hiss.

Sidheon's eyes went wide as his fingers loosed their hold on the driftwood and it tumbled to the damp sand at the water's edge. "How? How did you...?"

"My woman may not be the only one who can make modified rounds, but I bet she is the only one smart enough to reverse engineer an antidote to your serum, you scum." Bix rolled to his feet as Sidheon dropped to his knees, clutching his rapidly deteriorating chest, his lifeblood flowing between his fingers to pool in the cool grains underneath his failing body. Bix pumped several rounds into Sidheon's twitching flesh for good measure and watched the north wind carry the ash away.

Retrieving his katana, he wiped the blade on his ruined coat and slipped it into the sheath.

On his way back to the house he tensed when his wife barreled into his mind.

"Bix, where are you? Are you all right?"

She was worried. Or maybe she was hurt? Damn it, he should never have left her. Carin was a strong woman, but she was just mastering her new skills and abilities. He wasn't concerned about her ability to take Natasha down, but there were bigger and badder vamps in the house besides.

"I'm on my way back. Are you all right? Are you hurt? I'm coming, baby."

"Bix, I'm fine..."

But he wasn't listening. He was tearing his way towards the house at full speed to reach his mate. A few more strides and he'd be back with his woman.

The earpiece to his secure cell phone vibrated. He answered without slowing.

"Bixler here."

"The surviving rogues were secured on Stealth One and are on the way to headquarters. The Iudex judges accompanied them, declaring their sentences as they boarded. Stealth Two is waiting for the rest of us."

"What about Natasha and the others?"

"I don't have a status on Natasha, but Dr. Carin had Alaan call us to put the sick vampires on Stealth Two. She insists on keeping an eye on them and assist them if possible. They're all ready to go."

"Thanks, Randall." Bix spoke in hushed tones into his mouthpiece, and calmed. At least he knew Carin was safe. She'd probably tried to tell him she was fine, but the moment he heard the panic in her voice his brain shut down and all he could think about was getting to her.

He pushed through the front door into the foyer where he'd last seen his wife. Wounds, sore chest and all, he laughed his ass off when he found Carin sitting on an unconscious Natasha, whistling as she examined and reassured a few of the frail vamps.

Carin took one look at him, grabbed him by the arm and tugged him into the ruined dining room. He found himself seated next to a grumbling Alaan. His friend sat stiffly at the oversized table while Tameth fussed over a small gash across his forehead. The woman threatened to skewer him if he didn't sit still and let her tend him. Bix hid a grin at Alaan's deep answering growl as he stayed perfectly still. After all, Tameth was a Clan Serati Seeker. Since the mission was technically over, she was no longer subordinate to Bix as the team lead, nor Alaan as his Second, Clan Elders' sons or not.

Bix stilled in an instant when Carin, scalpel in hand, informed him of his options—sit still or die. His coat pooled at his feet as she examined the ruined shirt. It hung in tatters over his chest where Sid's modified bullet had hit. The flesh was red and somewhat swollen, but no gaping hole, no ashed-over skin, no dead Bix. At Carin's amazed gasp, Tameth informed her they'd found not only her modified bullets, but also the antidote she'd been working on to counteract Sidheon's serum. Kenoe and Dr. Lyons had administered the dose noted in her documentation before they boarded the jet. Bix knew several of the team should have left this earth at least twice over, their remains nothing more than piles of charred ash. Including himself. Instead he sported a single, puckered wound where he'd allowed Carin to dig out the bullet slug. That, and a bit of swelling on his chest and down his arm.

The woman was so happy she buried her face against his chest and bawled like a baby. He felt every wracking sob down to the depths of his soul. Didn't last long. If he thought she had a good set of lungs before, he soon realized he'd had no idea how good. The breath she took was deep enough to scuba dive with because she was soon screeching non-stop. She erupted at the top of her lungs, telling him how foolish he'd been to use an untested antidote, and what would she have done if he'd been hurt?

"Damn it, Bix, what if something had gone wrong, you muscle brained clod! What if the antidote hadn't been measured out correctly? What if...Mmmph..."

There was, after all, one way to stop an angry woman from talking. He pulled her down into his lap and groaned into her mouth as she responded hungrily to his kiss. She had no shame, wrapped her arms around his neck and pulled his bottom lip into her mouth. Leaning her back over his arm, Bix couldn't plunder her enough, feast enough, taste enough. A few annoying "a-hems" cut short their love play. No problem. He rose with Carin in his arms, and without a word walked right out the door to the car waiting to take them to the jet. He would never let her out of his sight again.

The mop-up team arrived and within two hours and right on schedule, there was no trace of the night's activities, with the exception of the broken glass panes. Those would be taken care of first thing in the morning.

Sidheon was destroyed. The mole was in custody along with all of the contacts stupid enough to be in this house during the raid. The rest were headed for the V.C.O.E. Most Wanted list. In the end, Carin was safe and they'd rescued a number of altered vamp hostages. Job well done.

ഇൻങ

The V.C.O.E. was thankful to Carin for her assistance. It had taken some time but she'd managed to develop a drug to undo Sidheon's handiwork on the vampires he'd used as servants. In appreciation, they'd given her the pick of any of the Council's estates. This particular property in Savannah, Georgia came complete with horses, as did the countryside manor in Wychnor Park, England.

Loving the feel of her mount underneath her, she urged it to go faster as Bix chased her across the rolling hills. For a woman who'd never ridden as a child, she'd caught on in no time. Even with the increased travel demands of her new Council position Carin made a habit of getting out to ride almost every day no matter where they happened to be.

They burst into the stables and Bix was off his horse in a flash. He'd pulled her out of the saddle and into his eager arms before she could get her foot out of the stirrup.

"Are you sure we can't stay another week?" she asked between hot little kisses.

"Sorry, love." He planted a loud smack against her neck. "You start a new project in sunny Charlotte, North Carolina in two weeks. We'll head to our ranch in Montana in the morning where I can make sure you get enough rest before then."

"Oh, come on, Bix, I don't make you rest before any of your secret Seeker gigs," she argued.

"But I'm not five months pregnant, am I?"

Her fist found its way to her hip and her left booted foot tapped on the stable room floor. "You know I'm not going for this crap, Bix."

With a sly smile he turned his back, removed the horses' bits and drawled, "No problem. Alaana will be close enough to..."

"Fine, fine, I'll take it easy. Just don't call *her*. Since I got pregnant, she won't let me do anything fun. It's like having a new mother." Carin scrunched up her face on a frown and shuddered.

She reached into the trough attached to the stall doors and threw a handful of hay at Bix while he laughed at her. Alaana, along with Alaan and his father, Ralen, spoiled Carin. She knew she was a damned brat, but hell if she was going to ask them to stop. In fact, Alaan had officially declared Carin his little sister and an adopted daughter of Clan Serati. And it was kind of nice to have a mom again. Well, more of a veritable dragon of a long-lived mom.

"You adore Matriarch Serati and all her mother-henning ways."

"And your point is?" Carin snapped and hauled back her arm to throw another handful of hay. Before she could toss it, Bix blurred from his spot near a hitching post, lifted her underneath her arms and pressed her up against the wall.

"Not sure about yours, but here's my point." He ground his hips against her and her legs automatically circled his waist. An unmistakable, mouth-watering erection pressed between her thighs.

"Mmm, it's a very nice point, too," she murmured with a husky sigh, opening for his kiss.

The groomsmen didn't bat an eye when Bix walked from the stables, up through the rear gardens and into the house with Carin's legs wrapped around his waist. They exchanged sizzling kisses as they went.

Yep, she thought, *there's a lot to be said for being mated to a vampire.*

"You've got that right."

"Bix, will you get out of my h...? Oooh! Oh my God. Mmm, never mind."

About the Author

Born into a musically eclectic family, TJ Michaels' first love is singing, even outside of the shower. Also an avid book lover, her eBook reader is shown no mercy, forced to entertain her at all hours of the day or night. Even in the dark you'll find her head buried in a story, whether it's her own creation or something snagged from the local bookstore.

So, where does this writing stuff come in? TJ taps her over fifteen years experience in technology to create realistic stories with out-of-this-world characters. And with an imagination expanded beyond belief since the birth of her two now teen-aged children (she'll never be sane again), spinning life's experiences into tales is a blast.

With more books in the works, TJ hasn't lost steam. Her mind? Yep, that's gone, but steam there is aplenty. As a true Taurus, TJ has no intention of slowing down and is definitely too stubborn to stop when she sees the fence.

To learn more about TJ Michaels, please visit www.tjmichaels.com.

Send an email to TJ at tj@tjmichaels.com or sign her guestbook on her website and the crew will be sure to keep you updated on the latest endeavors.

Look for these titles

Coming Soon:

Serati's Flame

*Sometimes magic is the only way to break down
the barriers to love.*

If Wishes Came True
© *2006 Cassandra Kane*

Maddy Langton has been in lust with fellow undercover
detective, Rafe West, for two years. Although they enjoyed a
brief sexual encounter during an undercover surveillance,
Maddy ran from Rafe before her lust for him jeopardized her
career...and because bad boy Rafe loves his women blonde and
gorgeous—everything she's not.

When Maddy helps a couple of Buddhist monks, the
grateful monks give Maddy a ring and ask her to make a wish.
Maddy wishes to be the blonde with Rafe. And when she puts
on the ring, that's what she suddenly becomes.

Willing to do anything to spend a night with him, Maddy
lets Rafe believe she's his beautiful companion. But does Rafe
really want her or the beautiful blonde she's become?

Available now in ebook from Samhain Publishing.

Enjoy the following excerpt from Scorch....:

And just like that, he was gone, leaving me alone with Dr. Naran.

"Come."

She turned and entered the inner office. I had never been here before and I didn't like the look of the place at all. The room wasn't very large. Off to the side was something that looked like a cross between a bed of nails and a clam. There were obvious protrusions on both the top and the bottom, suspended in some sort of gray cushion. The other side of the room consisted of a large panel, hosting a number of buttons, levers and dials, which obviously controlled the table.

"Get undressed."

I began to unbutton my shirt. She watched, focusing on me in a way that made me most uncomfortable. I shrugged the shirt from my shoulders and pulled it off. Her eyes never wavered. I wondered if this is what women felt like when they stripped for me.

Of course, this woman was a complete stranger. I didn't know her at all, had never seen her before our recent introduction. I couldn't remember the last time I'd been embarrassed undressing in front of a woman. I had thought those days were behind me, but I was wrong.

She must have sensed my mood, for she spoke. "There is nothing to be embarrassed about, Frank. During the next couple of weeks, I'm going to be working with your body and your mind, inside and out. You will have no secrets from me. I will share your darkest nightmares and your most intimate experiences. I will know you better than you even know yourself. I will surf your most secret thoughts and mold them to my will. When I am done with you, you will be what I want you to be, no more, no less."

I didn't say anything, but noticed my hand shaking as I placed it on the strips that held up my pants. It amazed me that after all these years, men's trousers were still fastened in this manner. I jerked and the sound of my fly coming undone tore through the room. It was the only act of defiance I would be allowed. I let my pants drop to the floor and stepped from them.

"All of it."

I shrugged, bent over and slid off my briefs. Then I rose and stood before her, the very act almost a defiance in and of itself. I would not cower or act embarrassed. Nor would I allow her to make me her toy. I had a will and would use it.

"Now what?" I asked.

She gestured to the machine. "Make yourself comfortable."

I turned to regard it. I had a feeling this would be horribly unpleasant, but then, disobeying a direct order would be worse. I approached it and reached out a hand. The foam was comfortable and even the protrusions were softer than I'd thought they would be. Without wasting any more time, I sat on the edge of the table, then lay down. I felt my naked body sink into the foam.

Dr. Naran walked to her control panel and pressed a button. The top half of the machine closed over me until my body was engulfed. I wondered how I'd breathe. I couldn't speak. I felt a moment of profound claustrophobia and fought it down. I soon realized I could feel nothing, see nothing, hear nothing. I had once been in a sensory deprivation chamber and it was much like this.

I seemed to have no trouble breathing, which was something of a relief. Still, I felt anything but relaxed. Then Dr. Naran's voice entered my mind.

"Hello, Frank. Ah, good, I see you can hear me. I'm going to run a few tests on you. Primarily responses to different stimuli. I need to know what makes you react and how. Some of this will, no doubt, be painful. At other times you may feel pleasure. Just relax and let yourself go. The more you fight, the longer this session will last."

I found myself holding my breath and released it. What seemed like a long time later, I felt the temperature drop. An icy wind passed through my entire body, starting with my toes and working its way up. It was as if someone had decided to pull a sheet of frost over me. Then, just as suddenly, it was gone.

It grew hot. Perspiration coated my body. I wanted nothing more than to withdraw from the sensation, but that wasn't allowed and in fact, after a short while, the heat increased in intensity until I could no longer stand it. My muffled screams didn't alter the level of pain, but I was powerless to struggle. Even if the machine didn't hold me in place, it seemed I had no control over my muscles. I mentally writhed in agony, until, many minutes later, the heat faded, leaving me gasping and sobbing.

For a long time, nothing happened. Then I felt tiny electric shocks touch various portions of my anatomy. My fingers, toes, nipples. Here and there, as if some tiny flying insect were circling my body, irritating me each time it landed. The charges increased in both frequency and power and it was more than just irritation. The back of my neck, behind my left eye, my right knee, my left testicle. The sensation grew more unpleasant, bordering on painful and the intensity continued to increase. Each new shock took me to a higher level of pain, until I thought I would die from it. This time, however, I found I could not scream. I had to lie motionless and endure it. I had no way to measure the passage of time, but I was sure it went on for hours. When it stopped, I was no longer certain I was within the boundaries of sanity.

I felt my body shudder and felt my cock begin to harden. I didn't want it to and fought the sensation. It was uncomfortable, considering it was pointing in the wrong direction. I could feel it pushing up into the foam. But as it grew harder, I felt my desire grow as well, until I couldn't think of anything but release. I found myself gasping for air and uselessly tried to grab my cock. I had never known such desire and when it ended, I wept as I'd never wept before. But this was only the beginning of the torment.

"I can see your thoughts, Frank. You're angry with me. You want to hurt me, but you can't. You're powerless to do anything against me."

The next voice that spoke was that of my mother, who had died when I was ten. "Frankie, you know better than that. Behave yourself, young man."

Then I heard a new voice, belonging to one of my teachers. She had taught Interstellar History and I'd barely been able to concentrate, as I'd been distracted by her large, firm breasts and narrow waist. Her long brown hair reached almost all the way to her nicely rounded ass. I couldn't even remember her name, but I recognized her voice immediately.

"I know you want me, Frank. Why don't you come here. That's a good boy. Suck on my tit, Frank. Suck! Suck hard! Ohhh yes, that's good. Suck it, boy. Suck my tit!"

In my altered state of consciousness, I almost didn't recognize this as one of my own adolescent fantasies. My cock grew hard again, as hard as before and I sucked and sucked, as she bade me. On some level I knew I was still in the machine, but that no longer mattered. I finally had my tutor where I'd always wanted her. I sucked even harder, hands sliding down over her curves.

Her own hands responded, touching me, trailing down my cheek, neck, chest, lower and lower, until I thought I would die from anticipation. She touched my cock and I felt it jump. I moaned and tried to fight the sensation. I was still in the clam and Dr. Naran was still watching. I wondered if she was doing anything else. I wondered what her body looked like, beneath that white lab coat.

Then my teacher's hand grabbed my cock more firmly and I was returned to the moment. Her eyes glazed over as she stroked, up and down. I clenched my teeth, but couldn't stop myself from thrusting into her.

"That's very good, Frank. Sooo good."

Her hand moved harder and faster, until I was panting. I couldn't think anymore. I could barely see. The only sensation in the world was that of her fingers on my cock, stroking and squeezing. I needed to come more than I'd ever needed anything in my life.